THE
TRIAL

JO SPAIN

QUERCUS

First published in Great Britain in 2024 by

QUERCUS

Quercus Editions Ltd
Carmelite House
50 Victoria Embankment
London EC4Y 0DZ

An Hachette UK company

Copyright © 2024 Joanne Spain

The moral right of Joanne Spain to be
identified as the author of this work has been
asserted in accordance with the Copyright,
Designs and Patents Act, 1988.

All rights reserved. No part of this publication
may be reproduced or transmitted in any form
or by any means, electronic or mechanical,
including photocopy, recording, or any
information storage and retrieval system,
without permission in writing from the publisher.

A CIP catalogue record for this book is available
from the British Library

HB ISBN 978 1 52941 922 1
TPB ISBN 978 1 52941 923 8
EBOOK ISBN 978 1 52941 924 5

This book is a work of fiction. Names, characters,
businesses, organizations, places and events are
either the product of the author's imagination
or used fictitiously. Any resemblance to
actual persons, living or dead, events or
locales is entirely coincidental.

10 9 8 7 6 5 4 3 2 1

Typeset by CC Book Production

Printed and bound in Great Britain by Clays Ltd, Elcograf S.p.A.

Papers used by Quercus Editions Ltd are from well-managed forests and other responsible sources.

Dedicated to Julie and Maureen, my grandmothers.
And to Kathleen, whom I never met but wish I had.

Author's note

This is a work of fiction and as such, any similarities or resemblances to real-life people, situations or locations are entirely coincidental and unintentional. While I undertook research into the treatment of Alzheimer's, the reference in this work to a potential 'cure' is fictional and purely for dramatic use.

Prologue

2014

Theo dresses as quietly as possible, desperate not to wake Dani.

He's leaving a few personal belongings in her room. T-shirts she now sleeps in. Spare boxers, a toothbrush, though she has no problem with him using hers. A couple of CDs. His Jeff Buckley, the one she listens to on repeat even while he's allegedly the bigger fan. One of the books from his course, a weighty tome that he's supposed to know back to front.

None of it matters to him any more.

He woke in the night, utterly certain of what he had to do.

But now, looking down at Dani as she sleeps, he feels unsure.

She looks peaceful. Her hair is fanned across the pillow of the single bed they share when he stays over. She has one hand tucked under her cheek, the other cupped beneath her chin. She always curls into herself when she's asleep. It's one of the things he loves about her. He's a head taller than her and he can envelop her whole body when he lies behind her. He likes the tickle of her hair against his chin and the rise and fall of her chest under his arm. He likes the smell of her skin and how her body is always hot, but her hands and feet are always cold.

Theo craves Dani. He has since he first met her.

He has to keep moving. He can't stop, can't talk himself out of these next steps.

The light from the lamps in the college square spill into the room through the bare windowpanes, helping him to find his shoes – one on the floor, one kicked under the bed. They'd been in a rush to make love; she was a little tipsy and horny, he needed to quieten his thoughts and lose himself in her.

He'd promised to look at her broken curtain pole if Maintenance didn't send somebody. Not that he's any use with tools. Not that he's remotely handy at all. But it felt like the manly thing to say. At twenty, Theo should have at least learned how to use a screwdriver, right? And yet, why would he, when he grew up with somebody always available to do menial tasks?

Dani stirs and Theo has to resist the urge to get back into bed with her, to wrap his arms around her and wait for her to wake.

He could tell her everything.

But that would mean dragging her into his crisis and he cannot do that. For many reasons.

Pain shared isn't pain halved. It's just pain distributed. That's what his father used to say.

Theo is meant to be the strong one.

He's fully dressed now, and Dani has started snoring lightly, her lips parted.

Twenty is too young to be this in love. They've both said it. And said that it doesn't matter. They can't get enough of each other. And it's been like that for eighteen months, from the moment their eyes first locked in the college bar.

He allows himself this one thing. He leans over her, silent as the grave, and breathes in as she exhales. Her breath is still minty from the toothpaste she used before bed, but there's a sweetness beneath. Cider. Her least favourite tipple, but one she can afford, and she always insists on paying for herself. He could buy her champagne, if the college bar even stocked such a thing. She deserves it. She deserves every good thing. But Dani won't allow it.

He looks at her one last time, taking a snapshot with his mind. Her long brown hair, her dark eyebrows and eyelashes, the little bump on the ridge of her nose, her cheekbones, the dimple on her left cheek, the tiny beauty spot near her lips.

I love you, Dani MacLochlainn, he thinks.

Then Theo walks to the door. His hand on the doorknob, he hesitates again. The dread is back, the feeling that maybe this isn't the best way, even if he thinks it's the only way.

Rational thinking kicks in. He's being stupidly emotional.

He turns the knob.

She'll understand eventually, he tells himself.

He closes the door softly behind him.

Theo has no idea it will be ten years before Dani sees him again.

April 2023

St Lawrence's Hospital, Dublin

Cecelia Vargas likes the hours after midnight.

Her shift starts at eight and the turnover with the other nurses is always frantic.

Then there's the bedtime routines; visits to the toilets and cleaning of bedpans; administering medication; talking patients out of their books or television programmes or, sometimes, their attempts to leave.

But after midnight, peace.

Not that it goes undisturbed.

There are accidents, crying; sometimes a little hand-holding is needed.

And then there are the deaths.

It's the nature of geriatric nursing.

Cecelia can hear the ragged breathing all the way along the corridor.

Her pumps squeak on the linoleum floor as she walks hurriedly towards the ward.

She already knows who the breaths belong to.

Dessie has been struggling all day.

Cecelia likes Dessie. He's forgetful with almost everyone else, but when he sees Cecelia, he immediately starts to flirt. She reminds him of a girl he used to fancy, he once told her. More and more, Dessie thinks she is that girl.

He used to be in the army. Peacekeeping, but he was stationed all over the world. Cecelia has only ever lived in Manila and now Dublin. But she'd like to travel and she likes it when Dessie tells her about Asia, a continent he's seen more of than she, born there, ever has or probably will.

She enters the ward as his breathing becomes more distressed.

She's only twenty-seven but she can already tell when it's a medical intervention situation and when it's end of life care.

Cecelia steels herself. Dessie is in the bed beside the window and the man next to him is sitting up. He looks at Cecelia, distressed. His name is Jim, and he's too far gone most of the time to know where he is or who he's with. But instinctively, he recognises death.

He points at Dessie.

'I know,' Cecelia says, in her most reassuring tone. 'It's okay, my love. I'll take care of him. You rest.'

Jim lies down, uncertain but willing to take guidance.

Cecelia stands by Dessie's side. His eyes are closed and the morphine he had earlier is letting him sleep while his body does what it must.

'I'm here,' she says, hoping her voice brings comfort. 'I'll stay with you.'

Cecelia takes his hand. With her other hand, she blesses herself.

She whispers the words of a Hail Mary as Dessie passes on to a better place.

When she's recorded the time of death and pressed the bell to alert the nurse at the desk, Cecelia rests Dessie's hands in a cross on his chest and gently places the top sheet over his face.

Dessie has no immediate family and his distant relatives never visit. Cecelia treats him with the care and respect she would her own grandfather.

She picks up his chart and begins to write the details of his passing.

She sees something then, something that jars.

The other nurse arrives and Cecelia is thrown into the routine tasks that accompany the removal of a deceased patient from the ward.

It's not until the following morning that Cecelia has time to consider what she saw on Dessie's chart.

She collects her coat and bag from her locker after she's handed over to the day shift.

Then she walks to Mr Rogan's office.

The senior physician is at his desk, perusing files, dapper as ever in his three-piece suit.

She knocks gently on the door and waits a moment until he looks up.

'Nurse Vargas,' he says.

He prides himself on knowing all their names, but he's never asked Cecelia anything about herself. He doesn't know that she's wanted to be a nurse her whole life, or that she's one of seven children and longs for home almost every minute of every day, or that she lives in a bedsit because she sends almost every cent she earns back to Manila.

Dessie knew all these things about Cecelia.

Mr Rogan just knows her name.

'How can I help you?' he says.

'One of my patients passed last night,' she says.

'Yes, I'm aware. Poor soul.'

Mr Rogan narrows his eyes and studies her.

Sometimes, geriatric nursing gets the better of staff. Seeing the isolation and loneliness that is so cruelly inflicted with age, the helplessness, having to bear witness to the end . . .

Cecelia knows he's wondering if she's had enough and is going to ask for a transfer.

'I noticed something on his chart,' she says.

'Such as?'

Cecelia hesitates.

'He was taking the same medication as my other patient, the one who passed a couple of weeks ago. Kitty Sheridan.'

Mr Rogan frowns.

'And?' he says.

'I just . . . wondered if the medicine could be connected. I know it's different and—'

'Your patient last night was quite advanced with his illness. We had done our best. But, along with his age . . . his death was expected.'

'I know—'

'His medication was neither here nor there.'

Cecelia has lived in Ireland for five years and she still doesn't know what that expression means.

Mr Rogan is looking at her impatiently now. Cecelia doesn't know what to add.

How can she articulate the vague suspicion she has? He's right. Dessie and Kitty were always going to die. The fact they were taking the same medication is irrelevant.

And yet . . .

Cecelia's gut tells her something is amiss. The carer in her — the professional in her — knows that when two patients are being given the same new drug and they both die in a similar fashion, somebody should ask the question.

She meets Mr Rogan's eye. His expression is one of frustrated indulgence. He's offered her his learned ear and his valuable time and she's been found wanting.

Cecelia bites her lip.

Because behind that expression, she sees something else.

A warning.

Don't open Pandora's box.

It sends a shiver through her.

'It's probably nothing,' she says.

Mr Rogan smiles now.

'It's never nothing,' he says warmly. 'You must always voice any concerns. Even if they are, in this instance, unfounded. Have a good day, Nurse Vargas.'

Cecelia smiles in return.

It's something she's learned to do. As a woman, as a foreigner, as a person of colour. Sometimes, she must just smile.

In the near future, she'll write down her concerns. She'll email an official in the Department of Health. But she won't know that, by going to her supervisor, she's already set in train a series of events over which she has no control.

Cecelia knows something is wrong.

She took an oath. Do no harm.

And she wants to know if what she's been administering to her patients has done them harm.

DUBLIN DAILY

10 May 2023

Gardaí are investigating the cause of a fatal accident in the Royal Canal yesterday evening.

Emergency services were called to the scene when a car was seen skidding from the road and entering the water.

Several passers-by entered the canal and tried to rescue the driver of the vehicle but were unsuccessful.

A recovery operation was later put in place to retrieve the driver, who was pronounced dead at the scene. The car was subsequently removed from the water.

The victim has been named as Cecelia Vargas, a 27-year-old nurse at St Lawrence's Hospital in Foxrock.

Miss Vargas had lived in Ireland for the past five years. The Philippine Embassy has been in contact with her family, and the hospital and Department of Health have also sent condolences.

A representative of St Lawrence's today said that Miss Vargas was a valued member of staff and much loved by her fellow employees and patients.

The Gardaí have yet to release their official finding, but a source has confirmed the incident is believed to be a tragic accident and will be recorded as misadventure.

September 2024

Before Dani MacLochlainn drives to the college, she heads to the lake in the Dublin mountains.

It's quiet. The September lull. School has resumed, parents no longer have to entertain their children every day.

The lake, which is often busy with day trippers, is deserted.

Dani stands at the edge, near the rocks where the life she thought she knew both ended and began again.

And she looks out over the water and thinks about what lies beneath its still surface.

I don't know if I can do this, she says to herself.

But even as she thinks it, she knows she will.

She knows she can.

She's always been strong.

It just gets tiring, sometimes, being the one who copes.

She crouches down, picks up a shore pebble and puts it into her pocket.

For luck, she tells herself.

The college was once a seminary for priests.

Three hundred years ago, the Order of St Edmund set about designing its grand residence on the edge of the small market town of Rathlow in County Kildare, Ireland.

For at least two hundred of those years, the property only

consisted of the main building, with the rest of the land used for farming. The seminary itself was an impressive four-storey grey-stone building, surrounding a large courtyard. The courtyard was planted with oak saplings that over time would become the trees the college was renowned for.

The seminary existed in harmony with Rathlow. While being in many ways self-sufficient – the young priests grew their own veg-etables and raised and slaughtered their own animals – a symbiotic way of living developed. The townspeople looked to the seminary for trade and spiritual guidance. The seminary bought from the town anything it couldn't grow or fashion itself.

When the seminary became a full-time college in 1905, a religious and lay-member board was formed. Newer buildings sprang up on the land beside St Edmund's, housing modern facilities for science and sport and technology.

Barely twenty miles outside Dublin, the once rural college became an elite centre of education. The demand for college places meant increases in fees and the resulting financial boost meant an increase in the quality of teaching.

St Edmund's became the university of choice in Ireland.

And the original seminary building, overlooking the pretty courtyard, is the place where every student and lecturer still wants to be housed when they attend.

Except for Dani MacLochlainn.

She stands, right now, in front of an exasperated woman in the staff administrative office. She can almost feel her heels digging in.

'I'm not saying I'm not grateful for the offer,' Dani says.

'You do appreciate how highly sought after the west halls are?' the woman replies. Dani has guessed her name is Bridget, if the

'Bridget's mug' cup on the desk is anything to go by. She's in her forties and one of those beautiful women who look like they're perfectly turned out from the moment they get out of bed. Unlike Dani, whose cardigan keeps slipping off her shoulders, and whose recently grown-out fringe won't stay tucked into her ponytail so her hair looks perpetually untidy.

'I know the west halls are in demand,' Dani says. 'But I don't want to be in the same building as my students. I don't want to give them any opportunities to blur the lines.'

'The staff are on an entirely different floor. And the students here know that out of hours is out of hours. You don't need to worry about them—'

'Is there any accommodation available off the main residence?' Dani is holding firm. 'Aren't there new studios over by the sports and science blocks?'

Bridget, or maybe just the current holder of Bridget's mug, casts her eye back at her computer screen. After the longest minute of awkward silence, she sees something that seems to enthuse her.

'I have a possible solution,' she says. 'It's still in the main building, but it's on the opposite side of the square. The east wing—'

'Isn't that where the heads of departments are housed?'

'Yes. The late head of humanities lived there and it's badly in need of a refurb. We were going to get some tradesmen in . . .'

'I'll take it,' Dani says.

Being on the courtyard at all is not ideal but the east wing she can cope with.

'Are you sure?' Bridget says. 'It's very old-fashioned. He never let us in to do any work and I had a look when we moved his belongings out . . .'

'Honestly, I'm not fussy,' Dani says.

She and Bridget make eye contact, both trying to ignore the irony in that statement.

Dani emerges from the administration office satisfied.

There was no way she could let herself be housed in the west halls.

She knows that's where the junior professors usually stay. On the floor above the students. She's known that since she attended this college herself.

But no. To have been near her old room would have been too much for her.

She's here to do a job. She can't focus on that job if she's reminded of the past every waking moment.

Dani jumps when the college bell starts to toll for the hour. She'd forgotten how loud it is.

Her heart rate slows as it reaches the end of its ringing.

The courtyard is relatively empty. A couple of early comers make their way across the diagonal pathway and around the edges of the lawns. They're mainly professors or tutors or admin staff, all of whom will form the operating core of the college in a couple of days' time, when lectures begin and the student body arrives.

Nobody notices Dani as she glances over at the building wing that she could have been staying in. Her eyes travel up to the second floor, and across, to the window nearest the corner.

Dani shudders before she hoists her bright blue rucksack back on to her shoulder and pulls up the handle on her wheeled suitcase.

She walks towards the opposite end of the courtyard, to the east wing, where she'll stay while she's lecturing at St Edmund's.

Her old alma mater, a place she swore she'd never return to.

The apartment is everything Bridget warned her it would be.

Dani lets herself in and takes a moment to survey her new home.

The carpet is almost threadbare, but odd patches reveal it was once a hideous orange and brown colour. There's an old, toxic-looking gas fire as a centrepiece in the sitting room, under a mantle heaving with dark, heavy ornaments and an antiquated clock. The wallpaper is straight from the set of a 1960s horror movie. And the lighting is . . . Dani turns the switch on and off to make sure it's not on dimmer settings. No. It really is that dark.

Dani wanders into the kitchen – a galley so cluttered she can't see the countertops; into the bathroom – a blue monstrosity of a room; and then the bedroom – thankfully boasting a new bed, at least, something to counter the bizarre shade of yellow on the walls.

She returns to the sitting room to reflect on her life choices.

There are positives.

There's a good solid desk in the corner and the bookshelves Dani might have chosen herself.

She can ask Admin to get the Facilities team to sort out the light fittings and throw down a good rug. She might even have them take out that gas fire – there'll be an open fire behind it, like all the other rooms in this old building.

She walks to the window. Some of the apartments on this side of the courtyard have their views obscured by the trees outside. This one does not.

Dani can see right over to her old room on the west wing.

She pulls the curtains closed.

She can't bear to look at the place where her heart was shattered.

It's an Indian summer.

The light is starting to fade when Dani enters the Admin office for the second time that day. But the high temperature has lingered, and she barely needs the sweater she's thrown on.

Bridget Armstrong, her full name, introduces herself properly this time. She has her coat on, is done up to the nines and mentions she's going for a nice dinner with friends, which makes her far more predisposed to Dani's requests than she'd been earlier.

'That's all very doable,' she says. 'To be honest, the Facilities department will be thrilled they don't have to completely renovate it.'

'Thanks. And I'm sorry for being so awkward earlier. I guess I'm just nervous about starting here. It feels like I've barely left.'

Bridget assures Dani that's perfectly normal, and it will all work out wonderfully, before offering to bring her for a drink sometime and then taking her leave.

Dani, hungry now, heads to the dining hall. A wave of nostalgia hits her as she enters. It's exactly as she remembers it, frozen in time.

The walls are wood-panelled, the tables long, and at this time of the year, mostly bereft of patrons.

At the top of the hall, there's a self-service area staffed by two dinner ladies.

Dani settles for a plate of Irish stew. The catering lady ladles food on to the plate like she's taking Dani's natural slenderness personally.

'I'll put this apple tart on the side,' she says, without asking Dani's permission. 'They call it apple pie back there, the chefs, you know.

Pie, my eye. All those American names for perfectly normal food. A tart is a tart.'

'As my mother used to say about the woman who lived next door,' Dani adds dryly. The catering lady cracks up, then adds a dollop of extra cream.

Always make friends with the servers and secretaries. That's something else Dani's mother always said.

Dani sits down at the far end of one of the staff tables. She looks at some of the other diners to see if she recognises any. Most are on their own, like her. She exchanges polite glances with some of them, then takes a book from her bag. She's brushing up on the Habsburg empire, but she can't bring herself to do it through dry texts, so she's reading a biography of the Empress Sisi. As good a source as any, to be fair.

Dani is on to her apple tart and Sisi's hair routine when she accidentally knocks over her bottle of water. The cap is unscrewed and it spills across the table and on to Dani's jeans.

She starts to dry the mess with her napkin when a man from further along the table approaches. He's attractive, with sandy blond hair, a nice tan, and dimples.

He makes an offering of extra serviettes.

'Thank you,' she says.

'I've been that soldier,' he replies. 'Head stuck in a book and living dangerously with my bottle lid not screwed tight.'

Dani laughs.

'Colm Ahern,' he says, extending his hand.

Dani shakes it.

'Dani MacLochlainn.'

'You're new?' he asks.

'Shiny.'

'Thought I hadn't seen you before. I've a good head for faces, terrible with names. What department?'

'History. Yourself?'

'School of Medical Research. I'm not a lecturer. Just tutoring while I get my PhD.'

Dani tenses when he names his faculty, but she tries not to show it.

'So, you're a genius who's going to help us all live forever,' she says.

Colm raises an eyebrow, bemused.

'I wouldn't say that. I'm a genius who's trying to cure you all temporarily.'

'Impressive,' Dani says. 'As a history professor, there is literally nothing new I can offer.'

Colm laughs.

'I'm going to get a coffee,' he says. 'Would you like me to get you one?'

Dani considers it but shakes her head.

'It's a bit late for me and coffee. I'm planning an early night.'

'On your first evening? That seems a bit—'

'Pathetic. I know.'

'The bar is open,' he suggests.

Dani smiles. It's as much of a push as she needs.

When they're outside the dining hall, Dani takes a right. Colm seems surprised.

'Do you have a homing device for alcohol?' he asks.

'I used to be a student here. Ten years ago.'

'No way! I'm surprised our paths didn't cross.'

'Did you do your degree here, too?'

'No. I interned for a semester in the research school. I wasn't clever enough to get into Edmund's through the front door.'

'You're doing your PhD here. You're clever enough.'

'Clever enough,' Colm laughs. 'I'll take it.'

Dani smiles again. She senses she's going to like Colm Ahern.

There may not be an awful lot of people on campus yet but of those who are, the majority are in the bar.

'How very Irish,' Dani observes.

'What's your poison?' Colm asks.

'G&T.'

Dani makes her way to a table by the window. The lamps have come on across the campus now that evening has fallen properly. The bar staff have lit the large fire in the corner and it's already flanked by several senior professors, two of whom are drinking whiskey and arguing heatedly in a manner that tells everyone around them that the debate has been taking place for years.

The bar has always been the one place where staff and students mingle without noticeable segregation, but like everywhere else in St Edmund's, everybody has marked their space. The lecturers get the best spots by the fire and the windows; the students own the vertigo-inducing tall tables and bar stools.

Dani has just sat down and is looking out over the woods to the rear of the college when a woman sits at the table behind her. Her chair knocks against Dani's as she pulls it out.

'Oh, sorry,' she says in an American accent.

'Don't worry about it,' Dani replies.

She decides to grasp the nettle and make another friend.

'I'm Dani MacLochlainn. History department.'

The other woman shakes her hand.

'Sharona Davies.'

Dani waits, but Sharona doesn't add any more and once they've shaken hands, she smiles politely and turns back to her own table.

Dani looks at the back of her head, bemused.

Colm returns. He nods at Sharona like he knows her, before placing a bowl-like G&T in front of Dani. He sits across from her.

'Where'd they put you?' he asks.

'East wing. I'm in an apartment that's just been vacated by the head of humanities.'

'They'd nowhere on the west?'

Dani shrugs.

'Do you live on campus?' she asks him.

'I have an apartment over by the research school,' he says. 'It's part of the package so they can feel better about screwing me on the tutor wage.'

'Ah. They're still at that lark?'

Colm lifts his Guinness, an air of resignation to the sip he takes.

'I'll be finished with my PhD this year. Then I'll get to be a serf in the private sector.'

'You don't want to stay in academia?'

'I'd really like to be able to eat something other than beans eventually.'

They both laugh.

'You're, what, thirty?' he says. 'That's the same age as me. Pretty impressive to be lecturing already.'

'It's a bit different to medical research,' she says. 'I did my degree and master's and was already lecturing during my PhD. But I'm only a junior professor. Trust me, we're not treated a whole lot different to the tutors.'

'Still. It's an achievement.'

Dani shrugs. 'Where are you from?'

'Galway. Yourself?'

'I'm a Dub.'

'You don't have a Dublin accent,' he says.

'I do. I'm just not thick northside or posh southside. Anyway, your accent is completely flat.'

'Nonsense. I'm full culchie. Galway city was a metropolis as far as I was concerned. So, what are you lecturing in? In history, I mean?'

'Mid-nineteenth-century Europe. Politics and aristocrats.'

'Ah. Modern history.'

Dani laughs again. The history course at St Edmund's begins in the Early Christian Ireland period, circa 400 AD. The nineteenth-century module has been a joyful relief for students for decades. Not to mention the field trips to Versailles and the Schönbrunn, a lot more enjoyable than the days out in the cold Irish countryside discussing early monastic towers.

Colm looks up. Somebody has just come into the bar and caught his attention. Dani has her back to the door, so doesn't see who, but she does see her companion's face light up.

'Would you excuse me for a moment?' he says. 'The boss has just come in.'

'Sure.'

Colm stands up quickly. Dani gives it a few seconds before she turns around to see who Colm is greeting.

He's joined two newcomers at the bar, and for a moment, Dani can only see the backs of their heads.

At the same time, she feels the woman in the chair behind her move. Sharona Davies gets up and walks to the bar and one of the newcomers turns and greets her.

Professor Declan Graham looks just as he did ten years ago.

The same tan, the same easy smile, the same startlingly blue eyes.

Dani turns away quickly, before he spots her.

She's not ready to have a conversation with him yet.

She takes a large sip of her drink.

Then she picks up her phone. She angles it as though she's reading something on it and quickly takes a photo of the group at the bar counter.

When it's done, she stands and leaves.

Colm is going to think she's odd, but she'll deal with that another time.

Outside, Dani looks at the photograph on her phone.

She knew she was going to see Declan. She wants to see him, in fact.

So why does she feel so uneasy?

And then she stares a little harder at the photograph.

The other man, the one who didn't turn around.

Dani looks at the back of his head. The dark, wavy hair. The wide shoulders.

He looks familiar.

Where does she know him from?

He may have been somebody she knows, she thinks, or he might just have been the ghost of somebody she remembers.

She'll have to get used to that.

She suspects she's going to be thinking about Theo Laurent a lot, now she's back in the place where he walked out on her.

2014

Two weeks have passed since Dani woke up to find Theo gone.

That first morning, she thinks nothing of it. They've both done it before. Crept out to early lectures, leaving quietly so the other can sleep on.

She tries to find him later that day, but he doesn't answer her texts, his room is locked and she doesn't spot him in any of their usual haunts. Still, she doesn't worry. She has a paper to deliver; Theo is prepping for mid-term exams. She assumes he has his head stuck in a book and has lost track of time. She sends him a *Goodnight, love you* text, starts outlining her essay on the Medicis and falls asleep.

The next morning, the absence of a reply text from Theo sows the first seed of discontent.

She calls over to his room again, and this time, his neighbour gives her his spare key.

Theo isn't there. In fact, his room has the distinct feel of somewhere that has been unlived in for a few days. Which makes sense because he's slept in Dani's almost every night this week.

Except for last night. So where is he?

She doesn't search the room – she doesn't want to invade his privacy – but her fingers are itching to pull out drawers and open the wardrobe.

She leaves and returns the key to Theo's neighbour.

As she walks back towards the main college building, she tries calling again.

It goes straight to voicemail.

'Theo, call me,' she says.

And still, she tamps down her concerns.

She doesn't want to overreact; she knows her imagination can be dangerously creative. Theo noted that once and she explained that having her father die so young meant she had the capacity to go to dark places in her head very quickly. When the worst thing happens, you're always waiting for it to happen again.

But that's irrational. Theo is somewhere. If anything had happened to him, somebody would have told her. Everyone knows they're an item and Theo has no family in Ireland.

Two days later, Dani is extremely worried. It's so unlike Theo to go silent like this. They talk every day, bar the very exceptional ones.

None of his friends from his course have seen him and none of Dani's friends either.

She racks her brain for reasons he might be avoiding her. Had she said something to upset him? They've never had a proper fight, but they've bickered lots about little things. Theo has a tendency to think he's always right and he's like a dog with a bone when he wants to prove his point. Maybe what she considered to be something small, he thought was much bigger?

She can't believe that's true, though. She knows this man. He's not the sort to go off in a huff because of a slight.

And yet, she's felt he's been a bit quieter lately. A little bit distracted and in himself, which she put down to exam prep.

Could it have been something more?

Was he already annoyed with her for something?

When they'd made love the other night, he certainly hadn't seemed irritated. He'd lost himself in her. She could tell.

When she's exhausted all the routine possibilities, Dani starts to consider the more extreme reasons he might be missing.

She gets it into her head that Theo has had a family emergency and had to rush home. She tells herself that it's so bad, he's not been able to let her know what's happened. He probably keeps meaning to call her.

She'll be cross at him for leaving her in the dark like this, but on the scale of things, if one of his parents has died (the first place her head was always going to go), she can hardly make the situation about her. At some point in the future, she'll ask him to try not to do that to her again, but she won't make a big deal of it.

Four days later, Dani is consumed with worry.

Even if there is some huge drama in France, does she mean so little to Theo that he can't turn his phone on and send her a one-word text message?

When five days have passed, Dani calls into the Student Liaison office.

The secretary on the desk hasn't had any correspondence from Theo. He suggests she try the School of Medical Research, in case Theo checked in with his lecturers and they haven't passed on the absence report.

Dani goes straight to the Admin office in Theo's school.

The secretary there tells her Theo has been marked absent for the last five days and they've not received any communication from him. He has been issued with an email asking him to explain his lack of attendance and if he doesn't reply by Monday, he will receive his first disciplinary note. The college expects students to act like responsible adults. They won't chase students to attend but if you fail to respect the timetable, you're held to account. Only illness or family matters are seen as mitigating factors.

That Sunday, Dani phones the number Theo once gave her.

He told her to only use it in an emergency.

A man answers with a curt, '*Oui?*'

'Um, *bonjour. Parlez-vous anglais?*'

'Yes.'

He already sounds hostile and she's not even introduced herself. Dani takes a deep breath.

'I apologise for calling out of the blue, Mr Laurent. My name is Dani MacLochlainn—'

'How did you get this number?'

'Your son gave it to me.'

There's silence at the other end of the line. Then:

'What do you want?'

'Is Theo there?'

'He is not.'

Dani feels panic rising.

'Do you know where he is?'

'Yes.'

She closes her eyes. God, the relief. She reminds herself to breathe.

'Can you tell me where he is?' she asks.

'Who are you?'

'I'm . . . I'm his friend. We're both at St Edmund's.'

'You're his *friend* and my son gave you my personal number?'

'Yes. But only for emergencies.'

'And why do you think this is an emergency?'

'Because he's gone. I haven't spoken to him all week. He's missed lectures; nobody has seen him. And I thought, I hoped, he might have had to go home. And now I know he has.'

'He has not come home.'

Dani's breath catches.

'I thought you said you knew where he was.'

'I do. But if he has not told you, I do not see why I should be his messenger.'

Dani senses the call is about to end abruptly and without her receiving any satisfaction.

'Please!' she chokes out. 'You don't have to tell me exactly where he is if you don't want to. I just want to know he's safe. We're . . . close and I'm worried about him.'

There's a sigh from the other end of the phone.

'It sounds like he has disappointed you in the same way he once disappointed me. Theo has left St Edmund's.'

'Left?' Dani is stunned. 'Why? Where has he gone?'

'He has decided to travel. That's what he said.'

Now Dani feels completely at sea. None of this makes sense.

'Travel where?' she asks. 'I don't understand. He didn't say anything to me.'

'I have ceased trying to understand my son, young lady. It was his choice to study in Ireland and now it is his choice to abandon his studies. I cannot tell you any more. You must wait for him to communicate his reasons to you. If he gives you that courtesy.'

Dani knows Theo's father is ready to hang up now. She has seconds.

'When he spoke to you this time, though,' she says, 'did he say anything about where he might be going? I'd like to reach out to him.'

'He didn't *say* anything. He deigned to send an email. Now, if you will excuse me, there's nothing more I can help you with.'

Dani is left listening to the dial tone.

The bottom has just fallen out of her world.

2024

It's a weird feeling, standing at the top of a lecture hall that you were once a student in.

Dani needs to get her bearings, so she arrives ahead of her class. Unusual for a professor, she knows. The young men and women who'll fill this hall in a few minutes will be expecting her to sweep in, superior and grand, a statement that will remind them of the pecking order.

But Dani needs these few minutes to talk herself into believing she's not a fraud. That she has every right to be here, facing the students and not in one of the seats.

She glances at her introduction. Just a few notes she's jotted down. She wants to take it easy in this first lecture – give them a brief overview of her course, then introduce herself and get to know them. As much as she can. There are seventy students signed up for this second-year module, and she suspects, given it's one of the easier courses, most of them will stay.

They begin to trickle in. Ones and twos and the larger gangs of friends. They're a noisy, excited bunch. Some of them glance down at Dani, curious about this new lecturer. Most ignore her. She's but a means to an end. A young man and woman hold hands as they walk towards the back of the room. Dani watches them, trying to ignore her chest constricting. She and Theo didn't share

28

lessons, but they spent almost every moment they were together on campus holding hands.

When the hall is more or less full, and the college bell strikes the hour, Dani walks to the large wooden doors at the side of the hall and pulls them shut.

The noise of them closing helps to settle down the students.

Dani returns to her podium and takes a deep breath.

'Good morning,' she says. 'My name is Dani MacLochlainn. You may call me Dani, Professor, whatever comes naturally, but if that's *Mac*, use your inside voice. I had an uncle called Mac and he was duller than early Irish Christianity, so I won't take kindly to it.'

The ice is broken. The students laugh, appreciating immediately the revelation that she has a lighter side.

'So, you guys and girls have chosen an excellent second-year module. The nineteenth century was for Europe what 5G has become for online clothes shopping. Revolutionary. Human and civil rights, strides in democracy, culture, art – these are all areas we're going to cover.'

Dani takes a breath.

'But we're also going to look at the expansion of empires, the extension and solidifying of colonies, and the brutality that came along with it. We'll look at the atrocities carried out in countries overseen by European powers, countries that helped to build Europe. The Congo, where severed hands became part and parcel of the rubber trade, where young soldiers were brutalised to the point of being forced to rape their own mothers and sisters.'

Dani takes a moment to look at the students. They're all leaning forward, utterly enthralled by the horror. And why wouldn't they be? She's not leading with the more technical, boring parts of the course. She's going straight for the riveting jugular.

'And we'll study all that alongside the jewels the Empress Sisi wore in her notoriously heavy hair; the targeting of Oscar Wilde for his sexual orientation; the invention of the telegraph . . . We have a busy year ahead.'

The students are still with her, still engaged. She's got them. She's done her job.

'But for today,' she says, 'let's start by introducing ourselves and getting to know one another a little better. I'll start by telling you I was a student here, on this very course, ten years ago.'

There are surprised smiles around the hall.

So, she's just like them. She's their possible future.

Dani is off to a good start.

They like her.

And they never have to know that she's just given them more or less the same speech she was given when she took this module ten years ago.

She didn't have the time to come up with a new one. She's not here for them. She's here for something else altogether.

It takes Dani a while to get over to the dining hall. A few of her new students come up to talk to her outside and then in the courtyard as she tries to make her way across it. She's happy they're enthused, and equally happy she put her foot down about not staying in the same building as many of them.

Before she arrives at her destination, she hesitates.

For a moment, she thinks she feels somebody's eyes on her.

She spins on her heel and looks back at where she's just come from.

She sees, or thinks she sees, the shadow of somebody who's just turned the corner.

He's gone now, but she suspects she knows who it is.

She knew he'd be watching her. She just didn't think he'd start this soon.

In the dining hall, she makes her way to the self-service coffee area. She's just milking her cup of coffee when she sees Colm come in. He looks over; she raises her cup and an empty one. He hesitates for a moment, then nods.

Dani joins him after a few moments with the two cups.

'I got you black and brought you some sugar sachets in case,' she says.

'Thanks.'

'About the other night,' Dani says.

'There's no need. To explain, I mean. I figured you got a call or something.'

'I did. But it was rude of me to just leave like that, especially when you'd bought me a drink. I promise, I'm not usually so flaky. I'll buy you two to make up for it.'

Colm shrugs and smiles. Dani is glad to see he's not the sort to hold a grudge. She's explained, he's forgiven her, they can move on.

Her phone starts to buzz, the ringer turned off. Dani takes it out of her bag and glances at the withheld ID. She knocks it off and places it on the table.

Colm says nothing but Dani feels the need to fill the silence.

'They'll leave a message,' she says.

Colm nods.

'That man you were talking to in the bar,' Dani adds. 'I think I recognised him.'

'Which one?'

'The sandy-haired guy.'

'Declan Graham?'

'That's it. I remember him from when I was here. I'd a friend in medical research. I think he was a lecturer at the time?'

'Now he's head of the department. I guess when you work in the leading college in the country, it's a bit pointless to move elsewhere. Luckily for me.'

Dani sips her coffee. She's trying not to look overly interested.

'Luckily for you?' she asks.

'He's my mentor on our current project,' Colm answers. 'And the reason I did that semester here all those years ago.'

Dani raises her eyebrows, naturally curious.

'We're trialling a new drug here,' he says, seeing she's intrigued. 'The company could have chosen any college to lead, but they chose St Edmund's. Mainly because of Declan, I reckon.'

'Oh. Yeah. That sounds . . . huge.'

'It is. It's in partnership with one of the biggest pharmaceutical companies in the world.'

'And Declan is in charge of the whole thing?'

'Well, of our team, yes. He brought me in on the project. He had dozens of students to choose from, but he gave me a chance.'

Her phone starts to buzz again.

'Maybe you should get it?' Colm suggests.

Dani shakes her head.

'It'll be some marketing firm.'

She takes a beat.

'It sounds like Declan has done really well for himself,' she says. 'And for the college.'

'He has. I'll introduce you if you like. There'll be drinks organ-ised soon. Start of term and all that.'

'Terrific. The other man you were talking to, does he work here as well?'

Colm frowns.

'Who? Oh. No. I don't know him. He's from the pharma com-pany the college is liaising with.'

Dani wants to press for more. She wants to know the man's name.

But she doesn't know how to phrase the question in an innocent way and Colm looks clueless anyway.

Move on.

'So, when are these drinks?' she asks.

Colm fills her in.

She watches him as he speaks.

He doesn't look anything like Theo, but she can't help but see Theo in him. A similar age, a similar passion.

Dani gives herself a mental shake.

She has to keep her focus.

She's not here for Theo.

Theo is the past.

Her concerns lie in the present.

She swore she'd do her job here properly. She can't fuck it up.

Not this time.

2014

Dani is pleasantly surprised at how well she's been treated by the Guards. The officer at the desk listened to her carefully once he realised she wasn't one of the many cranks who turn up routinely at police stations. And after taking the initial report, he brought her into this interview room. He even offered her a tea or coffee.

After a few minutes, the door opens and a woman with short brown hair comes in. She's reading something in a file but looks up at Dani once she's closed the door. Her features are hardened by what Dani can only assume are years in a tough job, but her face softens when she smiles, as she's doing now.

'Sorry for the wait, love. Got myself a lad down the corridor who's refusing to admit to something we have him on camera committing. You know those funny videos where the kid's mouth is covered in chocolate and they're insisting they didn't eat the chocolate? That's him.'

'Oh. Right. Thank you for making time for me.'

The woman puts down the file and sits across from Dani, placing both elbows on the table and lacing her fingers in prayer. She has a way of looking at Dani that feels both searching and reassuring. Dani can trust this woman.

'I'm Sonia Wall. I'm one of the detectives. And you're a student at St Edmund's?'

'Yes.'

'What are you studying?'

'History.'

'You're a Dub?'

'Drumcondra.'

'I used to share a flat in Drumcondra. Good pubs out that way.' Sonia pauses.

'So, you're worried about your boyfriend. Theo Laurent.'

Dani nods.

'He's a student there, too,' the detective confirms. 'And he's twenty years of age?'

'Yes. And he's been missing for eight days.'

Dani can hear the distress slipping into her voice and, evidently, so can the detective, because she reaches over and gives Dani's hand a squeeze.

'Okay, love. Tell me from the start. You last spoke to him . . .'

'Thursday night, last week. He stayed over in my room and when I woke up the next day, he was gone. I figured he had an early lecture, or he was studying in the library. I didn't panic. Not until I hadn't spoken to him for a couple of days. We talk every day. Even on busy days, we send a goodnight text.'

The detective cocks her head.

'You're really in love with this chap.'

Dani can't bring herself to say any words. She just nods. The detective looks even more sympathetic.

Then she grows serious.

'I don't mean this to sound dismissive or condescending, but there was no fight, no problems leading up to this, nothing in his character that would make you think he's just piddled off in a fit of pique?'

'No,' Dani says. 'Honestly, I understand why you're asking, and if I thought there was even a hint of him being like that . . . Well, look, I wouldn't be here. Theo is not . . . he's not immature. If anything, he's older than his years. He's kind and he's thoughtful and he's smart. He's studying medical research in St Edmund's. It's one of the top courses in the world. He's a good guy.'

The detective takes it all in.

'And you didn't notice any change in his mood? Is there a possibility he could have been feeling down about something and he decided not to tell you?'

Dani takes a sharp breath.

'He hasn't harmed himself,' she says. 'He tells me everything.'

'Everything? That would be a little unusual.'

Dani knows the detective is testing her. She also knows she shouldn't sound naïve.

'I don't mean it that way,' she says. 'He tells me the most important things. I'm sure he has his private thoughts, and he does have a tendency to try to deal with stress on his own. But he confides in me. Like, his family didn't want him to study in Ireland, but he came anyway. I guess what I'm saying is, he might not tell me every little thing, but he does talk to me about the big stuff.'

The detective narrows her eyes.

'Why didn't his family want him studying here?'

'The Laurents are very wealthy. His dad is – I don't really know the ins and outs, but – an investor of some sort. He makes his money in medical devices. Theo is his only son – his only child, in fact. And he was meant to follow in his dad's footsteps. But Theo is not like his dad. He wants to make medicine to help others, not just to make money. He wants to do something good for the world.'

'Hmm.'

The detective is studying Dani now. The compassionate expression has slipped, just a little, and Dani can't figure out why, but she can feel her cheeks starting to burn.

'So,' the detective says, 'Theo *is* capable of going off and doing his own thing, if it's what he wants. He has a history of it.'

Dani swallows, realising her error.

'Not like that. He didn't just come to Ireland on a whim. He fought with his father about it. For a long time. And they knew where he was going when he did leave.'

The detective sits back, her arms crossed.

'Okay. So, he is a good chap, he's responsible, he's smart. And you say he has no history of depression?'

'None at all. And that's why I'm so worried. Theo would have called by now if he could have. He'd have sent an email or something. Something is wrong.'

'I can see you're very worried,' Sonia says. 'I just need to rule out the obvious. In situations like this, especially with young men . . . Well, I'm sure you know what I mean.'

Dani nods. But not Theo. She knows Theo wouldn't harm himself. Even if they say you can never know, she knows.

'And I imagine with his family being abroad, you feel the weight of responsibility for him,' the detective adds. 'I presume he doesn't really talk to them that much, if things played out as you say.'

'No,' Dani agrees. 'His relationship with them is very strained.'

'Okay. Normally in a situation involving an adult, we would only take a report like this from a family member. But given Theo is a French national living here without family, and nobody has heard from him . . .'

37

The detective trails off.

Dani's mum always says her daughter's face is very expressive.

Sonia leans forward.

'Nobody *has* heard from him, right?' she says.

'Um . . . well, his dad.'

'What about his dad?'

'He said he had an email.'

'An email.'

'Yes.'

'From Theo?'

'Yes, but that's the thing. He said Theo sent an email saying he was going travelling, but that is so unlike Theo— Wait, you need to listen to me.'

The detective stands, her demeanour oozing exasperation.

'Dani, this is a busy Garda station and I'm a busy detective. You should have led with the fact your boyfriend had let his family know when he was pissing off on his holidays.'

'Please,' Dani pleads. 'I'm not wasting your time. Something has happened to Theo. He wouldn't email his father and not tell me where he was going, that he was going at all—'

Sonia has her hand on the doorknob. She hesitates and Dani's hope surges.

'Look, you seem like a nice girl,' she says, 'and I appreciate you're probably a little bit heartbroken at the moment. So, I'm not going to caution you for wasting police time. But I'm going to leave now and you're going to get yourself back to college and drop this. Take my advice: the next time you hook up with a chap, make sure you take the red flags seriously. Telling your whole family to fuck off because you want to live out some Harry Potter fantasy in Ireland? That was your first clue.'

The detective leaves.

Dani slumps back on to her chair, her head in her hands.

When she straightens up, her eyes are wet with tears of frustration.

She slaps the table so hard, her hands sting.

Why won't anybody listen to her?

2024

The tradesmen have been in working on her apartment all week, and their efforts – changing the carpets, taking out the old fire, switching the lights and curtains and taking away some of the clutter – have transformed the living space.

Dani guesses that if any of her more senior colleagues saw the apartment as it looks now, they might not be too happy with her staying there, as opposed to over in the west halls where the other junior professors are housed.

Earlier, Dani brought a bottle of wine and some chocolates to the Admin office to thank Bridget.

Bridget laughed and told her they were going to be friends for life.

Tonight, with a fire lit in the newly opened grate, the evening sun setting outside the mullioned window, and a throw over her knees, Dani wonders how she can use that friendship with Bridget to her advantage.

She has her laptop open and it's resting on top of the throw.

There's a photo of Declan Graham staring back at her from her screen.

She's reading an article published in the college newsletter the previous May. It's a short history of the School of Medical Research's programmes and achievements over the years. The school is listed as leading the way in studying the genetics of human disease, facilitating key breakthroughs in understanding neurological disorders, and investigating the immune system's role in illnesses such as asthma and eczema.

On and on. The school's catalogue of success is exhaustive and impressive, and much of that is attributed to its current department head.

The article includes a short bio, and Dani's eyes scan it.

From Dublin originally, Declan Graham studied medicine in St Edmund's, before leaving to achieve his master's in Stanford University. He returned to St Edmund's for his PhD, specialising in frontotemporal dementia.

Declan began lecturing in St Edmund's in 2011 and during his time in the college, he has published over fifty papers in the most renowned medical journals in the world. He was appointed head of the School of Medical Research in 2021. As well as continuing the school's existing research programme, Declan has put his own stamp on current projects, specifically in relation to preventative medicine for neurological degenerative illnesses.

Declan is an avid cyclist, a fan of classical music, a keen traveller, a passionate supporter of several charities, and a mentor and friend to many in the college.

Dani reaches the end of the article. She can taste bile in her mouth.

St Declan.

Dani's eyes flick back to the top.

Started lecturing in Edmund's 2011.

Theo and Dani's first year had been 2013. Declan back then, as described by Theo, was young, ambitious and energetic. He'd inspired Theo, made him feel that his choice of St Edmund's had been worth it. That all the anger and spite directed at him by his father was worth it.

Dani shuts down the laptop. She rests her head against the sofa's back and closes her eyes. Remembers better days.

Then she reaches over to the coffee table and picks up her phone.

The number is the last one she dialled. It usually is.

It rings three times before it's picked up by Sini.

'Good evening, Rose Hill Residential Centre. How can I help you?'

'Hi Sini. It's Dani. Can you put me on?'

'Sure. Give me a moment.'

There's a click as Sini puts the phone down in reception.

A minute later, there's another click as the nurse picks it up in the room that she's transferred the call to.

'Putting you on now, Danielle,' Sini says.

Dani closes her eyes as she listens to the phone rustle as it's placed against somebody's ear.

'Hello, love,' she says.

She waits in hope for a reply. There isn't one. Just the sound of breathing.

'I'm here,' she says. 'At St Edmund's. I started last week. They were going to put me on my old wing. You remember it? I said no. I managed to get a nice apartment across the courtyard. New start and all that.'

She might be mistaken, but Dani thinks the breathing she can hear down the other end of the phone has quickened.

'I saw Declan Graham,' she says. 'He's the head of the research school now.'

She's not mistaken. The breaths she hears sound ragged and harsh.

'I came back to do a job,' Dani says. 'But now I can't stop thinking about the past. There are still so many questions. I—'

There's the sound of movement and then Dani hears Sini's voice on the phone.

'I'm sorry, my dear. We seem to be having a difficult day today. Maybe tomorrow will be better?'

'Of course,' Dani says. 'I'm sorry, I won't be in for a few days. It will just be calls.'

'That's okay. It happens. Bye.'

Sini has put down the phone before Dani can defend herself. It's always the same. If she misses a visit she feels judged. Even if it's only her judging herself.

Dani gets up and fetches herself some wine. A deep burgundy. She sips some then she stokes the fire and tries to settle her thoughts.

When she's feeling calmer, she sits down and opens her laptop again.

This time she finds a file. It's footage from a camera in a car park.

Dani watches as a woman gets into her car and drives out of the car park.

She opens more files. This time, Dublin streets, filled with pedestrians. In one, the car from the garage emerges on to a busy road.

It's the umpteenth time she's watched these videos.

So why is it that this time, she feels like there's something she's not seeing?

She shakes her head with frustration.

What the hell is it?

Dani closes her eyes.

She won't see it tonight.

All she sees tonight is a young nurse getting into her car and driving to her death.

All she sees are Cecelia Vargas' last moments.

2014

Dani doesn't know what they do with a student's room when it's assumed they've left their course – whether they go in and pack stuff up for the student, or they wait for the student to return. She knows Theo's room will have been paid for the year, but if nobody's in it, and with the demand for accommodation so high, she doubts the college will leave it empty for long.

His neighbour still has Theo's key, which gives Dani hope.

And she's pleased to see that his room is, so far, untouched.

She's going to look for something that tells her where he's gone and what he was thinking when he left.

Her first blow comes when she opens his wardrobe.

Theo likes his fashion. He keeps his sweaters and T-shirts folded neatly, and his shirts are always carefully placed on hangers. Dani, who throws her clothes into her wardrobe higgledy-piggledy, has mocked Theo for his OCD wardrobe maintenance.

Of course, his clothes are all designer label, whereas Dani's are mainly from high-street chains.

Now, Theo's wardrobe looks very different. Most of the clothes have been pulled off the hangers and lie in a heap on the floor.

His drawers are the same. Things have been taken out and thrown back in.

His suitcase is still under his bed, but his rucksack is gone.

His books are still on his desk, along with his coursework folders.

But his laptop is nowhere to be found.

Dani sits on Theo's bed, and then she lies on it, turning her face into the pillow and smelling his scent.

He's taken his rucksack and his laptop.

He just hasn't taken her.

The messed clothes speak of a Theo she doesn't know.

But if he had been depressed and she'd not realised, if he'd been expert at hiding it and had in fact gone off to hurt himself, he'd hardly have taken his rucksack and laptop.

Something is wrong.

On her way back to her own room, Dani is stopped by her American history lecturer.

Professor Grace Byrne takes a lot of flak for her speciality, especially from the older professors who think the concept of American 'history' is laughable. Most of the students who take her course see it as an easy ride for a term. But Dani likes her. She enjoys the woman's passion for her subject and her devotion to her students.

'Dani, I'm glad I bumped into you,' the professor says. She tries to tuck the hair that's escaped from her massive curly ponytail behind her ears, but the wind has other ideas.

'Dear God, this weather,' she says. 'Step over here with me. You have a moment, don't you?'

Dani, who's just finished drying her eyes in Theo's, can't think of an excuse on the spot.

'Sure,' she says, and follows the professor over to the far side of the courtyard, where they seek shelter from the elements in an alcove.

'I just wanted to check you're okay,' Professor Byrne says.

It's this simple sentence that sets Dani off. She starts to cry again.

'Oh, dear.' The professor gives her an anguished look. She breaks all protocol and pulls Dani in for a hug. 'What's the matter, pet?' she asks. But Dani is sobbing too hard to answer. She's just grateful nobody else is around to witness her meltdown.

'Come on, let me get you inside and I'll make you some hot tea,' she says, when Dani still can't speak.

It's the prospect of this that jolts Dani into responding.

'No, no thanks,' she protests. Dani wipes her face roughly with the sleeve of her coat. She can't bear the idea of sharing her concerns again only to have another person in authority tell her she's cracked.

'It's just family stuff,' she says.

She tries to meet her professor's eye and look in control. It's a weak attempt but it works; Grace Byrne seems to relax a little, even if she's still watching Dani with a concerned expression.

'I see,' she says. 'I figured something was up. Your paper this week wasn't to your usual standard.'

'I'm sorry,' Dani says.

'You've nothing to apologise for. If I thought you weren't making the effort or you didn't like the course, I'd be worried, but we all have off periods. I just wanted to make sure you were okay and ask if there was anything I could do to help. Is there anything?'

'Really, I'm okay,' she says. 'My next paper will be better, I promise.'

The professor doesn't look like she wants to let Dani go but can also see Dani's not going to give her much more.

'Well, look,' she says, 'I'm always here to help. Whether it's to talk about personal stuff, or if you need a hand with coursework. You know if you want to revisit anything we've studied, you can access my personal planning notes for each session. I can give you the log-in details for my term folder. It's all in there and it'll save you printing out reams of paper . . .'

Dani smiles, trying to look grateful and in control. But she still feels on edge and she desperately wants to be on her own.

It's only when she's back in her room that Dani realises Grace Byrne has inadvertently helped by mentioning her log-in details.

Dani opens her laptop and signs out of her email provider.

She types in Theo's email address.

Then she stares at the log-in page.

What would Theo use for his password?

She tries his name and his birthday.

She tries her name and her birthday.

She tries Paris and his surname.

She tries them back to front.

She could be at this all night, she realises. Theo changes his password every six months; he told her that once. God knows how many password variations he's learned to come up with. It would be easier if she had his laptop, because for all his security consciousness, he leaves his log-in details saved there.

It's an hour later, an hour of frustrated thinking and typing, when Dani enters: *Theo&Dani2014.*

Theo's inbox appears.

Dani sits up straighter. She's barely noticed how dark it's become outside. The only light in the room is from her laptop and the lamplight cast in through her curtainless window.

She's torn between nerves and excitement as she looks at his messages. She's hoping to see something that will tell her where he's gone and, more importantly, why he's gone.

But within seconds, the excitement fades, replaced with that cold feeling of fear she's become familiar with.

Theo hasn't opened any of his emails, dating from the last evening she spent with him.

She checks back – there are various emails from professors, from the Admin office, from his course friends, from a friend in France called Louis, telling him he's thinking of visiting Ireland if Theo can't make it to France.

Nothing out of the ordinary, excluding the fact they've all sat there, unread.

Dani goes into the sent box.

The last two emails Theo sent are dated the day after he vanished.

The first email is to a lodging in a town in the south of France. Theo is inquiring if they have a room available for the next two weeks.

Dani recognises the name of the town. *Le Muy.* Theo mentioned it before. His aunt lives there. Aimee. And an uncle. She can't remember his name.

The second email is to his father.

She opens it, her fingers trembling on the keyboard.

Hi, I hope you are well. I'm writing to let you know that I've decided St Edmund's and medical research is not what I want to do. You were right. I'm going to take some time to work out what I want for the future. I think travelling might help.

I know our relationship has not been the best for the last number of years, but I don't want to leave and for you to worry about me. I am fine, this is just something I have to do. I would rather you didn't try to contact me. I need to work this out for myself.

Regards, Theo

Dani finishes reading the email, then rereads it.

When she's done, she stands up and rushes to the bathroom, where she vomits up the very little in her stomach.

It reads exactly like a message Theo would send his father. Curt and to the point.

There's only one glaring error, something that tells her Theo never wrote that email.

She's surprised Mr Laurent didn't mention it, though she's starting to suspect he didn't even read it – his secretary probably parsed it for him.

The email is written in English.

And Theo never spoke to his father in English.

2024

The start of term soirée for lecturers is held in the provost's apartment, and the invite says it's a casual affair, but both Colm and Bridget from Admin have informed Dani it's anything but.

Dani has rummaged through her limited wardrobe at length and settled on a plain, knee-length black dress that hugs her figure, paired with her mother's diamond earrings and a silver-threaded silk scarf. She ties her hair up and makes a quick assessment in the floor-length mirror that now stands in her bedroom.

She'll do. She's never been vain, though Theo always told her she was beautiful.

Dani had never thought she was beautiful, until she met Theo.

She shakes her head. She needs to stop thinking about him.

She checks she has essentials in her small bag. Phone, keys, lip gloss.

She has three missed calls on her phone.

She opens the text message the caller has sent.

Looking at the photo from the bar. Recognise Declan Graham. Will come back to you on the other guy. Check in, please.

She'll deal with that later.

Colm has agreed to meet her on the way to the provost's apartment, because Dani has told him she feels intimidated going in on her own. It's unusual for a PhD student to get an invite, even if he is a tutor, but apparently Declan Graham can move mountains. He's so well regarded, he's allowed to invite who he wants.

Colm greets Dani outside her building and she can tell immediately that he's more nervous than she is.

'Is this your first time going to one of these?' she asks him, suspecting she already knows the answer.

He tugs uncomfortably at his bow tie as he nods.

'Right,' Dani says. 'So, it's more me bringing you, than you bringing me?'

Colm laughs.

'It's just going to be cocktails and fancy food in tiny portions,' Dani says. 'All anybody will expect from you is for you to entertain them with fascinating, unique, hilarious tales and confirm your brilliance.'

'Is that all? There was I thinking I'd have to sing or something.'

Dani smiles.

'Come on,' she says.

The provost's apartment is already humming with people when they arrive.

In the entrance hall, there's a large self-portrait of the man himself.

Dani has to stop herself from laughing at his ego. She remembers Malachy Walsh from when she was a student here. He'd been appointed provost the previous year and his natural pomposity had grown larger with the title. She never met him during that time, but she'd heard plenty of tales describing him as a self-aggrandising twat. One of the tales had come from Theo, who had had the pleasure of meeting Walsh.

He swept into our lab in one of those lecture capes, you know the ones, like he thought he'd walked out of a Dickens' novel. And I swear, he acted

52

like he's responsible for everything the research school is doing. More or less telling us we're welcome. He reminded me of one of those surgeons who thinks he's God. Total asshole.

You don't think you're being a bit hard on him, Dani had said, laughing.

Wait until you meet him. You'll make up your own mind.

Theo had taken such a dislike to the man, Dani had decided she never wanted to meet him. And she hadn't.

Once inside, Dani grabs two martinis from a passing waiter's silver tray. She hands Colm one.

'Are you okay if I go let Declan know I've arrived?' Colm asks.

'I'm a grown-up,' Dani replies. 'Go on, I'll be fine.'

Dani stands at the side of the room for a few minutes to get her bearings.

The apartment has high ceilings and large open-plan rooms, so the crowd is easily absorbed. It screams money – old and new.

The provost's accommodation had been renovated not long after he got the job. Walsh was rumoured to have spent over one hundred thousand euro fitting out the old apartment with oak parquet floors, state-of-the-art lighting and an Italian marble-top kitchen.

He'd been forced to keep some of the original features after the heritage society in the college got wind of his plans.

Standing in the luxury apartment, Dani feels like the renovation was money well spent. Maybe he is unpleasant, but the provost has good taste.

As she surveys the crowd, she's joined by Bridget, who fits right in in her sleek midnight-blue cocktail dress.

'I didn't realise you were coming,' Dani says.

'Oh, I make sure I get on with Walsh's secretary,' Bridget says.

'And I never miss this one. Wait until they start circulating with the hors d'oeuvres. Your mind will be blown.'

'Not baskets of cocktail sausages, then?'

'Blinged blinis all the way.'

Dani smiles.

'Are you settling in okay?' Bridget asks.

'I am. I've got a lovely bunch of second years and I'm tutoring some smaller first-year groups.'

'I'm glad to hear it. If you need anything, let me know.'

Bridget squeezes Dani's arm, then wanders off.

Dani sips her martini and considers moving around the crowd herself. She could introduce herself to people, but she's not sure she wants to engage in endless small talk.

She's weighing up her options when she sees the head of her department, Grace Byrne, approaching with Malachy Walsh.

'Dani, so glad you could make it,' Grace says. She leans in for a hug. Dani gently squeezes the top of Grace's arm as they embrace, an acknowledgement of all the woman has done for her.

After all, she's responsible for Dani getting this job.

Dani releases her and watches as Grace tries to smile at Malachy.

Which is, Dani knows, a really difficult thing for Grace to do.

Grace hates this man. And for good reason.

'You know our provost,' she says.

Dani shakes Malachy's hand.

He hasn't lost the air of self-importance. They're roughly the same height, with Dani in heels, but he manages to look down on her.

'You'd just started as provost when I was a student here,' she says.

'Indeed,' he says. 'Dictators have shorter reigns.'

54

Dani laughs politely.

She understands it now, what Grace meant when she said she couldn't stomach the man, even before he did what he did.

Dani doesn't like the way Malachy is looking at her. Like she's his property and she's supposed to be thankful for it.

'I'm already hearing good things,' he says. 'Grace speaks very highly of you and I value her opinion. One of our best lecturers. I believe you have your students fully engaged already.'

'Thank you. May it last to exam time.'

Grace smiles. 'It will. You specialised well. Unlike me. American history and now the Reformation. I get duller by the topic.'

'I got ninety-five problems, but a pope ain't one,' Dani says.

Grace snorts her wine and laughs, genuinely. Dani is pleased to see her relax. This situation isn't easy for either of them.

Malachy beams at them both indulgently.

'Well, enjoy yourself tonight,' he says. 'I hope you find college life suits you, Dani.'

Dani flinches but she has no time to respond. He's already moved away.

'Are you okay?' Grace asks Dani in a hushed whisper.

'I'm fine,' Dani says. 'You?'

Grace nods.

The two women exchange a meaningful look.

Then, over Grace's shoulder, Dani sees that Colm has re-entered the room and is looking around for her.

'Go,' Grace says. 'Get to know everybody.'

'Of course,' Dani replies.

When Grace departs, Dani walks towards Colm.

She's almost reached him when she realises he hasn't come into the room alone. He's with the woman Dani saw in the college bar the time she and Colm went for the failed drink: Sharona Davies, the American.

But that's not where her focus is. It's on the man standing behind her, Declan Graham. He catches Dani staring and looks back with a mixture of confusion and surprise.

'Dani,' Colm says. 'I was just coming to find you.'

Dani tries to keep her expression blank.

'Dani MacLochlainn,' Declan says, smiling broadly. 'It's been a while.'

He really does look the same as he did back then. A little greyer, a little more lined around the eyes and mouth, but recognisable as the man who had the female students in his department aflutter and the male students in awe.

'Declan,' she says, trying to sound normal. 'Ten years, I believe.'

'And you're a fellow professor now. Gosh, it's hard to believe. When Colm said your name and that you'd come here, I presumed it was just a coincidence. I thought, that can't be the same Dani who studied history here all those years ago.'

He turns to Colm.

'You know that I used to teach Dani's boyfriend? Theo . . . Theo—'

'Laurent,' Dani says quietly, then quickly sips her martini.

'Ah, yes. Theo. Lovely guy. So sad, though, what happened.'

Dani takes a deep breath. She can't be doing a great job of hiding her discomfort because she can feel Colm's eyes on her.

She has to do something, or she's going to vomit.

She turns to Sharona.

'I think we said hello in the bar the other evening.'

Sharona smiles.

'We did.'

'Are you a lecturer in the medical research department, too?'

'No. I'm on liaison from my company in the States.'

Sharona is speaking politely, but Dani feels on edge. She has the impression that Sharona already doesn't like her, and that's confirmed when Sharona looks back at Declan, impatience on her face.

Declan's not taking the hint.

'So, you became a lecturer in the end,' he says. 'How unusual.'

'It's not really unusual, is it?' Colm says. 'I imagine most people who study here covet a professor job at some point.'

'I'm sure they do,' Declan says. 'I just wasn't sure Dani would keep up with history. Not after she dropped out.'

Dani's cheeks are burning.

'You dropped out?' Colm asks. Even Sharona seems more engaged now, looking at Dani curiously.

'Yes,' Dani says. 'I had . . . family stuff going on. I finished my degree abroad.'

'Well,' Declan says. 'I'm glad to see you went back to it. Most of the time when a student doesn't finish a course, they end up doing something completely different. But I do recall you were always a determined young woman.'

Dani doesn't let her emotions show.

'Declan, would you mind if I have that chat with the provost now?' Sharona interrupts. 'I need to hop on a call with my boss soon.'

'The horror of working for a company in a time zone that's eight hours behind,' Declan proclaims. 'We should get on.'

He holds out his hand. He's watching her, compassion and pity on his face.

Dani accepts it. She knows he can feel the clamminess of her palm.

'It's so lovely to see you again,' he says, with sincerity. 'Let's catch up properly another time. It's a delight to see you so successful and . . . doing well.'

Dani nods. She tries to make a noise that sounds like assent, then pulls her hand free. Her skin tingles.

Declan and Sharona move away. Sharona throws a backward glance at Dani like she's some sort of odd species she's just laid eyes on for the first time.

Colm remains behind. He's looking at her, too, concern on his face.

'Are you all right?' he asks. 'You've gone very pale.'

Dani takes a deep breath. She feels nauseous.

The entirety of the past and her memories come rushing at her.

'Dani,' Colm repeats, and his voice sounds like it's floating down a tunnel. 'Dani, are you okay?'

Dani feels the glass slip from her hand before she can stop it.

It's the sound of it smashing that shocks her into remembering where she is.

She opens her eyes and sees Colm and everybody else staring at her.

Declan and Sharona are looking too; Declan with that same look of concern on his face.

'It's the heat,' Dani says.

Colm nods. He guides her to the door.

Dani can't get away fast enough. She'd had no idea it was going to be this hard.

She'd never have agreed to come back if she'd realised.

How is she supposed to do her job here if she can't stop thinking about what happened back then?

2014

Dani thought she'd have to beg to get an appointment with Professor Graham. His secretary is affectionately known as Cerberus to students in the research department. Her ward is popular and in demand and she runs his office efficiently.

But hours after she's sent the email, Dani gets a call telling her to come over to the professor's office.

Dani arrives, out of breath and soaked to the skin. The March rain seems endless. It matches her current mood. Which has been made worse by the fact her first stop – at Professor Graham's regular office – was a pointless exercise. The professor's office is being renovated and he's in a temporary one upstairs. The head of the department's, as it transpires. He's on a sabbatical in another college for several months and Declan has benefitted from it.

Declan's secretary purses her lips when Dani arrives. She doesn't tell her to sit down, quite possibly because Dani would leave a puddle. She calmly takes a sip of tea from her mug. Dani watches silently, transfixed by the secretary's cool demeanour. She looks at the clinically maintained desk. It's spotless and everything on it looks like it's been placed with precision. There's only one personal photograph, presumably of the secretary's children. And just one Post-it stuck on the bottom of the computer screen.

When she's good and ready, the secretary stands up, pops her head into the professor's office, and a few moments later, tells Dani she may go in.

Professor Graham is at his desk, reading a paper. He's absorbed and she has a couple of seconds to watch him before he notices she's there. He's young, by lecturer standards. Mid-thirties, with sensibly cut sandy blond hair and glasses. His face is full of laughter lines, though, and the all-round image is one of a pleasant, friendly man.

Theo has spoken about his mentor in reverent tones. Professor Graham is considered a prodigy of St Edmund's and the college was extremely happy to have him back after his stint in the US.

We're so lucky to have him.

We? Dani had laughed. It sounds like I have a little competition.

I love the man's mind. Though the rest of him is okay, too. He's got these great eyes. You know the type. They sort of sparkle.

Jesus. Is there something you need to tell me?

Come to think of it, he has great hands too. I've watched him in the lab. He's so delicate with those vials.

Dani had straddled Theo then, one of her knees slipping off the edge of the bed, but the rest of her anchored by him.

I forbid you to leave me for Professor Graham. You live here now. Between my thighs.

God, I love it when you're bossy.

Professor Graham looks up and his legendary blue eyes immediately fill with concern.

'Oh, my God, you're drenched!'

The professor is clearly less concerned about Dani causing a mess than his secretary. He ushers her over to the side of the office and makes her stand in front of a radiator while he hangs her coat. He leaves the office and returns with a towel for her hair, then tells her that his secretary is fetching tea.

'But I think you'll need something stiffer,' he says. 'I don't want you catching a cold.'

He walks towards a large cabinet and opens it.

'Our head of department has a problem,' he says, taking out a decanter filled with whiskey and a thick crystal glass. 'And his problem is, he didn't leave this cabinet locked when he said I could borrow his office.'

Dani manages a smile. She's shivering now, her fingers tingling as she holds them against the radiator.

She startles when a loud noise sounds. It's the college bell tolling, but electronically.

'Sorry,' Declan says. 'They pipe them into the building. Like they're not already loud enough.'

Dani winces with each clang.

'What possessed you to come out without an umbrella?' Declan asks, as he hands her the glass with a dash of whiskey in the bottom.

She looks at it hesitantly. She's not a spirit drinker.

'Medicinal,' he says, seeing her reaction. 'Don't worry. It's not a gateway to living under a canal bridge with a bottle in your pocket.'

'I know,' Dani says. 'Sorry. I just don't drink a lot. My dad used to have the odd whiskey.'

She knocks it back. It burns her throat and her eyes start to water.

'Well now,' Professor Graham says, looking impressed. 'I doubt your dad drank it like that. Grab a seat, go on.'

Dani feels herself warming up and warming to him. She understands now why Theo is such a fan. She feels at ease. Like she can tell this man what's on her mind and he won't judge her.

She sits down gingerly on the couch. He rolls his chair over from behind the desk and sits across from her.

'I'm just grateful you agreed to see me, Professor Graham. I know how busy you are.'

'Declan, please.'

'Declan.' Dani says his name, even though it feels weird.

'And I was always going to make time for you,' he says. 'I know who you are. You're Theo's girlfriend.'

Dani feels a rush of emotion. Just hearing Theo's name spoken in such normal terms by somebody else who knows him, as though Theo is just next door, or in a lecture, and that she's known as Theo's girlfriend . . . it makes everything normal again, for a few moments.

'Yes,' she says, nodding eagerly. 'So, you know why I'm here. He's gone.'

Professor Graham – Declan, she reminds herself – looks confused.

'I know,' he says. 'I was hoping you might be here to tell me he's having second thoughts.'

'What?'

The momentary calm Dani felt is dissipating. She feels queasy and the whiskey she's just knocked back is not helping.

'Well, I assumed you'd spoken to him,' Declan says.

'No,' Dani replies. 'I haven't spoken to him in two weeks. He didn't . . .'

Dani can feel the now familiar lump in her throat and the sting in her eyes. The tears are coming.

'He didn't tell me he was leaving,' she manages to get out.

Declan's face fills with worry.

The door to his office opens and his secretary comes in with a tray of tea things. Even though Dani is looking at the floor, she can feel the secretary judging the situation, judging Dani. Theo has told her some of the female students in the research school are shameless in their pursuit of his mentor. Declan never entertains them, apparently, and still they come.

Theo has told Dani something else, too. Declan Graham has a male partner, something his legion of female followers would no doubt be devastated to learn.

Dani had asked Theo why the professor didn't just openly state his sexuality to avoid having to deal with hormonal, lustful ladies.

It's his business, Theo had shrugged. He's not secretive about it, he just doesn't broadcast it widely.

When the secretary departs, Declan reaches for the pot.

'I'd be useless without her,' he says, making tea without asking Dani's preference and putting it in her hands.

She clasps the mug like the life raft it is.

'I'm sorry,' Declan says. 'He didn't say anything to you at all before he left?'

Dani takes a deep breath.

'Not a call, not an email. I've been so worried. I – I went to the police.'

'The police?' Declan sounds shocked.

'Yes. But they didn't take it seriously because Theo sent an email to his father saying he was going travelling. But the email, it wasn't from Theo.'

'What do you mean?' Declan looks completely puzzled.

Dani takes a sip of the tea in an attempt to keep calm. It's sugared.

She knows that's meant to help but right now, it makes her want to gag.

'I mean, the email Theo sent was in English and Theo never wrote to his father in English.'

Declan sits forward, his elbows resting on his knees, his head in his hands.

'Dani, I'm not following. You think Theo hasn't gone travelling because he emailed his father in English, not French?'

'That's exactly what I'm saying.'

'But that doesn't make sense. Are you saying somebody else sent the email?'

'I know it's hard to fathom, but I know Theo,' Dani says. 'I don't know what's going on with him, but I do know he wouldn't email his father in English, and that he wouldn't just leave without telling me where he's going.'

And then it occurs to Dani – what did Declan mean when he said he was hoping Theo had changed his mind?

She doesn't have to ask him. He's already telling her.

'I do know what this course meant to him,' he says. 'Which is why I was so surprised when he told me he didn't want to take it any more. He said he was going to travel. He mentioned relatives in France—'

Dani's breath is sharp.

'He told *you* as well?' she says.

Declan nods. He looks embarrassed, almost in pain.

'I'm so sorry,' he says. 'I just assumed he'd told you, too. He spoke fondly of you and, well, I guess I'm surprised. That's why I thought you were here. To either tell me he'd changed his mind, or maybe ask for my help in convincing him to change it. I don't know what else to say. Honestly, I've been feeling a little disappointed in Theo. I shouldn't take it personally, it's not my place, but I expected more from him.'

Dani's shoulders slump.

All her theories, all her suppositions, fall flat in the face of what Declan has just told her.

Why would Theo tell his mentor and his father that he was leaving, but not her?

What did she do to deserve this?

'But, thinking about it afterwards,' Declan continues, 'I figured it was the pressure of the course and he was making a knee-jerk decision. That he might rethink it after a week or two. I tried calling him at the weekend, but his phone is off.'

'It's been off since he vanished,' Dani says, her voice leaden with defeat.

'I guess we just have to wait for him to contact us then,' Declan says. 'If he wants space, we have to give it to him. I know this can't be easy on you. You'd be well within your rights to tell him to, well, to tell him to fuck off when he gets back in touch.'

Dani places the tea on the floor and stands up. Declan stands too, uncertainty on his face.

'Is there anything I can do for you?' he asks. 'There's no need to rush off. If you want to talk—'

Dani shakes her head. She retrieves her coat. It's still wet. She doesn't care.

She pauses as her arm slips into one of the sleeves.

'You don't think . . . you don't think Theo would hurt himself, do you?' she asks, her voice small.

Declan's response is immediate and vehement.

'No,' he says. 'Absolutely not. That lad had his head completely screwed on. This is a blip, that's all.'

Dani nods. She wants to believe that.

She's zipping up her coat when something else occurs to her.

'You said you thought the pressure of the course was getting to him,' she says. 'I don't know why I'm surprised, but he never said he was struggling. I mean, he was on top of everything, wasn't he? He never stopped studying. And all his paper results were top of the class.'

'That *was* the pressure,' Declan says. 'Theo needed to stay on top and he told me it was getting to him. He said he felt overwhelmed. I should have taken that more seriously but I, well . . . I thought he was blowing things out of proportion.'

Dani frowns.

There's something niggling at her, something she can't quite articulate. And she realises what it is.

Theo once told her that one of the things his father hated was any admission of weakness. In his employees, in his business peers, in his own family. When Theo was seven, he'd sat his Grade 1 piano assessment and failed, caving under the pressure of the exam. At seven. His father sat with him in every piano lesson for a month afterwards, forcing Theo to play in front of him until he could do it without messing up. He went to the rescheduled assessment and watched Theo perform, and pass, the exam.

Theo had told Dani that even though he was only seven, it was a lesson that stayed with him for life.

Never, ever admit weakness.

Theo rarely reveals or admits when he's under pressure.

Pain shared is just pain distributed, that's what Theo likes to say.

She stares at Declan.

'So, he told you he was under pressure?' she says. 'He actually said that?'

Declan shrugs, his face full of emotion.

'Yes,' he says.

Dani swallows.

He's convincing, that's not in doubt.

But suddenly she's not sure that she can trust Declan Graham.

She just can't figure out why on earth he'd lie to her.

2024

Dani stands outside the provost's apartment building and inhales deeply.

A few minutes pass and then she realises somebody is watching her.

It's the man from the bar, the one Declan Graham came in with that first night. It's the first time she's seen his face properly, but she recognises the slant of his shoulders, his hair.

Why does he look so familiar?

Dani has no time to figure it out before he's passing her, on his way into the provost's.

'Sorry,' she says, stepping aside. 'Do I know you?'

He shrugs.

'Don't think so,' he says, in an American accent.

He stares at her. Dani feels her skin start to crawl. The man's face is perfectly pleasant – she'd actually describe him as good-looking – but his eyes are dark and unblinking and she can't help but feel like he knows something about her, like they've met before but it meant more to him than to Dani.

'There you are.'

She turns to see Colm, a look of concern on his face. He's holding out her scarf, the one she forgot to take when she left upstairs in a hurry.

The man nods at Colm and walks inside.

'Who is that?' Dani asks.

'Some guy from the pharma company we're working with. He's a bit . . . weird.'

'I got that, too.'

Dani stares at the door the man has just walked through.

Colm is still looking at her.

She shakes her head and turns to face him.

'You don't really know me,' he says. 'And I don't know you very well. But you seem like a nice woman and you also seem to be dealing with something at the moment. No judgement here. But, I can be a friend. If that's overstepping, tell me and I'll back off.'

Dani hesitates.

It's a second too long. Colm presses the scarf into her hand and holds up his own in a half-wave.

'I'll leave you be,' he says.

'I do,' she says.

He hesitates.

'I need a friend.'

'Okay then. Drink? I'm not going to lie, I'd planned to get hammered tonight, so if you don't fancy going back in, grand, but I need alcohol.'

'I'd like a drink. Is there somewhere quiet? Do you have anything in your apartment?'

Now Colm looks uncertain.

'Only because I don't want to talk in the bar,' she says. 'I swear, it's safe to be alone with me.'

Colm half smiles.

'I have a bottle of port and a bottle of champagne that's not even in the fridge. A gift from my parents for my master's.'

'Ten minutes in the freezer and it'll be good to go. Then we can move on to you getting gout.'

'Fair enough.'

Colm holds out his arm. Dani links it.

She doesn't feel anything sexual for this guy and she's fairly certain he doesn't think that way about her. But he's right; she could do with a friend.

Him, in fact.

Colm's apartment is more basic than Dani's, and smaller, but it's modern and tasteful, like all the apartments near the research school.

Dani sits on the grey L-shaped couch as Colm prepares some drinks and nibbles in the small kitchen that forms part of the open-plan living area. There's a breakfast island which doubles as the dining table, but he's told her to sit on the couch because he's more comfortable with her not able to see what he's doing.

'I'm fingers and thumbs in the kitchen,' he says, by way of explanation. 'If I think somebody is watching me, I break the corks in bottles, cut myself on cheese knives, drop stuff on the floor. And I really don't want you to see that because I abide by the five-second rule. Ten, if I bless it.'

Dani smiles.

She sits back against the cushions and looks around the room. His desk is the main feature; his computer is sitting on it along with stacks of papers. The desk is surrounded by piles of books – there are no bookshelves, so he's formed perilous Jenga-type stacks. She squints so she can read some of the names on the spines. A mix of academia and actual reading.

'*Nineteen Eighty-Four*?' she says.

'What can I say, I love rats.'

She laughs.

There's a pop, then Colm comes around the breakfast island. He hands her a wine glass filled with champagne.

'I wouldn't say chilled to the perfect degree but I read somewhere that you're not meant to serve expensive champagne too cold. But not room temperature. There's a middling point. Sorry about the glass, by the way.'

Colm takes his own glass from the island and clinks hers.

'*Sláinte*,' he says.

'*Sláinte*,' she replies.

To their health.

She sips the bubbles.

Colm, she realises as the liquid hits her tongue, comes from money. That or his parents spent all their savings on this bottle. And Dani made him put it in the freezer.

He returns to the kitchen and comes back with a board filled with cheese and crackers.

'So,' she says. 'Go on. Ask me stuff.'

'You never finished your degree here?' he says.

Dani sighs. She takes another sip of champagne then puts down her glass.

'No,' she says. 'I dropped out.'

'Because?'

'I don't know where to begin. I was going through a tough time. I'd met a guy. My first few weeks in St Edmund's. He was Declan's student, the one he mentioned. Theo.'

'Theo.' Colm starts to spread brie on a cracker. 'I'm guessing from how you pronounce it that he's French?'

'He was.'

Colm frowns. 'Tall. Dark-haired. Intense-looking.'

Dani is startled.

'Yes,' she says. 'Did you know him?'

Colm shakes his head.

'No, but I think I knew of him. I saw him a few times, with Declan. They seemed to get on really well.' Colm blushes a little. 'I was probably jealous. Both of Theo and his relationship with the big man.'

'Most people were jealous of Theo. He had that effect.'

There's a moment of silence. Dani lets Theo fill her head. For a moment, she can smell him, hear him, taste him.

Then she gives herself a shake.

'Things didn't go to plan?' Colm says.

Dani exhales heavily.

'No. Not exactly.'

Dani picks up her glass. The bubbles are still rising gently but there's no massive fizz, no extravagant froth. There never is with the most expensive vintages.

'You fall hard when you're young.'

Dani nods.

'Anyway,' Dani says. 'I struggled with the end of the relationship and there was stuff happening at home and I realised I needed to take a break. I guess coming back here now is dredging up a lot. I couldn't turn it down, it's such a huge opportunity lecturing in Edmund's, but . . . yeah. I've got baggage.'

Colm leans over and clinks her glass again.

'Baggage schmaggage,' he says. 'Look at you. We all hit bumps when we're young. You got over yours, got back on the field, and now you're here, with a job in one of the most prestigious colleges in the world. You're doing all right for yourself.'

Dani smiles. His positive attitude is infectious.

'What about you?' she asks. 'I'm being self-centred. I haven't asked you anything about yourself. Why medicine? Why research? Why here?'

'It's the best. I was brought up to be the best. My dad's a surgeon. My mother is a gynae. I don't know if I ever thought there was another route for me.'

'But you didn't want to practise? You went into the research end.'

Colm shrugs.

'I guess it was pick something in the family business, but I didn't want to pick the exact same thing, if that makes sense?'

Dani nods. It makes total sense.

'No girlfriends?' she asks. 'Or boyfriend?'

'Are you going to prey on me if I say I'm single?' he says.

'When you weren't looking, I stuck something in your glass.'

He picks it up.

'Well, it tastes the same. It smells the same. It looks the same. You know they've made most of the drugs used for date rape now blue-hued so they tinge the drink? So, if you've managed to drug me with an odourless, tasteless, colourless concoction, I've got a multinational I'd like to introduce you to.'

Dani laughs.

'I'm single,' Colm says. 'By choice. I love what I do and I've been really bloody ignorant to every girlfriend I've ever had, so it feels like I should keep my focus on this until I'm happy to share my time. Rather than be a dick.'

'Very sensible and very considerate. I've had a few boyfriends over the years who could have benefitted from the same approach.'

'You weren't the one breaking hearts?'

Dani shakes her head. It's a small lie. She's more like Colm than she'd care to admit. Career focused and not much else.

There's the sound of a phone ringing. The ringtone has been set to 'Ride of the Valkyries'. Colm looks around and spots his mobile on the breakfast island.

He stands and picks it up, frowning at the caller ID.

'Shitting hell,' he says. 'It's my dad.'

He looks at Dani.

'Do you think my apartment is bugged and he knows I froze the champagne?'

She shrugs, smiling.

'Would you mind if I take this?'

'Not at all.'

Colm walks in the direction of what Dani imagines is the bedroom.

'Help yourself to anything,' he says, as he leaves.

Dani nods. She listens as he moves down the small corridor and hears him answering with, 'Hi there.'

Then she hears a door close.

Dani stands up quickly. She walks over to the desk in the corner of the room.

This is what she's been waiting for since the moment Colm let her in the door.

She touches the keyboard and hopes against hope the screen is not password-protected.

Who protects their computer access when they live alone?

75

The screen comes to life.

Dani glances over her shoulder. The bedroom door still hasn't opened.

She looks at the computer desktop.

There are folders running down both sides.

Personal folders: tax year, photos, family stuff.

Then there are the academic folders.

Dani scans them quickly. Exams, tutorial notes, class prep, research methods, news items . . .

Her eyes land on the one she's looking for.

DG.

This one, she knows, is password-protected.

She knows because she's been told.

It's a shared folder from the School of Medical Research.

Dani closes her eyes and concentrates.

Then she types in a sequence of letters and numbers.

The file opens.

A list of Word documents appears. She uses the mouse to pull down the sidebar. There are hundreds of documents.

Dani sighs.

Nobody said it would be easy.

She opens the first one. It's just an article, copied and pasted from a medical journal.

She opens the next file.

It's an email from DG.

Declan Graham.

She starts to read.

She doesn't hear the bedroom door along the corridor open.

★

When Colm comes back into the room, Dani is standing at the desk, holding one of his books in her hand.

As soon as she heard his footsteps in the corridor, she quickly shut down the computer screen. Were he to touch it now, it would come to life, along with the file she's opened. But if she can keep him occupied and away from it, within a few minutes she knows the files will lock again. She's been told that's how the medical school's research files work.

'I don't know how you understand anything in these journals,' she says.

She flicks open a page.

'Gossypiboma. What?'

'Ah, yes. The medical term for when an item is accidentally left inside a patient during surgery.'

'*Whoopsies* wouldn't have done it?'

'It's important the patient never hears their doctor say whoopsies.'

They both laugh.

Another paper catches Dani's eye.

'Progressive neurological disorders,' she says. 'Like, MS?'

'Yep. Parkinson's, Huntington's, motor neurone, Alzheimer's. It's a long list.'

Dani looks at the other papers. There are several on the same topic.

'And this is what you specialise in,' she says.

'In one area in particular. Alzheimer's.'

A shiver runs through Dani.

'What do you know about it?' she asks.

'As much as there is to know,' he replies, shrugging. 'You know what Alzheimer's is, right?'

Dani nods. She's trying not to display any emotion, but it's difficult.

'Everybody does,' Colm says. 'But what doctors have spent the last few decades trying to figure out is what causes it. We believe now that it's an abnormal build-up of proteins around brain cells.'

Colm's face lights up as he's speaking. This is something he's passionate about, she can tell.

Dani's obviously not doing a very good job of looking dispassionate because Colm pauses, looking at her curiously.

'Are you okay?' he asks. 'I get carried away when I start talking about this stuff. It probably sounds like double Dutch to you.'

Dani shakes her head.

'I'm interested,' she says. 'I'm familiar with the disease.'

Colm looks surprised, then his face fills with compassion.

'I'm sorry to hear that,' he says. 'Family?'

Dani nods. She's hoping Colm won't ask her to be specific and he doesn't. She's grateful. She really doesn't want to open up that can of pain tonight. She's dealing with enough.

'We don't have to talk about what I do,' he says gently. 'But, if you thought it would help, I could explain the disease to you? The college is working with leading researchers in the field. We're at the fore of, well, honestly, trying to find a way of preventing it. A way of slowing it down, at least. We're in the middle of something very exciting, as it happens. That's what the clinical trial is about.'

'I'd like to hear about it,' she says quickly. 'I'm not sure I'll understand it all, but I think it would help. Knowing what it is. In my experience, most doctors tend to describe it in a way that . . .'

She trails off, not really knowing how to finish that sentence.

'Infantilises the patient?' Colm offers.

'Exactly that. *Oh, you're getting a bit forgetful, it's just old-timers.* That sort of thing.'

'I know,' he says. 'It doesn't help. There's something reassuring about being able to discuss the actual medical terms, knowing what's potentially causing it. Because if we know what causes it—'

'You can find a way to cure it.'

'Exactly,' he says. 'And that might not be as far away as some people think.'

Dani looks surprised.

'I can talk to you about it,' Colm adds. 'But the real expert is Declan Graham. You should talk to him. We're lucky to have him.'

Dani forces a smile.

Theo used to say the same thing.

2014

It's the first time Dani has gone home since Theo disappeared. She doesn't want to face the inevitable questions but it's Easter and she hates leaving her mother alone on the major holidays. Cora could go to Dani's uncle and aunt, Tom and Leanne, but Dani knows that Cora has never wanted to be too reliant on her brother-in-law's family.

What makes it worse is that Theo had started joining them for these events. Their little family of two had expanded and he was a welcome addition.

Cora has always liked Dani's friends and even her previously short-lived boyfriends. But she had a special place in her heart for Theo. Dani realised that when, the previous Christmas, Cora had asked Theo to sit at the head of the table, something that both amused and terrified him.

'Don't be nervous, honey,' she'd told him. 'It's just so I know somebody is in charge of carving when I get too drunk to do it. That's you, by the way. You're in charge now.'

Theo had laughed and saw to the small turkey with gusto.

He loved Dani's house, even though he'd grown up in what Dani realised quickly was essentially a chateau.

It was a big, expensive house, Theo had said. *You and your mother have a home. And I'd have swapped all the chateaus and chauffeured limos and ski trips and catered dinners for a home.*

Dani thinks of that now as she sticks rosemary skewers into the lamb shoulder.

Then she hastily wipes the tears from her eyes.

Her mother comes into the kitchen with the pot of potatoes she's been peeling in the sitting room while watching TV. Every Easter, Cora finds some old movie about the crucifixion, usually about three hours long and utterly melodramatic. Dani's mother is not even religious, it's just part of her Easter tradition.

She places the potatoes on the counter, then wraps her arms around Dani's waist from behind, and gives her a squeeze.

'I miss him too, love,' she says.

It's all Dani can do not to sob.

She pats her mother's hand, then finishes the lamb and places it in the middle oven. The kitchen is tiny but they renovated it years ago, using the lump sum paid out by Dani's father's job after he died. A health and safety accident, they called it. He'd been stacking boxes with a forklift in the factory he worked in when the pile had toppled, sending the forklift on its side and leaving her father trapped beneath it.

He was fifty years of age. Cora was only forty-eight, his daughter sixteen.

Cora had wanted to keep all the money for Dani's education but Dani had insisted the bulk of it be used to bring their little home up to scratch. Her parents had bought the two-up, two-down when they'd first married, and while it was in a terrific location, close to the city centre, it was quite dated and they'd never been in a position to do anything about that. Dani got a weekend job in a bar in town, and worked some evenings too, and between that and her student grant, St Edmund's was a manageable option without having to use her dad's legacy.

Dani sits at the table across from Cora, who pours her a cup of tea. She insists on making tea in a pot. Cora has no time for one-cup-teabag wastage, as she calls it.

'Drink that now,' she says. 'That lamb will be hours. I'll stick some carrots in with it in a while. Let them slow-cook.'

Dani adds milk and sips the tea, realising it's the first thing she's had all day. She's had a knot in her stomach since this morning.

'So,' her mother says, 'I assume if you'd heard anything, you'd have told me by now.'

A week after Theo left, Dani had called her mother to tell her what had happened. Cora had listened to all Dani's theories and she was equally suspicious when Dani then told her how Theo had allegedly told Declan Graham that he was under pressure.

Can't see Theo saying that, Cora had said. *Not Theo.*

'There's been nothing,' Dani says now. 'But, um, I've been thinking about something.'

'What?'

'I'm considering going to France. To that village where his aunt lives. Le Muy.'

'You think he might be there?'

'I don't know. He was looking for a room there so, maybe. I have to do something. Sitting here, waiting, it's killing me.'

Cora is watching her with concern.

'Can you afford to go?'

'My budget has been good all year and I haven't exactly been going out these last few weeks,' Dani says. What she doesn't add is that the money she saved up last summer so she wouldn't have to work during college term has stretched much further than she thought because Theo always insisted on buying things. She resisted, of course she did, but when he just arrived with things for her room, bread and milk and toothpaste and so on, saying he practically lived there too . . . well, it was hard to stop him.

'I've looked at the flights and they're not too expensive,' she says. 'And if I just go over for a couple of days . . . I can get cheap lodging, as well.'

Cora looks troubled.

'What?' Dani asks.

'Will you be safe, travelling on your own like that?'

'Of course I will. It's only France.'

Dani shakes her head, bemused. Cora still looks like there's something on her mind.

'What is it really, Mam?' Dani asks.

Cora sighs.

'I guess there's a little part of me that worries Theo doesn't want to be found,' Cora says. 'And if you do find him, it could be very upsetting for you.'

Dani stares at Cora.

'Mam, that's exactly what I want to happen. Don't you get it? I have to think that. I don't care if he's angry when I find him. I can live with that. What I can't live with is thinking something bad has happened to him. He can hate me, he can be the biggest bastard in the world and I just never realised. But I need him to be . . .'

'Alive?' Cora says what Dani can't.

Dani bites the inside of her cheek. The stress and fear she's felt for the last few weeks has become routine to her, but hearing it aloud, saying it aloud – that she's worried Theo is dead – it's unbearable.

Cora clasps her daughter's hand.

'I understand, love. And I really hope you're right. I've never

83

wanted to be so wrong about a person as I do about Theo. I want him to be a selfish so-and-so. I want to be really angry at him. Because I can't believe the young man I know would do this to you willingly.'

Dani is grateful for the squeeze her mother is giving her hand. It's the only thing keeping her tethered.

'But I'm also worried that if something bad has happened to him . . . it could be dangerous for you.'

Dani shivers a little.

'I'm not in danger, Mam.'

'You said Theo's father has money. People with that sort of money, sometimes they're targeted, Dani. No, don't roll your eyes at me. This isn't a world we know. But I know of it. I read enough, I watch enough. And you said he's not concerned about his son. That doesn't sit right with me. What if he knows more and he isn't telling you, to keep you safe? Isn't that a possibility?'

'What, like Theo has been kidnapped or something? Well, if that's what's happened, I still need to know.'

Cora watches her daughter for a few seconds, then looks away.

She glances over at the cooker.

'I'll stick some carrots in with that lamb in a while,' she says. 'Let them slow-cook.'

Dani frowns.

'You already said that.'

'Did I? Jesus! I'm getting old.'

Old, my eye, Dani thinks. Her mother is just trying to change the subject.

Cora gazes out the window, lost in thought. Then she spots something.

'Sugar. There's that tart out in her back garden again.'

'Her name is Maureen, Mam.'

'Did I ever tell you about that time she practically pushed your father's face into her cleavage at her New Year's Eve party?'

'Many times.'

Cora stands and kisses Dani on the top of her head. She leaves the kitchen and goes out to the back garden. Dani watches her mother talking to their neighbour over the low fence and she knows in about five minutes' time, she's going to have to go next door for a nip of sherry with Maureen.

Dani hates bloody sherry.

Theo would have loved the sherry. He would have loved their crazy, flirty neighbour. He'd have loved the lamb. He'd have loved everything about today.

Maybe Cora is on to something. Maybe Theo's father does know more. But it doesn't matter if he's trying to keep her out of it.

Dani is going to do everything in her power to find Theo.

2024

There are several bars in Rathlow village and Dani has been in most of them, but she's pretty sure she's not been in this one. Or if she was, twenty years ago, it's had a makeover since.

The waitress sits her in a reserved snug in the back. The tables are oak, the sofas a soft leather. There's a single tall candle in the centre of each table and the waitress puts a wine list in front of Dani that starts at eleven euros per glass of wine.

Definitely not student-friendly.

She asks for a Pinot Grigio and reads the news headlines on her phone as she waits. She's taken all the social media apps off. In fact, she's deleted her online presence permanently.

Instead, she has various news apps. She's never been more informed about the world.

She's absorbed in an article on Google Pocket about jaywalking, when he enters the snug and sits across from her.

George O'Shea looks irritated, and that's hard for him to do because he has one of those smiling faces that means even when he's angry, he's so inoffensive-looking, it's hard for him to convey it.

'Hey there,' she says.

He swipes at the raindrops in his wavy dark hair and sighs heavily.

'You've been taking the piss,' he says. 'Ten times I phoned.'

'I know. And I told you that I'd reach out when I had something to report. I couldn't just answer my phone every time. I've been doing stuff. Giving lectures. Immersing myself in college life. Being a professor.'

'I needed to check you were okay. This *isn't* a usual operation.'

'I know how unusual it is. I told you that when *you* insisted that I take it.'

The waitress appears.

'Would you like to order a drink?' she asks George.

He glances at the menu.

'Holy fuck,' he says. 'Did you milk this wine from the tit of a golden goose?'

'What?' the waitress replies.

'He'll have a Malbec,' Dani interjects.

The waitress departs hastily.

'Eleven quid. That's scandalous. We should call the Guards.'

'Why do you insist on sounding like a stingy old man? You know it's on expenses.'

'Expenses are meant to be submitted at normal rates. A fiver for a pint. That sort of thing. This isn't an episode of *Succession*. Fuck. We're meeting in McDonald's next time.'

'You said a bar, I picked a bar.'

George gives her a *you're still taking the piss* look.

'How are you?' she asks. 'How's the wife?'

'Still ex and still screwing me from a height. Her lawyer wants me to cede my half of the house and give her alimony in perpetuity.'

'Alimony? I thought that was for kids. You don't have any kids.'

'Au contraire. I married a child.'

'She does realise you're on a civil service salary, right?'

The waitress arrives with the Malbec. George drinks half of it in one gulp.

Eleven-euro wine, two-euro wine, it wouldn't matter to George.

'She doesn't care about the money, Dani. She cares about hurting me.'

Dani studies him. He sounds glib but she knows he's in pain. He'd told her at last year's Christmas party he still hadn't gotten over the shock that he was getting divorced. They'd been childhood sweethearts and, sure, they'd probably married too young, but he hadn't thought that at the time. The relationship had become strained in their thirties. When his wife hit forty, she decided she wanted to get something out of her system. That something being an affair with a work colleague. George had seen it as a line crossed. She expected him to forgive her, and when he couldn't do it, she decided to hurt him on the way out.

'I'm sorry,' Dani says.

'Not your fault.'

'I know, but I mean it. She did a shitty thing. I'm sorry she's making it shittier.'

He shrugs.

Dani considers giving him a hug but thinks better of it. She's always been careful not to be physical in any way with George.

Despite the fact she's had a crush on him for quite some time.

'So,' he says. 'How are you getting on?'

'I've successfully targeted one of our suggested contacts. Colm Ahern.'

'Declan Graham's little PhD prodigy?'

'Yep.'

'How did you land him?'

'I screwed him a few times.'

'Dani.'

'I'm kidding. We're *friends*. Same age, two newish faculty members, plus my charm and good looks . . . Anyway, I had access to his computer last night and to the research school shared file.'

'Did the password work?'

'Yes. By the way, how did we get all those in-house passwords—'

'Stop asking the same questions.'

'You'll tell me one day. Anyway, he came back into the room before I could look at it properly. But that's just his home computer. I'll need to try to access the one in the lab, too. I just need a little time. Unless you're going to let me recruit him.'

'Time is what we're short on.' George sighs deeply. 'Turner Pharma is pushing the schedule. This trial could all be over in a matter of months.'

'Months?' Dani blinks rapidly. 'I thought we had the college year, at least?'

'We did. That's what we thought, anyway. But Turner is saying the Phase 3 data so far is consistent with the previous two phases and that results are so compelling, it would be unethical to hold back on the drug's release. They've told the FDA they're confident they'll be presenting the full results in the New Year.'

'And that's not ringing any alarm bells?'

'What do you think?'

Dani lifts her glass. She takes a sip; it does nothing for her. In fact, the liquid is bitter on her tongue. She pushes the glass away.

'I can't do it,' she says, looking up. 'I'm ingratiating myself as fast as I can, but I'll need help to make that timeline.'

George observes her.

'Such as?'

'Like I said – either a recruit from within or our whistle-blower.

I presume they're the one who got me the password for those trial folders and they know what's going on.'

George shakes his head.

'It's a non-starter,' he says. 'They've given us what they can. It's up to us now.'

Dani bites back her frustration.

'This is impossible,' she says.

George eyes her.

'I'll keep going.' She sighs.

'Good,' George replies. 'I have every faith in you. But next time, answer your phone when I call.'

'If I can. That photo, by the way?'

George shifts awkwardly. She could sense there was something more from the moment he sat down.

'You took a picture of the back of his head.'

'Yes, but I've seen him from the front now as well. And so have you, because you've been on that campus a few times.'

'How do you know?'

'The other day, dodging around the corner before I caught sight of you?'

'I'm worried about you.'

'You sent me in to be undercover. You stalking me could blow my cover.'

'Like I said, I'm worried about you. And his name is Ron Perry. Former LAPD.'

'A cop?' Dani says, surprised.

'Former. He works for Turner now. Security.'

Dani frowns.

'Why do they need a security guy in St Edmund's?'

George shrugs.

'I don't know. I doubt he's there to protect Sharona Davies. She's just a cog.'

'Something is up,' Dani says. 'Do you think they're on to us? On to the task force, I mean?'

'No. I think they have invested hundreds of millions, if not more, in this drug passing this trial and they're not taking any chances.'

Dani mulls on that.

'I feel like . . .' Dani trails off for a moment. 'I feel like I know him. Ron Perry. Like I've seen him before.'

George studies her.

'Don't get on his radar,' he says. 'We don't want them to find you suspicious. It's enough you've made friends with this Colm guy. That will have been noted.'

Dani nods.

George drains his wine, makes a disgusted face, and stands up.

'Give me one thing,' Dani says quickly.

'What?'

'I want Declan Graham's file.'

'That's not part of your remit. You have one task. Try to get access to the original trial data.'

'I know,' she says. 'But this guy is at the top of the pyramid, isn't he? If he's that clever, he's going to be careful about who he shares the complete trial data with. Maybe I need to target him directly.'

George considers her. She can tell he's suspicious of the ask. She meets his eye.

'I'll think about it,' he says. 'But you need to remember, your role is just one part of all this. An essential part, but specific. Stay in your lane, MacLochlainn. You won't be bringing down Declan Graham. You just need to get us those files.'

'And Cecelia Vargas? Anything else on her death?'

'It's still being recorded as accidental.'

'It wasn't,' she says.

'I know.'

George leaves.

He's not even bothered to pay.

Sometimes, she doesn't know what she sees in him.

She was fucking crazy to accept this job.

October 2023

Garda Síochána Headquarters, Dublin
Interpol NCB presentation room

Dani's coffee is lukewarm but she can't taste it anyway. She's smothering with a cold and hasn't been able to taste anything in about three days. It's a miracle she's in work at all, and when the notice for this presentation landed in her emails, she was determined to avoid it. The subject title alone gave her shivers.

But most of her colleagues seem to be intrigued, if the amount of people in the room is anything to go by.

It's the break from the norm that's appealing to them. Interpol presentations are usually about organised crime and anybody who's worked on that front becomes very weary, very quickly, of that Sisyphean challenge.

An interjurisdictional force tackling big pharma corruption is something different. Something potentially rewarding.

But Dani isn't interested.

She's only there because she's been ordered to go.

She could have played the illness card but . . . it was George who'd done the ordering. And she has a terrible soft spot for him.

Dani grabs a seat near the front of the hall. She spots George standing at the side of the room and gives him a small, belligerent wave. *I'm here, see. Dragged myself from my sick bed.* He waves back. He looks smug.

He's her immediate boss since she transferred to the international crime unit, but they've known each other since Garda training college. He was her superior there too.

He's a good-looking man but, sadly for her, he's also a happily married man. Has been since his early twenties. Childhood sweethearts. Everyone else finds it ridiculous. Dani finds it romantic.

She's had a few boyfriends over the years but not one of them appealed to her as a long-term prospect, and if she was honest, she's never looked for anything serious.

She and Theo, they could have married.

She shakes her head, dispelling the *what if*.

Also dispelling the *what if* when it comes to George.

He's older than her. He doesn't see her like that.

He has a wife.

It's never going to happen. Much as she'd like it to. It's probably why she fancies him so much. The knowledge it just can't go there.

A woman takes to the podium and smiles at them. Dani recognises her from previous presentations. Lucia Russo. An Italian Interpol agent stationed in Dublin for a few years now as part of the National Central Bureau.

They're all a little in love with Lucia.

Dani watches with admiration as Lucia tucks her long chestnut hair behind her ears and rolls up the sleeves of her shirt. A woman that beautiful should be aware everybody is watching her every move, but Lucia's gestures are entirely lacking in self-consciousness.

'Jesus, it's warm in here,' she says into the microphone. 'I don't think we were expecting quite so many bodies. Who knew pharma could be so sexy? You guys know this isn't about Viagra, right?'

The laughs are louder than the comment warrants. Everything Lucia does is charming, but the accent – Italian mixed with Irish – is also endearing.

'So,' she says, 'let me begin. You know what we are looking at today. Organised corruption and criminal activity undertaken by big pharma. Now, you might wonder how, after several large scandals, pharmaceuticals are still managing to work around the many, many laws and regulations that are meant to police their industry. The truth is, these multinational corporations are better at circumventing the rule of law than most of the gangs at the top of the organised-crime food chart.'

Lucia turns and points a clicker at the screen set up behind her. It fills with a list of corporation names. Dani recognises most of them. Several from the backs of drug packets she has in her medicine cabinet, others because she's heard about them on the news.

There are figures beside each company name.

Settlements.

Lucia points a red light at each one as she describes them.

'Limvest: $300 million in fines after they misbranded a drug as a treatment for nausea in cancer patients. Their drug contributed to 594 deaths worldwide before it was discovered to rapidly increase the growth of cancerous cells.'

There are audible murmurs of disgust in the room. Lucia points to the next name.

'Matley: $600 million settlement after 20,000 complaints were filed in a class action suit against their clotting factor drug. The drug caused internal bleeding in most of its recipients, many of whom were haemophiliacs.

'Cusher. Their drug was labelled to treat psychotic episodes. It caused heart attacks in 300 patients, but not before several of them had suffered severe psychosis and, in some cases, physically harmed members of their own families. Cusher was fined $200 million. It spent $100 million alone on its marketing campaign for the drug, which included flying the doctors who prescribed their product to the Canaries for a little holiday.'

Dani takes a deep breath. Everybody in the room is utterly transfixed by the information.

'A litany of pain brought about by the very companies who claim they want to take care of us,' Lucia says. 'But, as we know, these companies are mainly about profits, and like any industry invested in profit-making, they will seek ways to generate money. Sometimes, at any cost. Which is why the State often has to intervene in drug development and safety issues. I think I will give you a little background into the sort of money we're talking about so you can understand me better, yes?'

Lucia doesn't wait for any replies. She has everybody in the room enthralled.

She clicks the next slide. It contains a graph of numbers that makes Dani's head spin.

'What you need to know is that from conception to market, a drug can cost a pharma company anything from $160 million to $2 billion,' Lucia says. 'You can imagine that when a company has invested this much, it is desperate for the drug to become a sellable commodity. But just because the company wants to sell it, doesn't mean they can. They need to prove it literally does what it will say on the tin. That is when clinical trials kick in.'

Lucia introduces the next slide.

'Sometimes,' she says, 'a company can get away with one clinical trial for a new drug. That's usually when there's a pressing need for the drug – as in, it is deemed essential by national governments. Usually in the event of, for example, a global pandemic. Like Covid.

'However, in normal circumstances, a drug must undergo three trials. Big pharma organises the trials, funds the trials and, sometimes, cherry-picks the data they want from the trials. And governments are aware of that.'

Lucia looks out to make sure everyone is following.

An officer a couple of seats down from Dani puts his hand up.

'Why don't governments run their own trials, if they don't trust the pharmaceutical companies to do it? I mean, it has to be cheaper than the amount of healthcare issues a bad drug throws up and the litigation that follows?'

Lucia holds her hands out in an *it makes sense* way.

'They do,' she says. 'But big pharma outstrips and outspends them. In America in 2014, big pharma paid for approximately 6,500 trials. The National Institute of Health paid for just over 1,000. You can see the disparity. Governments just do not have the finances to conduct independent studies for the amount of drugs out there.'

Dani is on tenterhooks.

She suspects she knows what's coming.

She, more than most in the room, has already dipped her toe into this arena.

'So,' Lucia continues, 'people are more and more aware of the potential for corruption. Paying off researchers, skewing trials, and promoting drugs for off-label use – that's when a drug is approved for one treatment but actively encouraged for use in a treatment it's not approved for.'

Lucia waits for them all to nod in agreement, which they do.

'What happens then,' Lucia says, 'when a pharma company gets an independent university involved in running their clinical trials? This would add reinforcement that the drug is safe, yes? The gold standard. The FDA in the States would probably accept the trial results as an honest representation and pass it. Doctors would feel confident that this wasn't a drug trialled in-house and they'd be more inclined to prescribe it.'

People are interested again now. They sense an angle coming.

'Everybody would know and accept that the college would not undertake the trials for free,' Lucia continues. 'They would seek expenses. But not profit-making expenses. They would cover the time of their researchers, but the real gift to the college would be the involvement in a trial that could be potentially ground-breaking and educational. Sounds like a win for everyone, yes?'

Lucia pulls up the next slide.

Dani's heart almost stops.

It's a photo of St Edmund's, her old university.

The building that changed her entire life.

The building that made her join the police.

She turns and stares at George.

Everyone is watching Lucia, but he's watching her.

'St Edmund's,' Lucia says. 'One of Ireland's most – if not *the* most – prestigious universities. St Edmund's School of Medical Research has won awards for its in-depth analyses. It has even played a part – in an independent, not-for-profit capacity – in the development of some of the world's most revolutionary new drugs.'

Lucia looks at the slide for a few moments.

'Ireland has a long-established, excellent reputation in healthcare,' she says. 'Its universities, en masse, are respected and renowned for their highly educated graduates and transparent, effective research procedures.'

Lucia pauses for effect.

'But now,' she says, 'we believe this university is being used to deliver results in a clinical trial on behalf of the Turner Pharma global group that may be based on corrupted data. And by that, I mean the college is corrupting the data at Turner's request.'

Dani's chest is tight.

'A number of incidents have drawn us to look closer at this situation,' Lucia continues. 'A few months ago, an email was received by the Irish Medical Board which didn't mean a lot at the time. A nurse on a geriatric ward had noted two deaths in patients who had both been prescribed a new trial drug.'

Lucia takes a breath.

'The nurse was involved in a fatal accident on the same evening that the email was sent, which would lead us to believe, if she was targeted, that those responsible for her death didn't realise she'd already managed to bring her concerns to the authorities.'

The atmosphere in the room changes. They're all reaching the same conclusion.

'Even though they failed to silence her, the nurse's concerns weren't treated with the seriousness they warranted. The two individual deaths she'd highlighted were both recorded as originating from different causes, so the medical board didn't consider the matter worth investigating. Story over.'

Lucia leans into the microphone.

'But then, two months ago, we were contacted by a whistle-blower who has inside knowledge of the clinical trial Turner Pharma is undertaking with St Edmund's. The trial of a drug that both of that nurse's patients were in receipt of before they died. And our whistle-blower asserted that the trial taking place right now is recording inaccurate information and, therefore, is illegal. Those patients should never have been on those drugs. Nobody should.'

Dani can barely breathe.

'This war against big pharma has to be fought one battle at a time,' Lucia says. 'And in St Edmund's, we think we have a battle we can actually win.'

2024

Dani knows what her real job in St Edmund's is, but to maintain her cover, she needs to make sure she's performing as a lecturer.

The Garda undercover unit did an excellent job of faking Dani's qualifications. A degree in history in Glasgow, followed by a master's in Queens. A few years' lecturing in Queens, then back to Glasgow. The paper trail is impeccable and the contact numbers for her employment references go straight to a designated line in Garda HQ. But Dani's team went further. They secured cooperation from trusted contacts in all three universities, just in case somebody wanted to do a little more digging.

All new professors are assessed at the end of their first term and so far, she thinks she's hitting all the right notes. But it won't be her teaching methods that are ultimately scrutinised. It will be her students' Christmas exam results. And her class is only as strong as its weakest link, which is, in this instance, extremely weak.

She's in her office, rereading Stephen Mulligan's latest paper, when he arrives for his scheduled appointment ten minutes late.

'Sorry, Prof,' he says. 'Got stuck into a workout in the gym. Totally lost track of time, then had to shower so I didn't come here ponging.'

He flashes her what she suspects he thinks is his most disarming smile. Dani doesn't return it. She indicates with a nod of her head that he should take the seat on the other side of the desk.

She's met kids like Stephen Mulligan before. And she says 'kid' even though he's twenty. It's going to be a long number of years before he makes the leap to adulthood, if ever.

Stephen, Dani suspects, has had the best of everything. Fee-paying schools, a large allowance from Mummy and Daddy, a fancy house, nice holidays to the Caribbean in the summer, skiing in the winter. He's popular with females and his male peers alike. He works out in a way that's given him that odd-shaped triangular body – muscular on top, skinny legs. He's cocky but thinks he's charming enough to pull it off.

She can't fathom why Stephen chose a history degree. She can only imagine that he was expected to go to the best college – that he's always been bright, but not clever enough for the more demanding subjects like maths or medicine. But maybe he has a good memory and got away with cramming dates and facts in school-level history.

At third-level, he's expected to have a more analytical and nuanced perspective when analysing historical scenarios.

Stephen wants a degree he can use to coast into a job, probably in his dad's or one of Daddy's friends' firms.

He glances now at the paper in front of Dani, a thinly disguised smirk on his face.

'Let me guess,' he says. 'Too controversial?'

Dani sits back in her chair. She resists the urge to cross her arms; it would only betray her hostility.

'Why do you say that?' she asks.

'Well, it's not very woke, is it? I haven't jumped to Oscar Wilde's defence. I just thought I'd come at it from left field. Something original.'

'You assert that Wilde is responsible for his own downfall.'

'Yeah. Look, I do say up top that it isn't a reflection of my personal beliefs. I've no problem with homosexuality or bi- or asexuality or whatever. Live and let live. But history is all "blame the Marquess of Queensbury", "blame the British press", "blame the laws of the time", "blame the defence attorney". It's ignoring the obvious, isn't it?'

'Is it?'

'Wilde married so he'd fit in, and then he lived a life of decadence. He pursued a man fifteen, sixteen years younger than himself. A love that dare not speak its name, but Wilde was speaking it by shagging everything around him.'

'Okay. Let's leave aside what some might say is the blatant homophobia in that statement. As you say in your paper, he was advised by his friends on multiple occasions to go to France. Where homosexuality was decriminalised.'

'Exactly.'

Stephen is starting to relax now. Dani suspects he thought he was coming in for a bollocking, but now thinks he's going to be told his essay is unusual, and he reckons he can support it.

'All of that is an interesting take,' Dani says. 'And God knows, I believe in looking at all the angles when it comes to history. There's never just one version of any event.'

'Yeah, right? That's what I believe too.'

Stephen nods eagerly, thrilled with himself.

·'So did the original author of this essay,' Dani says. 'Charles Parr.'

'What?'

Confusion for a moment. But she can almost see the second Stephen realises he's been rumbled and starts to get ready to defend himself.

'You lifted it off the web,' Dani says. 'Look, don't bother denying it. I recognised it.'

Coincidentally, it was one of the ones she'd read recently. When she'd been studying her way back into the course.

'And even if I hadn't, you must know that there's software now that lets you run an essay against a programme so we can see if it's been lifted word for word or just plagiarised in spirit.'

Stephen's mouth has twisted from a smirk into a sullen grimace. Now he looks like a toddler who's been caught with his fingers in the sweet cupboard.

'You didn't give us enough time for the assignment,' he says. 'We're all under pressure, you know.'

'You're in the second year of a four-year degree. It only gets more pressurised.'

'That's not much help.'

Dani sighs. In the wider scheme of things, Stephen is not her problem. Or her responsibility. But she swore when she took this job that she wouldn't let any of the students suffer in their education. She felt confident she could do that. Dani never stopped loving history; she never stopped reading it, on her own time. Her lesson plans and coursework are all following a standard year programme as signed off by the head of department. She's neither pushing her students too hard nor letting them off easy.

For any professor, Stephen Mulligan would be a problem.

But he does have an advantage. Dani doesn't want any extra attention on her teaching or her class. She needs to deal with this in-house, in a way that doesn't ring any alarm bells.

'I understand,' she says. 'The course gets tougher in year two, you're correct. We've moved beyond the macro into the micro, and that level of detail and examination and the personal thought required is difficult. But this isn't going to fly.'

Dani taps the essay.

'I'm happy to give you a second shot,' she says. And she means it, though the way he's looking at her, she'd prefer to give him a smack in the ear.

'You want me to write another paper?' he asks incredulously.

'You didn't write this one,' she says. She really can't believe the gumption of this guy. Most students would have fallen on their swords at this point. They'd be begging for mercy.

'For when?' he says.

'Same timeline as last time. End of the week.'

He sighs.

'Fine,' he says.

'I think you mean "thank you, Professor, and it won't happen again".'

He looks like he wants to tell her to fuck off, but instead he manages to choke out a thank you.

Dani watches him go.

He's going to be trouble.

He's just left her office when she gets a text. It's from George.

Ran BG on Ron Perry, the security guy. He's bad news. Steer clear. Enforcer for Turner.

Dani frowns at his words.

She knows what enforcers are capable of. She's met them before. She's seen them protect their employers at all costs.

So why is a man who may be capable of anything on the grounds of St Edmund's?

Turner would only send him if they felt their plans were under threat.

Dani sits back uneasily.

She believes her cover is safe. So, if Perry is here to watch somebody, it's unlikely to be her. It's more likely to be somebody involved in the trial.

She doesn't know who yet, but she feels anxious.

There's more at play here, she thinks. And she's slap bang, on her own, in the middle of it. After working so hard to get control of her life, for the first time in a long number of years, Dani feels like she may be out of her depth.

2014

The flight to Nice was the most turbulent Dani has ever been on, and a two-hour bus ride later, she's still not back to herself.

She knew things were bad when the flight attendant started to dump all the teas and coffees that had just been poured into a bin before most of them had even been sipped.

It was the sort of flight you don't need when your stomach is already in your throat.

Dani gets off the bus in the centre of Le Muy – if it can be called a centre – and thanks God that at least the weather is pleasant. She's only brought an overnight onboard bag to save on an additional luggage fee and if it had been cold in France, her spring coat wouldn't have withstood it.

But it's warmer here than Ireland and for a few moments, Dani stands still and enjoys it, her face tilted to the sun, inhaling the April air.

Until the bus driver flings her bag at her from the undercarriage of the vehicle.

'*Merci*,' she says.

He grunts in response.

When the bus pulls off, Dani realises her fellow passengers have dispersed without her even noticing. She looks around the empty street. It's just her and the dust kicked up by her departing transport.

The buildings are all old stone with thick walls and shuttered windows. They look residential. Dani wonders if there's a main street where she can find somewhere to eat. For all she knows, this is the main street, just unlike one she's seen before.

She takes out her phone and opens Maps. She barely has 3G and even that is taking an age to load the location pin for her lodgings.

She's chosen the same *pension* Theo sent a request to.

She doesn't know why, with his aunt living here, he decided to stay in a B&B, but she reckons if she follows his steps, she might be able to work it all out.

Dani hoists her bag on her back and starts to walk.

At the end of the street, she takes a left, drawn by the sound of soft chatter.

Up a cobbled lane, she sees tables outside a restaurant, a few old men sitting at them and drinking wine.

Dani approaches and the conversation lulls.

'*Pardon,*' she says. '*Anglais?*'

Theo has taught her some French but she's not confident using it in France, which is deeply ironic.

One of the men stands up.

'*Oui.* How can I help?'

'Oh. Thank you. I'm looking for *Le Maison de Madame Allez?*'

'Ah. The accent. You are Irish.'

'Yes.'

'You have arrived,' the man says.

He points up at a small plaque on the wall, which Dani now sees is a signpost for the lodging she's looking for. She blushes, mortified.

The man holds out his hand. Dani shakes it.

'Your bag, *mademoiselle,*' he says.

The other men laugh.

'Oh. Right.'

Dani hands him her bag and follows him inside the restaurant, still blushing.

When she's checked in by a girl who Dani can only guess is Madame Allez's daughter, given she looks about sixteen and appears to be there under duress, Dani asks if there are any other guests staying in the accommodation.

The girl shakes her head.

Dani feels that wisp of hope evaporate.

Then she asks if she can book a table for dinner.

The girl points at the empty tables inside the dark restaurant and snorts.

Dani takes that to mean yes.

Upstairs, she finds her room small and comfortable. The bed is springy with a wrought-iron headboard and a floral duvet. A vase of tulips has been placed in the window. There's a small closet with a toilet and the narrowest shower Dani has ever seen.

She feels a strange sense of pride in herself. It's the first time she's travelled alone and so far, everything is going to plan.

She splashes water on her face, knots her hair into a bun, then looks at herself in the mirror.

She's beginning to wonder if Theo stayed here at all.

'Where are you?' she whispers.

Downstairs, the man who helped her outside is lighting candles on the tables indoors. With the interior lit better, Dani can see the old beams in the ceiling and the bouquets of dried lavender tucked in various nooks and crannies.

'Irish,' he says. 'I have reserved for you our best table.'

Dani follows him to the table in the centre of the empty room.

'We are very busy in the summer,' he tells her. 'This month, not so much. Only locals and they come and go when they please.'

He hands Dani a menu. She freezes a little when she sees it's all in French.

He notices the look of panic on her face.

'This is your first time in France?' he asks.

She nods.

'And not Paris or Marseilles. You come to Le Muy. So, you have good taste, and you are courageous.'

Dani smiles.

'I'm looking for somebody,' she says.

'Aren't we all?' he replies.

Dani doesn't have a response for that.

'Would you like me to bring you what is good?' he says.

'I don't follow . . .'

'From the kitchen? Will I decide for you?'

He points at the menu.

'Oh. Yes, please.'

'You are not one of these strange young people who does not eat meat?'

'I eat meat.'

'Excellent. My granddaughter, she exists on lentils and potato chips. It is a tragedy for our chef.'

He turns to go, but stalls.

'We will talk, after you have eaten. You will tell me who you are looking for. I am Anton and in the absence of a single other guest, you are now my most important reviewer.'

Dani smiles again.

Later, after she's filled up on the most delicious stew she's ever eaten, Anton sits across from her. He hands her an espresso and pours himself a glass of wine from a carafe.

'So, young Irish. Whom do you seek?'

'My boyfriend has family here,' she says. 'I think.'

'I see.' He frowns. 'He is here? No, he has sent you.'

'Not exactly,' Dani replies. 'Something has . . . I think something has happened to him.'

Anton sits back. He takes another sip of his wine.

'I see,' he says. 'What age are you?'

'Twenty.'

'Twenty, and you are undertaking this mission alone. That is very difficult. What is his family's name?'

'Laurent.'

He frowns again.

'I know everybody in this village,' he says. 'There are no Laurents.'

Dani's shoulders sag.

Has she come all this way for nothing?

'Is his name familiar?' she asks. 'He's Theo Laurent. He inquired about a room here a few weeks ago. By email.'

'Email?'

'There was a reply, saying you had availability, but he didn't reply to that one. Would your . . . Would Madame Allez have spoken to him?'

'Madame Allez was my mother. My own wife has passed on also. My son handles reservations, but he did not tell me anybody was coming of that name. We get inquiries, but if somebody is coming, we will wait for their booking form to be filled out before we confirm them as a guest. I do not remember a Theo Laurent.'

Dani picks up her coffee. She's spent hundreds from her savings to come here and now . . .

'Laurent,' Anton says, pondering. 'Laurent. First names?'

'His aunt is Aimee. I can't remember his uncle's name.'

Anton closes his eyes, deep in thought.

Dani waits for what feels like an age, the coffee bitter on her tongue, the only part of her left that appears able to feel something.

Anton stands up. He leaves the restaurant and goes outside. Dani realises, as she looks through the open door in his wake, that the men from earlier are back outside, at the same tables they were sitting at this afternoon.

After a few moments, Anton returns.

He looks content, a man who's just solved a puzzle.

'It's her maiden name. That is why I did not think of it. But yes, we have a Laurent in the village. She is now Madame Aimee Bennani. I can tell you where she lives.'

'Thank you,' Dani says, stunned. '*Merci.*'

He waves his hand dismissively.

'No, really,' she says. 'You didn't have to help me. You didn't have to be so kind.'

'Of course I did. If my granddaughter was in a foreign country, I hope that somebody would be so kind to her.'

Dani blinks rapidly before he can see her tears of gratitude.

The next morning, after a call with her mother, followed by a decadent breakfast of hot chocolate and croissants, Dani sets out, following the directions Anton has given her.

The village is bigger, prettier and busier than Dani was led to believe when the bus let her off yesterday on the outskirts. She wonders now if perhaps Theo just picked a place nearest to the bus drop-off point, which no doubt would have popped up on Google Maps.

Why not choose a place close to his aunt's?

She passes by some restaurants and stores, a few already populated by spring tourists who haven't yet found their way to Madame Allez's place of residence.

Dani stops and checks she's taken the right path every now and again but Anton's directions are easy to follow.

On a quiet street not far from the centre of the village, Dani finds Madame Bennani's house. There's a garden in full spring bloom to the front, and a man tending to it. Dani watches for a few seconds as he ties jasmine stems to training rods.

He looks up when he realises he's being watched. He's in his fifties, dark-haired and dark-skinned, and his eyes are the most beautiful shade of golden brown.

'Can I help you?' he says, his expression quizzical but welcoming. He addresses her in English.

'I'm looking for Madame Bennani,' she says. 'Does she live here?'

The man is frowning, studying her.

'Wait,' he says. 'I know who you are.'

'You do?'

Now he's smiling.

'You're Dani!' he proclaims.

Dani has never felt so much relief in her life.

'Yes!' she says. 'That's me. You're . . . are you Fadoul? Theo's uncle?' She is relieved that his name has come to her at last.

'Yes, yes! Of course! Come in, come in. Meet his aunt. Aimee!'

Dani lets herself be ushered into the house. Her spirit is soaring with what this might mean – that Theo is here or has been here and has been talking about her. Maybe he even left a message explaining what's happened.

How else would his uncle know so clearly who she is? Why would he react as though it's completely normal she's there?

Dani follows Theo's uncle through to a large, country-style kitchen. Dani doesn't need an introduction to the woman there to know she is Theo's aunt. She has the same full lips, the same blue eyes, the same crease in her forehead. His whole family must share these features, Dani thinks. She'd looked up his father once and found images on the web that made him and Theo look like before and after models.

Aimee is kneading dough in a bowl and startles when her husband and Dani walk in. Then her expression, too, fills with surprise and happiness.

'Dani?' she says.

Dani nods eagerly.

'My goodness,' she says. 'You're just like your photo.'

Aimee grabs the tea towel and rubs her hands clean, then comes around the table to face Dani. Before Dani can say anything, Aimee envelops her in a big hug.

'You are so welcome, my dear,' she says.

'Thank you,' Dani says, her voice almost a sob. 'Is he here?'

Aimee frowns.

'Is who here?'

Aimee and Fadoul stare at her.

'Theo? Is he here?'

Aimee shakes her head, looks back at Fadoul, then shakes her head again.

'Isn't he with you?' she says.

It might be the dashing of hope or maybe the fatigue caused by endless worry for the last few weeks; whatever it is, when Dani tries to answer Aimee, the words can't come out. She hears a rushing behind her ears, a heat builds in her neck and face and then . . .

She falls to her knees and starts to sob.

A short time later, Dani is sitting on a comfortable sofa on the far side of the kitchen. Aimee is beside her and Fadoul is at the cooker, brewing something in a pot.

He pours the liquid into a cup and approaches.

'Drink this,' Fadoul says, pressing the cup into her hands.

It's a tea of some sort, sugary and smelling of something else, some herb that Dani doesn't recognise, but when she inhales it, she already feels calmer.

'None of it makes sense,' Aimee says. 'He's disappeared?'

'It's been four weeks,' Dani says. 'And nobody is taking it seriously because he emailed his father and told his professor that he was going travelling.' She tells them about the email and the phone calls.

'Who is this professor?'

'Declan Graham. And when I heard that, I hacked into Theo's emails – I'm sorry, but I had to see – and he'd contacted some place here, asking about accommodation. I'm staying there now but according to the guy who runs it, Theo was never there.'

Aimee mulls on what Dani's told her. She starts to shake her head.

'He would never do that,' she says. 'Never. Theo loved his course, he loved Dublin. He loved you. And if he planned to come to Le

Muy, he would tell me. He would stay here. This is not the Theo I know.'

Dani's eyes fill with tears.

'And this man,' Aimee says. 'His *professor*. Is he trustworthy?'

'I don't know,' Dani says truthfully. 'He claimed Theo had told him he was under pressure, but that didn't sound right. There might be things I don't know about Theo, but I know that he never admits to being under pressure.'

'Oh, I am well aware, my dear,' Aimee says. 'That was a lesson my brother instilled in me, too.'

She hesitates.

'That man, his professor?' Aimee says. 'I believe Theo had begun to dislike him.'

'What do you mean?'

'Did you read all his emails?'

'Not all of them. Only the ones from the last few weeks. I didn't . . . It seemed okay to read his recent ones, to see if anything had changed. I didn't want to read all his correspondence. It didn't feel right.'

'So, you didn't see the email he sent me three months ago?'

Dani frowns, thinking. She'd read a few of the emails between Theo and Aimee, but they'd been mainly small talk, updates about his course, his life in Dublin. There was nothing in them of note and she'd not seen any emails in the run-up to him booking accommodation in Le Muy.

'No,' she says. 'I don't remember seeing any emails that were of concern.'

'Now, it makes sense,' Aimee says.

'What does? What did he say?'

His aunt hesitates.

'Drink your tea,' she says. 'Then you will freshen up and we will talk some more.'

As the evening wears on, they move to the garden. Aimee brings them blankets for their knees and hot coffee. It's not as cold as Ireland but there's an evening nip in the air.

Still, it's a pleasant night, if anything about Dani's current situation could be considered pleasant.

'He used to come here on holidays, when he was younger, didn't he?' Dani says.

'Yes. When he was a boy, his mother organised for him to visit a few times,' Aimee says. 'Obviously my brother wasn't as keen. You say you've spoken to Alexandre?'

'Mr Laurent?'

'Yes.'

Dani nods.

'And I imagine Theo has told you a little of what Alexandre is like.'

'I know he went against his father's wishes to come to Ireland and pursue medical research. I know he finds his father . . . difficult.'

'Difficult is something you can work with. Alexandre is impossible. We are estranged, sadly. He pushes everybody away, in the end. Unless you work for him. Then you have to put up with him because he pays you.'

'I'm sorry,' Dani says. 'I didn't realise there were other people in the family that Theo's father had fallen out with. I mean, everything Theo has said has made me think his dad is quite – cold, I guess. But I know father and son relationships can be hard. I assumed they'd make up one day.'

'When I met Fadoul, I didn't tell Alexandre at first. I had to be sure that Fadoul was the one. Our parents had both died by the time Alexandre was in his twenties and I was in my teens. We had been raised very conservatively, very much in a Catholic manner. The bishop used to come to family dinners regularly. After our mother passed, Alexandre took over my upbringing, in a way. We were left with a lot of wealth and resources. There were nannies and tutors, but I suppose he saw his role as paternal. And I did – I do – love him. But when I told him Fadoul and I were to be married . . . he didn't want to speak to me again.'

'Because you hadn't told him you had a boyfriend?'

'No.' Aimee laughs harshly. 'Because Fadoul is French–Moroccan. My brother is a snob. I agree with him on many political and societal matters but not that one. And it is not even race. It is purely because marrying Fadoul would make others look at our family with contempt.'

Dani shakes her head in disbelief.

'He'd rather lose his own sister than accept her choice of husband?' she says.

'Yes,' Aimee says. 'But, thankfully, Theo's mother was always a little more . . . well, let us use the word "relaxed". And by that, I mean intoxicated. She didn't stop me from seeing my nephew. She allowed Theo to spend a few weeks with me in the summer when his father was away for business. It got him out from under her feet. It suited us both. Then Alexandre decided Theo should go to boarding school and he wouldn't let him visit any more during the holidays.'

'I'm sorry,' Dani says again.

'It is not your fault. And Theo escaped in the end. Liberation.

Going to Ireland set him free from his father. I felt the same when I walked away from Paris. But I think what Theo did was much braver. He could have gone to a college here of Alexandre's choosing and then straight to work in one of his father's firms. Alexandre invests in everything. Especially in the medical world. Theo could have followed his passion with Alexandre paying for everything, but he chose to do it alone. That was courage.'

Aimee looks very grave, suddenly.

'So, I believe you, Dani,' she says. 'Theo would not email Alexandre to tell him he was leaving his studies to go travelling. He wouldn't bother to tell his father anything unless he had to. And he certainly wouldn't have sent it in English. I agree with you. I doubt Alexandre even read the email. I imagine one of his employees informed him of the correspondence.'

Dani agrees.

'But that only leaves us with one conclusion,' Aimee continues. 'If Theo didn't send that email to his father, or the email inquiring about accommodation . . .'

'Somebody else sent them,' Dani finishes the sentence.

'Somebody wants us to think that Theo has left of his own volition,' Aimee says. 'Somebody who is covering their tracks. Who would do such a thing?'

'What you said about Declan Graham,' Dani says. 'Why did you say Theo had started to dislike him? Did he tell you that?'

'The first time he mentioned that professor, Theo said he was brilliant and inspirational,' Aimee answers. 'That he'd pursued the career Theo wanted to have. But a few months ago, he stopped talking about him. I inquired after him and Theo brushed it off.'

Dani's brow furrows.

'He never told me anything was amiss.'

Aimee hesitates.

'That man, Graham, is a homosexual, no?'

Dani nods. She doesn't see the relevance. But she realises, from the look on Aimee's face, that Theo's aunt thinks differently.

Aimee shrugs.

'Perhaps he tried something with Theo?'

'I don't think so,' Dani says. 'He would have told me.'

Aimee purses her lips.

Dani frowns.

She likes Aimee and they share a love of Theo, and she has her own suspicions that Declan Graham isn't telling her everything. But what Aimee said about being raised Catholic and conservatively . . . Dani wonders now if that's clouding the woman's judgement.

'Whatever happened, he stopped talking about him,' Aimee says. 'And then, three months ago, he sent me that email. Maybe I am being old-fashioned. Yes, I know, I hear it too. But our family is not exactly what you would call progressive. And I do believe Theo had some problem with this Graham man.'

Dani sits up straighter.

'What was in the email he sent you?' she asks.

'A request. He asked for the number for the Fox,' Aimee says.

'What?' Dani is completely confused.

'The Fox. Alexandre's man.'

'Aimee, I don't understand. His father has a man called Fox?'

'No, the Fox is his nickname. Always has been. Alexandre said once it is because his hair is red, but I always thought it's because he sneaks around so much.'

'Right, so there's a man called the Fox and Theo asked for his number,' Dani repeats, trying to process what she's hearing. 'But why?'

'The Fox fixes things,' Aimee says. 'He's a man who can find out anything and he protects Alexandre.'

'So . . . was Theo asking to be protected from something? That could make sense, right? If he thought that he was in danger and this man could fix something for him— What could it have been? Did he say any more?'

'No.' Aimee shakes her head. 'Because I reminded him – if he asks the Fox to do something, he's asking his father to do it. That's how it works. And after trying so hard to get away, Theo would be right back in Alexandre's grip.'

Dani tries to absorb this. It's so alien to her: people who *fix* things.

It's a part of Theo's world she knows nothing about. Just like her mother said. And without even being told, she senses it's a dangerous part.

She wonders if that's why he kept it from her.

'Did you give him the number?' she asks.

Aimee remains silent for a few moments.

'Yes,' she says eventually. 'And now, I regret it.'

'Why?'

'Because it's not the Fox's job to protect Theo, Dani. It's his job to protect Alexandre. And if Theo had done something or found out something that might damage his father . . . the Fox wouldn't let the fact they're family stand in his way.'

Dani feels a shiver run right through her. Aimee's voice is filled with something Dani recognises very well these days.

Hard, cold fear.

'Where is he?' Dani asks.

She doesn't need to specify who she means. Aimee already knows.

'Paris,' she says. 'But you cannot go near him. Do you understand me, Dani? He is not a man who helps people. Fadoul and I know that very well.'

Dani doesn't reply.

She's already calculating if her budget will take her to Paris.

2024

The street Dani has come to is not a million miles from where she grew up. Close to Dublin city centre, the rows of red-brick houses are so small and contained you could almost drop from the second-floor windows to the pavement beneath without hurting yourself. And all around, the ever-growing apartment and office blocks cast these old Dublin streets into shadow.

It feels weird, to think Cecelia Vargas lived so close to Dani's old stomping ground. It's only a few years since her mother sold her house, and given how long Cecelia had lived in Ireland, it's entirely possible that she and Dani crossed paths at one point.

Maybe on this very street.

Dani looks up and down the road, searching for the thing she's come for.

She's taken a risk. If there's even the slightest chance Turner suspects somebody is looking into the trial, they might be monitoring people who've come into contact with those charged with running it. Like Colm. And if she's being followed, how could she explain why she's visiting the place where Cecelia Vargas lived?

Dani pulls the visor of her baseball cap lower and starts to walk. She checks each house discreetly as she goes.

If any of the neighbours has what she's looking for, they've hidden it well.

And yet she knows somebody will. These houses only have street parking, and so close to town, their cars are constantly at risk of vandalism or being stolen.

She stops at a point of the road facing a house that she knows is split into three apartments. A tiny house, made even smaller.

Cecelia lived in the back of that house.

Officially, her case has not been declared a murder.

The detectives who looked at it at the time didn't find anything suspicious and so the coroner recorded it as an accident.

When the task force took over, Cecelia's death was considered just a little bit too coincidental, but a decision was made by the higher-ups to leave it alone for the time being.

If Turner were involved in her death, looking into it would only draw attention to the fact the police had their suspicions and that might encourage Turner to shut down their operation in Ireland.

Dani's both agitated by that decision and grateful for it. Grateful because it allows her to do her job in St Edmund's, hopefully unnoticed.

And agitated, because she believes Cecelia deserves justice and she knows that a thorough investigation could throw up any amount of evidence to bring her that. So far, all the police have done is retrieve the CCTV from the garage where Cecelia had parked her car, and the surrounding streets, to see if anybody nearby was acting suspiciously.

But they haven't ticked the usual boxes of a murder investigation.

Talked to neighbours, co-workers, established the patterns of Cecelia's life, tried to ascertain if anybody had been threatening or watching her.

And Dani's worried that by the time her lot do get round to it, evidence may have been lost.

She shouldn't be here, on this street, doing what she's about to do. But here she is.

She stares over at Cecelia's house for a few more moments. There are several cars parked on that side of the road, one of them filling the space Cecelia's would have once.

Dani turns and looks again at the houses she's standing in front of.

The one in front of her doesn't have what she's looking for. Nor the two to the left. But then she peers closer at the house on her right.

And there, tucked into the corner of the sitting room window, is a domestic security camera.

She walks towards the house and is about to knock on the door when she feels another hand on her shoulder.

She jumps, and spins around. It's George.

'What are you up to, MacLochlainn?' he says.

'For fuck's sake, you gave me a fright,' she answers.

'Not as much of a fright as you're giving me.'

He takes her arm and moves her away from the door of the house so they're standing closer to the road.

'Are you following me?'

Dani fills her words with an indignation she knows she has no right to possess.

'Of course I am,' he says. 'You're my biggest bloody asset in the most important investigation of my career and you're meant to be on St Edmund's grounds right now. So, care to explain?'

She glances at the window. He follows her eyeline, spots the camera.

'Ah, Dani,' he says. 'You know a decision was made . . .'

'Those cameras store cloud footage for six months, tops,' she says. 'If somebody was following Cecelia, they'll have spent time learning her daily routine. What time she left the house, the route she drove to work, where she parked there. They'd have made a decision about where and how to tamper with her car so they wouldn't be seen. Outside her house would have been too risky. Too much chance of a pedestrian passing or a neighbour popping out. But they'd have had to come here to see that.'

'We don't know she was murdered.'

'Bollocks. George, if there's evidence to be found, we have a duty of care.'

'We've a duty of care to all the people who could end up having their lives destroyed by a Turner drug,' he rebuts.

'I know! But it shouldn't be an either/or. Please. Just let me do this. And I swear, I'll go back to my job.'

George hesitates.

'Why now?' he says. 'I get it, six months, but what's changed to make you focus on this?'

Dani bites her lip.

'I can't tell you,' she says. 'It's just . . . a suspicion right now. But I want to get that footage. Are you going to let me?'

George studies her. Then, slowly, he shakes his head.

'I'm going back to HQ,' he says. 'Do what you need to, then go back to work. Dani, don't fuck this up. This operation, it's bigger than whatever is going on in your head. It's bigger than you.'

He looks at her for a few moments and Dani keeps eye contact for as long as she can before blinking and looking away.

He's disappointed in her.

She stares at the ground, knowing he's still watching her, but she doesn't raise her eyes to meet his again.

He has so much more to be disappointed about.

She hasn't told him the half of what went on ten years ago, what her time in St Edmund's was really like or what she did when Theo first went missing.

If he knew, he would never have asked her to go back there.

2014

Paris

Dani has been sitting in the café across the street for two hours now. She's barely taken her eyes off the large wooden doors that protect the entrance to the courtyard leading to what she knows is Alexandre Laurent's main Paris apartment.

Aimee may not be in contact with her brother, but she was able to tell Dani that when Alexandre is in Paris, he no longer stays at the family chateau but at his city-centre residence. His difficulties with his wife are ongoing, but being a very conservative, religious man, Alexandre refuses to divorce her.

He ignores her, instead.

Even though it's off-street and private, Dani can tell from the doors alone that Alexandre's second home is no less grand than his first.

The middle-aged waiter refills her coffee. He was irritated with her the first day when she managed to stretch out one pastry over four hours. But he warmed to her yesterday when he asked where she was from, and she told him Ireland. His curiosity about her country seems to have no bounds.

Dani isn't sure if there's any sense to this plan at all, but she doesn't have much else to go on. Aimee's told her that where Alexandre is,

128

the Fox surely follows. So, she's hoping if she watches the apartment, he will either turn up or leave at some point. But this is day three and so far, no sign. And she only has enough money for a couple more days at the hostel.

The hours pass and her bladder starts to make her uncomfortable.

She nods at the waiter, who nods back, an indication he'll watch her table while she pops to the loo. God know what he thinks she's waiting for every day.

Dani has just returned and is considering calling it a day when she spots movement across the street.

The wooden doors open and a red-haired man emerges. He's already striding down the street.

The Fox is exactly as Aimee had described.

Dani throws some euros on the table and grabs her bag.

She runs out the café door.

She looks in the direction the man took. She panics for a moment as she struggles to catch sight of him through the pedestrians. And then a gap appears and she spots his red hair.

Dani runs until she's almost caught up with him. He takes a left and she follows. She doesn't know these streets and she's hoping he doesn't get into a car at some point, because there are plenty parked along the road.

But he keeps going.

At the next crossroads, he doesn't bother waiting for the pedestrian lights. He dodges through the traffic. Dani panics. He might be used to Parisian traffic but she's not.

She stands on tiptoes, trying to keep her eye on him as she waits for the signal to cross. Her heart is racing.

She wants to ask him about Theo and whether he got in touch.

But there's a tiny part of her that hopes he may actually lead her to Theo, just by following him.

She can't lose sight of this man.

The lights change and she runs across the road, forcing her way through the mass of people coming from the other side. Luckily, he's stopped just up ahead and appears to be reading a text message on his phone. He starts off again, but she closes in as he makes his way towards a large, beautiful church. The Church of Saint-Germain-Des-Prés, a sign tells her.

The Fox goes inside. Dani frowns and follows. She has a vague memory of hearing the church's name before and she thinks somebody famous is buried here but she can't remember who.

Dani steps inside and everything becomes quieter.

She looks around. The layout and iconography tell her immediately that this is a Catholic church. She shivers a little. Neither of her parents were ever particularly religious so Dani has been in church sparingly, but the last time, the time that stands out in her memory, was her father's funeral.

There are a couple of tourists here and there, skirting the pews as they study the artwork and statues. A few elderly people sit and kneel in the rows, deep in prayer.

But she can't see the man she's following.

She knows he's in here somewhere.

She begins to walk along the side of the church. She checks the side chapels off the main body as she goes, in case he's ducked into one of those.

Dani is passing a large column and almost at the altar when she feels a hand cup her mouth and she's lifted off the ground. She can't make a sound and doesn't have the time to protest anyway before she's manhandled through a side door of the building.

On the other side of the door is a small room filled with storage equipment. She's pushed inside roughly and turns in time to see the Fox locking the door behind them.

'What are you doing?' she chokes out. She's so scared, she can barely breathe.

'You are following me,' he says. His accent surprises her; he sounds like he's well-to-do English, not French at all. Educated abroad, presumably. His expression is completely unreadable; he looks entirely placid, but his gaze makes her feel deeply uncomfortable.

'Yes,' she says, 'but I have a good reason.'

'And you have a good reason for watching my employer's apartment for the last three days?'

Dani baulks.

'How did you know?' she says.

'You talk too much,' he says. 'You gave the history of Ireland to that waiter.'

Dani's heart sinks. It never occurred to her that the waiter, who'd been so rude and then become friendly, could have meant any harm to her. She feels like an idiot.

'I guess you know who I am, then,' she says.

'I know,' he replies.

She looks at the door behind him, uneasy.

'Why did you grab me? I want to talk to you, but I'm not comfortable being locked in here.'

'I do not feel comfortable being followed by little girls who have no business being in Paris.'

Dani's fear is starting to subside and it's being replaced with something else: anger. Who is this man to make her feel so bloody scared when all she's done is come here to ask him for help?

He cocks his head as she's thinking this. She half suspects he knows what's going through her mind.

'Let me go,' she says.

'Then how will we get to know each other?' he replies. 'I need to know you are worth my time and effort.'

He takes a step towards her. She winces, not knowing what he plans to do.

He smiles. He can see she's frightened.

That pleasure in his expression. It spurs Dani on.

'I'm not afraid of you,' she snaps.

'No? You should be.'

'Well, I'm not. You're not going to hurt me. You just want to intimidate me. And I don't have time for that, so can we just talk?'

The Fox smiles again, but this time, he just looks amused.

Dani bites her lip.

'Theo asked Aimee for a contact for you,' she says. 'You know he's missing—'

'Travelling, according to his father. If he was missing, I would have been sent to find him.'

Dani doesn't have the patience for this.

'He's missing,' she says. 'And he wanted to talk to you. Did he?'

'If he wanted you to know, wouldn't he have told you?'

Dani clenches her fists.

'If you're not going to help me, let me go. I'm sick of not being taken seriously. I mean it. I'll scream. There are people out there, this room's not soundproof.'

The Fox studies her for a few seconds.

Dani senses some hesitation in his demeanour, a recalculation.

'Did he contact you?' she asks, her voice small.

'You know Descartes?' the Fox says.

Now she remembers. René Descartes, that's who's entombed in this church.

'The father of rational thinking,' the Fox says. 'Every thought must be examined through that prism. Fact, evidence, statistics. It makes sense, no? Speculation, paranoia, imagination, there is no room for this.'

Dani stares at him. What does that have to do with anything, she wonders.

'Theo contacted me,' he says.

Dani's heart rate slows so much she thinks she might have missed a beat.

'He wanted my help.'

'With what?'

'Nothing rational,' the Fox says. 'I like Theo, you see. I always have. He is a smart boy. A little stubborn, a little too sensitive, often arrogant. Always correct, in his head. But a good boy. My feelings don't come into it, however. I work for his father. I am not family; I'm not a friend.'

'What did he ask?' Dani says, unable to hide the desperation in her voice. Despite what she's told him, her fear is growing. Maybe Aimee was right. Maybe she should never have come here; she should never have approached this man and asked for help.

Because from the sounds of it, if Theo wanted help in dealing with anything to do with his father, this man would have chosen Alexandre over Theo every day of the week.

'He wanted to meet me,' the Fox says. 'He wanted to ask about a company called Amarita Medical.'

'I don't know who that is,' Dani says.

'You wouldn't. They are a small pharmaceutical company. Theo said he was considering working with them.'

'What? A job? When? He's only in his second year in college.'

'Yes. You see. Irrational. And then, he didn't turn up. If he had, I would have told him this pharma company is about to go out of business. They are too small, and the medicine they make, it is being made better by bigger firms. Firms his father could get him a job in when he qualifies, if he wishes to make amends with Alexandre.'

Dani looks at the man in front of her, filled with despair.

'So, you haven't seen him?'

'No. He changed his mind, obviously. He decided to travel instead.'

'He didn't!' Dani cries. 'For God's sake. He asked you for help and he didn't turn up and you aren't even worried. Why is nobody worried?'

The Fox says nothing. He merely looks back at her. Dani stares back, willing him to say something. It takes a few moments before she realises.

He does care, she thinks. It's why he let me follow him, it's why he's brought me in here, where nobody will see me talking to him. He's worried, but he doesn't want anybody to know yet.

'I think something bad has happened to him,' she says, closing her eyes in frustration.

She hears the turn of the key in the lock and a click. She opens her eyes.

The Fox has opened the door and he's about to leave, his body half turned away from her.

'He's not in Paris,' he says. 'And he hasn't left Ireland. If you want to keep looking for him, that's where he is.'

'Won't you help me?' she asks.

He gives his head a small shake.

'It's not my job until I'm told it's my job,' he says.

With that, he leaves.

Dani steps outside after a few moments. The church has emptied out.

She feels completely alone.

2024

Dani has taken the day off sick to go through the security footage from the home camera on Cecelia Vargas' street.

On the one hand, she's been lucky. The camera's recordings are stored in the cloud for as long as six months if the owner pays for the platinum package and this owner actually has. He didn't even realise what deal he was buying, he just signed up with the security company.

So, she's able to go right back to the day Cecelia died and to a couple of days before.

The camera is at an angle that's directly pointed at the parking spot outside its owner's house, but it captures Cecelia's front door and several houses to either side of hers. Dani reckons she has about fifty metres of street recorded.

She watches every single second of it in slow motion, trying to see if anybody walks past Cecelia's house or can be seen on the edge of the coverage – anything that might indicate the woman was being watched.

She watches Cecelia leave for work that morning and never come home.

When Dani fails to find anything on that day, she rewinds to the start of the footage and goes through the two days leading up to Cecelia's death.

She knows this could be a fool's errand. Even if somebody was watching Cecelia's house, they could have been standing on the same side of the street as the camera, which would mean they never appear. But she rules that out as quickly as she thinks it. They wouldn't be standing. Not on a residential street. There's no café or bar to sit inside, there's no bus stop to pretend to sit at. A stalker wouldn't want to stand out, so the only way to watch Cecelia would be by sitting in a car.

What Dani is hoping to see is Cecelia coming or going from her house and a car following.

Cecelia leaves and re-enters her house four times in the two days leading up to her death. Two of those times include going to and returning from work. On the first day, she goes out again that evening and returns with shopping bags. The second night, she leaves with a small gym bag and returns with her hair wet, looking fresh.

On each of those occasions, Dani watches the cars that go down the road immediately after Cecelia has left and returned.

She doesn't see the same car twice. She notes every one of the twenty cars she does see, including their registrations or partials when she can't see the whole plate.

Three Ford Escorts. Two Toyotas. Three BMWs. A Mercedes. Four Hyundais. Two Nissans. One Audi. One Volkswagen. Two Renaults. One Volvo.

She'll run the registrations anyway, but she knows the absence of a repeat car is telling. You don't stalk somebody once.

She stares at the drivers when she can see them properly, which isn't every time because the cars are passing at speed and, even paused, the security camera is not advanced enough to capture a perfect still.

It doesn't mean anything, she tells herself.

The person who killed her could have already established her routine. They could have been watching Cecelia for weeks and at that point, the plan was already in place.

But she knows that doesn't help. The detectives who worked on the original case couldn't find anything that showed Cecelia's car had been tampered with. Dani's discussed this with George and they both agree Cecelia's killer probably got lucky. The car didn't just crash, it crashed into a body of water, and by the time it was retrieved, it was difficult to establish what damage had been done before or after the accident.

By nine that evening, Dani shuts her laptop, defeated. She rubs her eyes, blurry from spending the day staring at her screen.

When she opens them, she sees the text from George.

Anything?

She's not surprised. He's just as curious as she is, no matter how much he's told her to leave this bit aside.

She texts back *No*.

Within seconds, he replies.

Get back to work.

She sighs.

The lecture hall that Dani teaches in is a traditional St Edmund's affair. Arena-like seating, a lower podium, artificial lighting and a distinct musty smell built up over decades.

The School of Medical Research's lecture halls and offices are far more modern. The building was constructed in the eighties to an exceptionally high standard and that standard has been maintained.

Dani looks around at the spotlessly clean, modern workstations, and the large airy space, and thinks that this part of the campus, compared to the original St Edmund's building, is night and day.

They're sitting at the workstation at the top of the class because Colm has just finished a tutorial. Dani waited by the door as the students streamed out, and as much as she tried not to, she saw the ghost of a young Theo in every single one of the boys.

It's happening more and more now.

She's finding it so hard to concentrate on the task at hand.

Colm is eating the ham salad sandwich Dani brought him. It's lunch time and this is the quid pro quo – she'll feed them both, he'll tell her about the college's research into Alzheimer's and the drug they're trialling.

'Okay, so you know essentially what the disease is, right?' Colm says, after swallowing his first bite.

'Sort of,' Dani says. 'Something happens in the brain to do with proteins and you start to lose the ability to remember things. I mean, that's the basic starting point, isn't it?'

'Pretty much. It's an abnormal build-up of proteins in our brain cells – amyloid, which forms what we call plaques around the brain cells, and tau, which makes what we call tangles within the brain cells. And when the brain cells become affected, our neuro-transmitters—'

'Which are?'

'Think of them like chemical signals that jump between our brain cells. They decrease. One of the neurotransmitters, acetyl-choline, well, the levels of that have been found to be particularly low in the brains of people with Alzheimer's disease.'

'Don't they say that the brain shrinks?'

'Yes. Different parts of it. And the first part affected is usually the area responsible for memories. Though, people can lose other functions, too.'

Dani nods.

Colm is watching her take all this in.

'Do you mind if I ask which of your family members has it?' he says. 'It's okay if you don't want to talk about it.'

'No, it's fine,' Dani says. 'My mam got it. When she was quite young, actually. She was only in her fifties. It came on in little ways. Forgetting small stuff, leaving the cooker on, that kind of thing. And then it got very aggressive.'

He puts his hand on hers and squeezes it.

'Thanks,' she says quietly. 'That's why it means a lot to me, you know. That a cure is found. Or prevention, or whatever it is. I guess I worry a lot that it might be hereditary. I don't want to go through what my mother went through.'

'I understand. Everybody wants the same. And there have been lots of leads over the years. Once medical scientists started to identify what they thought was causing the problem, they came at it from different angles. Some tried to target the neurotransmitter acetylcholine, attempting to artificially boost its levels to work around the attacking proteins. The problem is, no matter how good the neurotransmitter, if the brain cells are dying because they're under attack, then there's nothing to transmit to.'

'Why not go after the proteins?' Dani asks.

'They've done that, too. There are these drugs called monoclonal antibodies that aim to prevent the plaques from what we call *clumping* in the brain cells. There are a few drugs in the States now, FDA approved, that seem to be slowing the clumping.'

'FDA is like, what . . . the government?'

She has to feign ignorance about a lot of this.

Dani knows what the FDA is. She knows how Alzheimer's works and she certainly knows about all the research and the many drugs that are out there.

This is all about ingratiating herself with Colm.

Making him trust her by showing she trusts him.

Colm was one of the targets chosen specifically by the task force because he's specialising in Alzheimer's for his PhD. The logic being, Colm is in this for a cure, not just for the money. Unlike Turner.

So, in a way, Dani does trust him. But she also wants to use him.

'The Food and Drug Administration,' Colm says. 'It's government-run. They have to approve a drug before it can be used. They're reviewing some of the Alzheimer's treatments at the moment, the ones that are having little or no effect. But they also get to sign off when a drug is purported to be useful for Alzheimer's but it's off-label.'

'I don't understand,' Dani says. 'What does off-label mean?'

'Off-label prescription. A drug that has been approved to treat one thing but is found to be having a positive side effect on another disease. There's a drug at the moment designed for cancer patients that the industry believes is effectively reducing plaques around brain cells, the very ones contributing to Alzheimer's. And there's another cancer drug that they think might be able to reverse, to an extent, the loss of memory. They experimented on mice and found the drug turned off a protein, which allowed synapses to start working again.'

'But all that's not enough?' Dani asks.

'No. Because the plaques are just part of the problem. We also have to find a way to stop the tau from tangling.'

'The tau from tangling. It sounds comedic.'

'I know.' He smiles gently. 'And there's research into it, but the closest we've got so far in terms of actual approved drugs is a tau aggregation inhibitor.'

'I'm going to pretend I know what that means,' Dani says.

'Ha! There's so much more research. Some scientists believe the brain cells of sufferers are particularly inflamed, so they are looking at anti-inflammatory drugs as part of the treatment. There's an idea that insulin might slow the deterioration, though that's not gone anywhere yet. And there's a whole body of research looking at the heart and head connection – that dysfunction in the heart might put extra strain on the brain cells. I mean, it goes on and on. Hormone studies, lifestyle . . . the point is, we have a general idea of what causes Alzheimer's but not an exact one. It's one of those diseases that we're really still quite in the dark about.'

'There can't be a cure, then,' Dani says.

'No. But, there's about to be a giant leap forward in slowing the disease. And if it can be slowed significantly, that will be a huge step in the right direction. We can even reclaim memory function, working with skilled therapists.'

'How is that going to happen?'

Colm grins smugly.

'St Edmund's,' he says. 'In cooperation with Turner Pharmaceuticals. Turner has done something really special. They've taken all of the areas we know the most about – the plaques, the taus, the inflammation – and they've created one drug that targets all of those things at the same time.'

Colm has become more animated. He's practically fizzing with excitement. Dani forces a smile.

This is what Interpol and the multi-jurisdictional task force and, more importantly, she is trying to stop.

'A saviour drug,' Dani says.

'Exactly that. And we've been running the trials on it. We're almost finished with the third trial. And the results are . . .'

Colm blows a puff of air and mimes an explosion with his hands.

'It's slowing down the disease?' Dani asks tentatively.

'Dramatically. On this trial, we're up to 5,000 adults across Europe with medium-advanced Alzheimer's. Sixty per cent of them have experienced a stall in the disease and a small number of them have recovered a level of memory retention that's never been seen in treatment before.'

'Oh, my God,' Dani says, 'that's incredible.'

And she means it.

She thinks of her mother and what life could have been like.

'I know,' Colm says. 'It's mind-blowing. And it's all thanks to Declan and the provost here.'

Dani frowns.

'The college didn't come up with the drug, though, did it?' she says. 'I mean, they're just running the trials.'

'Sure. But Declan was aware of Turner's early research; he'd already built a network with them because the college has done so much research in the area. And Malachy Walsh was the one who offered to form a coalition with Turner. Once they knew they'd be getting the talent and expertise of Edmund's attached, they started pouring money into their own research and ours. Those men are probably going to get a Nobel Prize when this all comes to pass. And I and the rest of the team are going to have worked on something that will change the way Alzheimer's is treated forever. Isn't it something else?'

Dani smiles at his enthusiasm.

She wants to feel happy for Colm. She can see his enthusiasm for Turner's drug comes from somewhere genuine and good.

Unlike Declan Graham.

Or Malachy Walsh.

But none of that is Colm's fault.

She just hopes he survives the fallout of what Dani is going to have to do.

This is why I'm back, she reminds herself.

Not for Theo.

To stop these monsters from giving people false hope.

2023

Phoenix Park, near Garda HQ

Dani finds George sitting on a bench near the tea rooms in the Phoenix Park. He's just unwrapped a sandwich from greaseproof paper, he has a can of Coke on the seat beside him, and he's turning the pages of a paperback, an old spy novel by the look of the cover.

Her shadow lands on the pages and he glances up with an air of resignation.

'MacLochlainn, I left HQ so I could eat this extremely limp and increasingly damp sandwich in peace.'

'Did you put the tomato in again?'

'I've nowhere else to put the tomato but in the sandwich.'

'You get a lunchbox and you put sliced tomatoes in foil in the side. Then you stick them in the sandwich when you're eating it.'

'And like I told you last time, I'm not buying a lunchbox because I'm not twelve.'

'Get your wife to buy one,' Dani says.

George bristles. Dani has noticed that a bit lately. She doesn't want to ask what it's about. Work is work and private life is private life. If it was any different, George would know she isn't as strong as she lets on and she's worked hard since she joined the Guards to create a new image for herself and leave her past behind.

She sits beside him on the bench, forcing him to move his Coke.

'What do you want, MacLochlainn?' he says.

'Why do you always call me MacLochlainn, George? Is it because you feel the need to impress your superiority on me? Does my brilliance threaten you?'

George puts his sandwich down.

'Just say it,' he says. 'Before I die of frustrated starvation.'

'You know why I'm here. I'm not doing it.'

'Doing what?'

'You're going to send somebody undercover into St Edmund's and you've decided it's me.'

'Is that so?'

'Mm-hm.'

'And what makes you think that?'

'Well, call me a detective, but you made me go to that briefing and you've cleared all my other cases.'

'What makes you think we need somebody undercover?'

Dani sighs.

'If you thought a warrant for their records and data would be of any use, you'd already have executed it. You wouldn't want them to see you coming. So, the fact you haven't tells me you don't know what you're looking for, you're worried they'll erase it before you can find anything anyway, and you're going to have to get creative in how you source your information.'

George turns and looks at her.

'We explored the option of an undercover officer,' he tells her. 'We started off thinking we needed somebody with a medical research background and some sort of academic qualifications. Somebody who can get a place on the clinical trials Turner is running.'

'You should do that,' Dani says.

'It's impossible. They need to have a police background and there are no cops who've become doctors and no doctors who've become cops.'

He takes a breath.

'And then we realised something,' he says. 'You went to St Edmund's.'

Dani stares straight ahead.

'That wasn't on my application when I applied to join the Guards.'

'It wasn't. But guess who else is a detective?'

'George, I was only there for two years. I dropped out.'

'And finished your course elsewhere.'

'No, I dropped out. I cared for my mother for two years and then I joined Garda training college.'

'Not what your new records will say. They'll say you finished your course elsewhere and went on to study further.'

Dani groans.

'I think you're missing the point of undercover?' she says. 'There will probably be people there who still recognise me.'

George doesn't say anything for a few seconds.

'True, it normally involves working under an assumed identity. We wouldn't be able to change your name. But you haven't kept in touch with anybody there. Not that we can see. You've removed it from your life. Why is that, Dani?'

Dani stares down at the ground. When she doesn't answer, George speaks for her.

'You don't need to answer that,' he says. 'I know it's because of what happened with your boyfriend. Theo, wasn't it? I'm sorry, Dani.'

She shakes her head.

'It was a long time ago and I was young.'

'Too young to go through that.'

She nods.

'Sometimes we have to do uncomfortable things,' he says. 'Go to places we don't want to go. You had a very bad experience there but now you have the chance to do something good in the same place. Something important.'

'I'm not a medical scientist.' Dani is still grasping. 'You can't fake that.'

'Nope. But St Edmund's recently advertised for a new history professor.'

Dani stiffens. She should have known it was something like this.

'And from what we've heard,' George continues, 'St Edmund's has always been more inclined to hire its own.'

'And like I said,' she replies, 'I never finished my degree. You could just as easily stick in a janitor or a gardener.'

'In the hope they have access to the senior staff and buildings and computers in the medical research facility? We have identified targets in there, Dani. People running the trial. How likely are they to make friends with a gardener? To go for drinks with them, to loosen up and reveal hugely fucking sensitive medical information or put them in a position where they'll have access to their private computers, let alone lab computers?'

'It's undoable,' Dani says.

'But if you were going to do it, how would you?' George prods. 'If we could make it look like you'd finished your degree, you had your PhD, you were a possible candidate for that job on paper . . . do you think you could succeed in an interview for the post?'

Dani doesn't answer for a few seconds.

'They hire their own because they know their own,' she says. 'Who's on the interview panel?'

And then he lands the nail in her coffin.

'Grace Byrne,' he says. 'The head of the history department. A couple of others, but we suspect she's the top gun. You know her? She was working there ten years ago, so we're guessing you do.'

Dani swallows. George sees it.

'She was there, she knows I dropped out,' Dani says.

She turns on the bench and faces him.

'I don't want this job,' she tells George. 'Pick somebody else.'

'Dani, you're it,' George says. 'You were it from the moment we realised what Turner's new drug is for. Of all of us, you're the one who understands this thing.'

He pauses.

'Your mother has Alzheimer's, doesn't she?'

And there it is.

What Dani knew was coming from the moment he told her to attend that briefing.

Did Lucia know too? Have they all been planning this?

Dani hangs her head.

'It's a long shot,' George says. 'But we believe in you, Dani. We don't know what Turner is hiding. But if we can get somebody in there to help us get the raw data from that trial, we can have our own experts ascertain what they're up to. And then we can issue warrants and come after them.'

'Illegally attained information. Sounds rock solid.'

'No. We'll come at it from the whistle-blower angle. Judges are a lot more amenable to that for the time being, anyway. Yes, we're not playing entirely by the book. But . . . nor are they, Dani. We won't be using what you find. That will just point us in the right direction with the warrants.'

Dani looks into the distance. There's a playground nearby, she can hear children squealing and the noise of equipment in use, but in her immediate eyeline, there's nothing but trees, their branches swaying softly in the wind.

'Why are you not surprised?' George asks.

'Surprised you've chosen me? Why would I be? Like you said, I went there—'

'No. Surprised that St Edmund's could be corrupt. That they could be involved in a medical fraud so large they've attracted the attention of a multi-jurisdictional task force. You've not even tried to defend them. Isn't there normally some innate loyalty thing people have for their old colleges?'

Dani hesitates.

Should she tell him? What she suspected all those years ago for all of five minutes?

But if she does that, she'll have to tell him about the rabbit hole she went down before she learned the truth about Theo.

She'll have to tell him just how far she'd gone into madness.

So, instead, she shrugs.

'The bigger the uni, the bigger the greed,' she says. 'There's always a risk, isn't there? Even I know that.'

George nods, watching her. He's determined she'll do this.

Dani realises she's going to have to try another approach.

'George, there's more. You know what happened to Theo. But . . . he was actually in the School of Medical Research. That was his topic. I . . . I knew some of his professors. Not properly—'

She winces at the lie, hoping he won't notice.

'Like, just in passing,' she continues. 'But they might still be there and know me and—'

'I know,' he says. 'That's what I'm hoping. Don't you see how perfect this is, Dani? You can walk right into that college for us. They know you, but they don't *know* you. You're the ideal candidate.'

She has one hope left.

That St Edmund's won't hire her. Even if Grace is on the panel, that's no guarantee she'll consider Dani suitable for the job.

There's every reason she shouldn't consider her suitable.

'There's, um, somebody I'd like you to talk to,' George says.

Dani looks up sharply.

'Who?'

George turns and looks behind them. And there, over by the trees, stands Grace Byrne. She looks older but she still has that wild curly hair, the kind, smart expression . . .

Dani gasps.

She turns back to George.

'You fucking arsehole! You knew I'd come out here, you knew I'd say no, and you had her waiting there . . . you fucking arsehole!'

'I think the words you're looking for are "you brilliant detective".'

George puts the remains of his sandwich down and closes his novel.

He stands up.

'You should talk to her. She doesn't know the details of why we want you in there, but she does know it's a police investigation and you'd be undercover. And she has very interesting things to say about Malachy Walsh. Listen to her, at least.'

★

They don't hug. Not physically, anyway. Grace puts her hand on Dani's arm and squeezes it. Their eyes say everything. How have you been, are you okay, it's good to see you.

Then they start to walk.

'Well, this is unexpected,' Dani says.

'More for me than you, I imagine,' Grace says. 'You must do this stuff all the time, now. I'm very proud of you, Dani. I know that's not my place to say. But to have gotten yourself here after everything you went through . . .'

'How much did he tell you?' Dani asks. She doesn't want to go over the past. There's only the present and this job that looks like it's about to be foisted on her.

'Just that you're part of a specialist investigative unit that some-times sends officers into workplaces in undercover roles.'

'That's true,' Dani says. 'And we usually try to find somebody on the inside to help us get in. How did you end up on his radar?'

It's Grace's turn to look uncomfortable.

'I made a complaint.'

'To whom?'

'To the Guards.'

Dani stops walking. They've arrived at a copse of trees where they're hidden from view, if anyone was to walk by.

'About somebody in the college?'

'Yes.' Grace tugs at her bottom lip with her teeth. 'Malachy Walsh.'

'The provost?' Dani is stunned. 'What did he do?'

'He's been sexually harassing me. Not only me. I'm just the latest.'

Dani assesses the situation. She realises now what George has done and she's not happy.

'So, you went straight to the Guards. You didn't report him to the college?'

'What would be the point?'

'Oh, Grace.'

There are no lengths to which her team won't go. Dani knew that already but she still finds this upsetting.

'You don't have to do this,' she says. 'If you want Malachy Walsh dealt with, he should be dealt with.'

'But he will be,' Grace says simply. 'That's what your boss says. It'll take a bit longer but I will have done something useful. He didn't say why they need you in the college and I know you can't tell me, but I've been speculating in my head. I can only imagine it's something financial and if that's the case, then Walsh will be up to his neck in it.'

Dani looks away.

'I know how hard it is to prove sexual harassment,' Grace continues. 'But if he's part of something bigger, something worse . . .'

'Sexual harassment is bad enough,' Dani says.

'Yes, it is, but it's not enough. If you and your team can get him for something . . .'

Grace trails off. She looks at Dani, her eyes pleading.

'I'm happy to help,' she says.

'You realise what you're risking?' Dani says. 'If it comes out that my qualifications are forged, that you were responsible for hiring me and you didn't check properly . . . you could be fired. Your complaint against him won't stand. It would be viewed with bias, in fact.'

Grace nods.

'Your boss explained everything. But Dani, I'm telling you what I told him. You were the most brilliant student in your year.'

'I quit my degree!' Dani almost laughs, she's so exasperated.

'And you and I know why,' Grace says. 'You were only twenty, Dani. It's okay to be human.'

Dani shakes her head.

Grace lets the silence hang for a few seconds.

'How much do they know?' she asks. 'About Theo? I didn't say anything.'

'They know what's in his file,' Dani says. 'I don't want to talk about him. I don't want to even think about him. I've built a good life for myself, Grace. I don't want to go backwards. And I don't want people knowing how bad things got for me in St Edmund's. About the things I did. I don't want to go back in there at all. But they're not going to give me a choice.'

Grace shakes her head now.

'You know it wasn't your fault, don't you, Dani? Everything that happened. It would have sent anybody into a spiral. You did nothing wrong.'

Dani can feel a sob building in her chest.

She did everything wrong and she's been running away from that fact ever since.

If she goes back to St Edmund's, she knows she'll have to confront that.

Grace takes her hand.

'Whatever happened before, you are obviously excellent at your job,' she says. 'I believe in you.'

Dani grimaces. George said the same thing just minutes ago.

Everybody believes in her.

It's only Dani who doubts herself.

2024

Rose Hill Residential Centre is surrounded by trees and now, fully into autumn, the driveway on either side is dotted with mounds of dead red and brown leaves.

Dani drives up to the visitor car park and manages to squeeze her GoCar into a tiny spot between a badly parked BMW and a set of bollards.

She walks the rest of the way, her grip tight on the bag from the chocolatier in Rathlow. She does this every time, brings something along, even though she knows her gifts are more for the nurses than who she's visiting.

Sini is on the desk. There hasn't actually been a time when Dani has visited here and that woman hasn't been working.

She's a saint in a little blue nurse's uniform.

'Danielle,' she says. Sini always uses Dani's full name. It's what was filled in on the admittance form for next-of-kin.

'Dani is too like Sini anyway,' Sini said, one time. 'If I had a beautiful name like yours, I wouldn't cut it in half.'

Dani has been Dani all her life and she's never thought of it as half a name. She's too fond of Sini, though, to protest.

'Go on through,' Sini says. 'I'm afraid it's another bad day.'

Dani doesn't respond to that. Every day has been a bad day for a long time. But she appreciates Sini's eternal optimism that there will be a good one in the future.

Dani has resolved to hope for a good moment.

She walks along the corridor, her runners squeaking on the scrubbed tiles. The doors are open to most of the rooms and Dani could look into each one as she passes, if she wanted to be nosy. But she doesn't. Each room is somebody else's pain and Dani barely has the capacity for her own.

She stops at the end of the corridor and puts her hand on the door handle. She steels herself, her usual routine of preparation. Some deep breathing, a reminder that she'll feel better for coming even if the visit is painful in the doing.

She opens the door.

The nurses have left the window slightly open to allow the air to circulate. It's a small room and needs fresh air, but it feels a little cold to Dani.

The figure in the bed is prone, lying facing the window, as though looking out.

'It's me, Mam,' she says.

The figure doesn't stir.

Dani walks around the bed and sits in the armchair on the other side.

Cora is staring straight ahead, no sign of recognition or response.

There was a period when Cora thought she knew who Dani was, even if she was mixing her up with somebody else. An old friend or one of Cora's cousins.

And then there were the moments of lucidity that had been at once distressing and comforting.

There's no more of that.

Dani puts the chocolates on the bedside locker. She looks around the room. The small, utterly pointless TV on the chest of drawers facing the bed. The washbasin in the far corner. The table, with its two magazines, the ones that have sat there for six months.

It takes a while before Dani can look at her mother. It's always the same.

When she does, she swallows, hard.

Then she reaches across and takes her mother's hand. It's a redundant gesture.

Cora's hand is cold. Even as Dani takes it, she shudders.

Her mother was always a warm woman. In every sense.

Her mother is no longer in there. That's what Dani tells herself every time she visits, every time she phones.

Except, now she's thinking something new. Something dangerous and awful and heart-breaking.

What if they could get some of Cora back?

What if Turner's drug actually worked?

What if there was a drug coming from anybody, anywhere, that could work?

Dani closes her eyes.

Enough. She can't think like that.

She leans across and strokes what's left of her mother's hair.

That was one of the things that, weirdly, upset Dani the most. One of Cora's favourite pastimes was getting her hair done.

Dani hates the hair salon. She'd cut her own hair if she could. She's never been able to make small talk with hairdressers. She feels completely intimidated by them. And yet, she's never comfortable not talking either. So, she ends up chatting mindlessly.

But Cora, she'd book in for every treatment under the sun and her hair was always beautifully shiny and healthy. The stringy grey strands there now are an affront.

Yet another middle finger from the disease that's stolen her life.

'How are you, sweetheart?' Dani says.

Some of the literature tells her she should talk to her mother like she's still there, like Cora understands everything she's saying.

Not because there's a glimmer of hope she does, but because thinking so will make Dani feel better.

So, with each visit, Dani tries to talk like everything is normal, like they're sitting in the kitchen of their small home having a cup of coffee like any other mother and daughter.

The home Dani was forced to sell to pay for this never-ending care.

When her mother was first diagnosed, the doctors told them the disease would be brutally aggressive and would shorten Cora's life expectancy drastically.

That wasn't the worst thing, even then they realised that. If they'd told Cora she had a terminal disease and could expect to live maybe only five to ten years, Cora would have eventually come to terms with having five to ten years, hoping for more.

It was the knowledge that Cora would live that long and for most of it . . . already be gone.

A living death.

'I don't want you to live with that,' she'd told Dani. 'Send me somewhere. Do what you have to. Forget about me. I can't bear the thought of burdening you.'

And even that hadn't been the worst of it.

Dani had cried her eyes out, angry that her mother would think she could just walk away, devastated because she knew she couldn't.

They'd tried every drug, every treatment. All the tools and exercises designed to try to keep the brain active for as long as possible.

The doctors had been right about one thing – the disease had attacked with speed and ferocity.

They'd been wrong about Cora's life expectancy. Cora is ten years into her diagnosis now.

For the last eight of those, she's barely been there.

'There's a drug,' Dani says, before she can stop herself. 'A new one. And somebody told me recently that they think it doesn't just stop the advance of Alzheimer's, it can actually reverse some of the damage. When I heard that, I thought of you, Mam. And I thought, I'd give anything to have you back. Just for five minutes. Just to see in your eyes that you remember me. To hear your voice, to hear you say you love me.'

Dani chokes back a sob.

Cora hasn't even blinked.

'But there's a problem with it,' Dani continues. 'My team, we're investigating it. We think the pharmaceutical company making it is lying to the FDA. That the drug has terrible side effects and the company is speeding through the clinical trials and hiding the adverse reactions they're finding. I'm supposed to be helping to find out what those are. But Mam . . . what if the drug does work? For some people?'

Dani shifts in her chair. She feels ill, nauseous for saying aloud the thoughts that have entered her head since she spoke to Colm.

It can't be true, she tells herself. The drug isn't a saviour drug. The drug is deadly. That's why they've zeroed in on it. Trying to pre-empt class action suits which cost plaintiffs and governments millions, not to mention the pain and damage inflicted before a drug is taken off the market.

The door opens and Sini comes in.

'Oof, it's cold in here, isn't it?' she says.

She crosses to the window and closes it. Then she walks to the bed and tightens the blankets around Cora's tiny frame.

'Will I get you a cuppa?' she asks Dani. 'We're about to do the teas.'

'No, thank you, Sini,' Dani says. 'I'm not staying long.'

'Of course,' Sini says.

There's no judgement in her voice. Dani feels it all the same.

She leaves and Dani is left alone with Cora again.

There's a tiny dribble at the side of Cora's mouth. Dani takes a tissue from the locker and wipes it. She turns to throw the tissue in the bin beside the locker.

She feels her mother stir a little and turns quickly to look at Cora.

Her mother's face is the same, her eyes still staring vacantly into the distance.

Dani leans closer. She can smell Cora's breath. It's stale, medicinal. She knows the nurses make sure she's hydrated but the smell builds all the time anyway, because Cora doesn't speak or eat or drink for herself.

'I miss you,' Dani says. 'I love you, Mam. I'm sorry if I didn't tell you that enough. I'm sorry for how I was back then. When I lost it. I shouldn't have wasted a second of my time with you.'

Dani sits back.

She'd wasted time on Theo then. And now she's doing it again, thinking about him when she has a job to do.

She needs to put him out of her head, for good.

2014

Dani's home for the weekend when it happens.

When he turns up outside her house.

She's not in good form, anyway. As soon as she got in the door, Cora suggested they head out for a Chinese meal. All Dani wanted to do was get her washing on, have a bath and go to bed early.

This seemed to irritate her mother and Dani couldn't understand why.

Was it too much to ask, with everything she's gone through, that her home be the one place where no pressure is applied?

Dani's upstairs rooting through her wardrobe for some old PJs when the doorbell rings.

She listens for a second to see if Cora's heard it, but the radio is blaring in the kitchen and there's no sound of any doors opening downstairs.

'I'll get it, so!' she calls out with irritation, even though nobody can hear her.

She opens the door and the man she knows as the Fox is standing there.

Dani can't speak for a moment. Then the words gush out.

'Is it him? Is everything okay? Have you heard something?'

'Somebody is here to see you.'

The Fox gestures at a car parked outside. A black Mercedes.

Dani stops breathing. She can see a figure sitting in the back.

She walks down the garden path in her stockinged feet.

As she reaches the gate, her heart falls. There's a man in the car but it's not Theo. It's an older version of Theo.

His father, Alexandre.

She turns and looks at the Fox.

'I'll wait here,' he says, gesturing at the car.

Dani gets into the car.

Alexandre looks at her, then looks away.

'I . . . Hello,' she says.

He continues to stare straight ahead.

'Is it bad news?' Dani rushes the words out.

'What?' he replies.

'You've come here to give me bad news,' she says. 'I presume. Otherwise, you would have just phoned.'

'I have not come here to give you news of Theo.'

'I don't understand.'

'You have become a problem for me.'

Dani doesn't know what to say to that.

'In several ways,' he continues. 'First, I learn that you have followed an employee of mine. And then, I hear from the gendarmerie. Because my sister has reported my son missing.'

So, Aimee did it. She went to the police.

'Good,' Dani says. 'I'm glad. It's about time somebody in his family did something for him. Seeing as you won't.'

Alexandre makes a sharp intake of breath. She guesses he isn't used to being spoken to like this.

'Miss MacLochlainn, when we spoke last, I told you where Theo was.'

'No. You told me what was in the email you believed Theo had sent.'

'The email I believed he sent?'

'Yes. I've seen that email and Theo didn't send it. It was written in English. Theo wouldn't have emailed you in English. Didn't that alarm you at all? And what kind of parent gets an email from his son saying he's dropping out of college and doesn't worry about that in the slightest?'

'Miss MacLochlainn—'

'I realise you weren't happy when he decided to come here to study, but for fuck's sake, it's one thing him being over here and you knowing where he is. For him to just up and leave like that and only send an email . . . why weren't you worried? Why don't you care? He's your son!'

Dani's voice has risen. She can sense his simmering anger but she's not going to take his feelings into consideration. Not when he cares so little about hers.

There's silence in the car for a few moments. Then, he turns and looks at her.

'Are you finished?'

The words feel like a slap. She doesn't know what she hoped for. Maybe, that her obvious distress might get through to him.

But it hasn't. His voice is cold. Furious.

'Yes,' she says.

'Then perhaps you will listen to me, now. And this time, hear me.'

Dani presses her lips together.

'You may have known my son, intimately, for all of, what, a year?'

Dani doesn't want to correct him. Eighteen months might feel longer to her but it will sound petty out loud.

'He is, as you have pointed out, my son,' Mr Laurent continues. 'I have known him all his life. And I know things about him that neither you, nor my sister, know.'

Dani bites her lip so hard, she draws blood.

She quickly wipes it away. Her heart is racing.

'Like what?' she says.

'Like nothing that is any of your business.'

Dani almost cries with frustration.

'No,' she shouts. 'That's not good enough. I'm the one who was with him here. I have a right to know what's happened.'

She stops, takes a breath. If she keeps going like this, he'll probably just tell her to fuck off and she really wants to know why he's here. Because there's no way a man like this flew all the way to Ireland just to put her in her place.

'Look,' she says, a little calmer. 'You're right, maybe I didn't know Theo as well as you. And I don't know you at all. But from what I did know of your son, he was a good man. A lovely, kind, intelligent man. And some of that *must* have been your doing. And I haven't spoken to him in over four weeks, and everything I know about him tells me that's something to be worried about. I can't stop thinking that he might have come to harm. That somebody hurt him or he had an accident or . . . I don't know. So, if there's something relevant to why he might have left, I'm asking you, I'm begging you . . . please tell me.'

She waits a few moments. She's starting to wonder if Mr Laurent is done with her, but then he speaks.

'I am used to my family having privacy, Miss MacLochlainn.

And now I have the police asking questions about matters that don't concern them. You may be angry at me, but it is nothing compared to how angry I feel towards you and my sister. But now I have a bigger problem.'

Dani holds her breath.

'My man is concerned about where Theo is. And unbeknownst to me, he has been looking for him. Prompted by you. Because I did not ask this of him. And I am not used to my employees going behind my back on matters that do not concern them.'

The Fox, Dani thinks. Always sneaking around, according to Aimee. And Dani is really, really grateful for it.

'Why are you here?' Dani interrupts. 'Is it just to have a go at me, or has *your* man found something?'

Mr Laurent returns his gaze to the front.

'No,' he says. 'He has not. And that is why I am here. To meet with the Irish police.'

Dani finally breathes.

At last.

'Why didn't you listen to me before?' she says. 'You've wasted weeks.'

'Like I said, you do not know Theo as well as I do. You don't know how stubborn the boy can be. I wasn't worried about him. And now, that worry has been forced on me.'

Dani shrugs. She doesn't feel any sympathy for him.

'Your role in this is finished,' he says. 'I will find my son.'

'He's still my—'

'You are nothing to him. When I find Theo, maybe he will decide to resume relations with you, maybe not. I suspect if he has ignored you this long, you do not mean as much to him as you believe you do. Good evening, Miss MacLochlainn.'

He stops talking.

Dani, stung, waits a few seconds, then gets out of the car.

The Fox looks at her sympathetically as she walks back to the gate.

She hesitates before passing him.

'Thank you,' she says.

'For what?'

'For making him take it seriously.'

He doesn't respond.

'What's your name?' she asks.

'I'm sure Aimee told you.'

There's a hint of bemusement in his voice.

Dani shakes her head.

'What did she refer to me as?' he asks.

'Just . . . a nickname.'

He smiles.

'Ah. I can guess. She means it in a derogatory fashion but I don't hear it as that. They're cunning, you know. Wily.'

'I know.'

'Louis,' he says.

It takes her a moment. Then she remembers.

'It was you.'

'Me what?'

'You emailed Theo. Said you were thinking of coming over to Ireland if he didn't make it to France. You're his old friend.'

'When he didn't turn up after contacting me, I became worried. I figured if he would not come to me, I would go to him.'

Dani nods.

Aimee was wrong. This man wouldn't harm Theo to keep Alexandre safe.

He cares for Theo.

'Will you tell me, if you find him? It doesn't matter if he doesn't want to speak to me. I just need to know.'

He nods curtly in return.

Then he leaves.

Dani walks into her house, in a daze.

What did Mr Laurent mean, she didn't know Theo?

Cora is in the living room, watching TV, but she's not really watching it. She's just staring at the screen vacantly. She doesn't seem to realise Dani was outside.

'Oh, have you changed your mind about going out?' she says. 'There's nothing on the telly . . .'

She trails off, staring at Dani.

'You've got blood on your lip,' Cora says. 'And across your cheek. Are you okay, love?'

Dani shakes her head.

'Theo's dad was outside,' she says.

'What? Outside? Why didn't you invite him in?'

Dani sits down, her legs feeling like jelly.

Cora places a hand to her chest.

'Oh, God,' she says. 'Is there news?'

'No. He's angry at me. He's going to report Theo missing. He told me this has nothing to do with me any more. That Theo obviously doesn't want anything to do with me. He's not worried something has happened to him, he just thinks he needs to be found.'

Cora purses her lips. Dani waits for her to say something and when she doesn't, Dani starts to get annoyed.

'Mam,' she says. 'Don't you think that's weird?'

Cora sighs.

'Dani, I don't know what to say to you. Maybe you just need to move on.'

Dani stares at her mother.

'Move on?' she says. 'You agreed with me. When Theo vanished, you said it was out of character. You know him, Mam.'

'I thought I did. And so did you. But Dani, sweetheart, if something had happened to the lad, you'd know by now. I think it's time you started to accept that he doesn't want to be found. His father must know him better than you ever thought you did . . .'

'Mam!'

Dani is close to tears. She looks at Cora beseechingly.

'This is the worst thing that's ever happened to me,' she says. 'I need you to be here for me.'

As soon as she says it, Dani regrets it. Cora looks appalled.

'I don't mean—' She starts to say.

'The worst thing!' Cora snaps. 'Your father died in the prime of his life and you think this is the worst thing?!'

'It came out wrong . . . I meant, not knowing where he's gone—'

'For God's sake, Dani, I didn't rear you to be so selfish. Theo was your boyfriend, that's all. Other people have problems in their lives. You've no idea. All I wanted tonight was a bloody break. A nice meal and a glass of wine. And instead, I have you whining about you, you, you and your conspiracy theories, and it's like having a fucking toddler in the house!'

Dani is lost for words. Her mother is glaring at her. She's never seen Cora like this. She's not sure she's ever even heard Cora curse before.

But before she can even process it, Cora's expression changes.

It's almost like she's surprised at her own outburst.

She clamps a hand over her mouth.

'Oh, love,' she says. 'I'm sorry.'

Dani shakes her head. She doesn't know what to say.

'Dani, I don't know what came over me. I've just had a few things going on . . .'

'What things?' Dani says. She's instantly ready to forgive Cora. The idea that her mother might be stressed about something and trying not to upset Dani with it is infinitely more comprehensible than Cora snapping at her for no good reason.

But Cora just shakes her head.

'Nothing important,' she says. 'I'm sorry, really. I shouldn't have gone off on one like that. I know you're worried. I'm just hoping there's nothing to be concerned about. Look, how about we order in? I'll open a bottle of wine.'

Dani wants to cry but she just nods.

Cora looks uncomfortable, like she needs to get away from Dani. She stands up.

'Where are those takeout menus?' she asks.

'Where they always are,' Dani says quietly. She can't meet Cora's eye. She's too upset.

'I'm getting old,' Cora says. 'I'd forget my own name.'

She leaves the living room.

Dani stares at the television. There's some documentary on about the Amazon river and how much fresh water it pumps into the sea.

Her phones beeps and she ignores it. She's checked it instantly every time it's gone off recently, filled with hope. But the last twenty minutes have just been too strange for Dani to even try to function normally.

She keeps watching the TV and it's a few minutes before she realises her mother left the room to look for the takeout menus, which are all in the drawer under the television stand.

Dani's about to call Cora when she realises Cora knows full well where those menus are. She obviously just wanted to get away from Dani.

And her whining.

Dani swallows the lump in her throat.

She takes out her phone. She's seriously considering checking the train timetables. It's a Friday night and there'll be plenty of trains back to Rathlow for the evening crowd.

The message on screen is from Mr Laurent's mobile number.

Dani opens it, bracing herself for another onslaught.

She's not prepared for what she reads.

I apologise if I sounded harsh but I am correct. You don't know my son. I have been advised that you may need some context. I doubt you know this, but Theo spent six months in juvenile detention when he was fifteen and then ran away. He has always been a complicated boy and this is not the first time he has done this. Accept that and move on with your life.

Dani stares at her phone.

What?

Juvenile detention?

Running away?

That can't be true. And if it is . . .

Why hadn't Theo told her?

2024

The dinner, Dani has told Colm, is a thank you for telling her about the Turner drug.

She's cooked lasagne and Colm has just agreed to a third glass of wine.

Dani has been watching her own alcohol intake, topping up her glass along with his but always when she has barely taken a few sips and his is fully empty.

'I visited my mam yesterday,' she says.

Colm stops eating. He looks surprised.

'I didn't realise. She's still alive?'

Dani nods.

'That's . . . unusual. Early-onset normally means . . .'

'I know. She proved them wrong. On that bit, at least.'

'That must be very hard. I'm sorry, Dani.'

'I'm sorry too. For my mam. She's a shell of herself. But, yesterday, I told her about the research you guys were doing and the trials—'

Colm's expression is panicked.

'Oh, God, I'm sorry. I should have said. The trial is full. We're not taking on any more participants. We're almost finished.'

'No, I didn't mean that,' Dani says.

He visibly relaxes.

'I just found myself talking about it and I suppose for the first time, I felt this glimmer of hope. I know that's silly. My mother is too far gone for there to ever be actual hope. And even if by some miracle she came back now . . . She's missed so much. I'd hate to see her have to deal with that.'

Colm's eyes are full of compassion.

'But I feel hope for others, if that makes sense? I thought, this is not something for us, but maybe other people won't have to go through what we've gone through.'

'That's my hope, too,' Colm says. 'I wish we could find the miracle cure. Even if it meant people having to accept those years were lost. But that's not going to happen. If we can prevent it, though, and get back some memory function, that's a start.'

Dani raises her glass. He does the same. They clink and they both drink the toast. Him, deeply. Her, a sip. Then, she fills his glass again.

'Are you trying to get me drunk, Professor MacLochlainn?' he laughs.

'I'm trying to get myself drunk, Tutor Ahern. You're just a casualty of war.'

Colm laughs. Dani smiles mirthlessly. Colm is a casualty of war and she feels deeply sorry for it.

'I don't care,' he says. 'Sunday tomorrow. I've been at it all week. I plan to sleep all the way through to, oh, I don't know, 8 a.m.'

'Sloth!'

Colm shrugs. He finishes his food and Dani takes his plate. When she returns from the kitchen, Colm is standing in front of the fire she's lit in the grate, his wine glass in hand.

'It's cosy, this place,' he says. 'I like hanging out here.'

'Why, thank you.'

'My apartment is just so functional compared to this.'

'Have you been in any of the apartments over this side?' she asks. 'Like Declan's? Doesn't he have one of the older apartments?'

'Not any more. He's over in the block near the research school, too.'

'I see.' Dani keeps her voice casual and fills his glass again. He tries to stop her, but she brushes his hand away.

'Go on. Sunday tomorrow, like you say. Don't let me be hung-over alone.'

'Well, this is the last. I'm already tipsy. And I think your fire is giving me first-degree burns.'

'Then sit down, idiot!'

Colm crosses back to his chair.

'Can I ask you one thing?' Dani says. 'About this drug you're testing?'

'Fire ahead. You see what I did there? *Fire* ahead.'

'You're a genius.' She laughs. Then she grows serious again. 'Are there any side effects? I always worry when there's a drug coming that sounds so positive. It seems too good to be true.'

'Nothing is too good to be true. Look at what medicine has done over the years. Think back a century ago and what people would have thought about radiation killing cancer cells. There are always side effects. It's about finding a way to minimise the amount of adverse reactions versus the good the drug is doing.'

'And in this one?'

'They've found the balance. The usual complaints are there – nausea, headaches, some vision impairment, dizziness, kidney infections . . . common symptoms.'

'And the more serious considerations?'

Colm shrugs.

'There's always a worry a drug that's operating on so many levels will have an undesirable effect elsewhere in the body. We were most concerned about other organs. The heart, mainly.'

'Like, heart attacks?'

'Well, yeah,' Colm says. 'That the drug could put too much strain on the patient and increase the heart rate to unsustainable levels. We monitored for it.'

'But it doesn't do that?'

'No. In the tiniest percentage, less than half a per cent, it put some pressure on the heart. As a result of other issues. Nothing that couldn't be monitored and alleviated. But the FDA will put a warning label on for doctors to not prescribe to patients who have severe heart problems. Just to be safe.'

'Well, that's normal, isn't it?' Dani says. 'I'm sure there are lots of things those patients can't have.'

'Sure. But Turner doesn't want to be responsible for killing anybody.'

Colm says it lightly. Dani smiles.

He believes what he's saying.

She almost wishes he was part of the problem. It would make this a whole lot easier.

Later, when he's passed out on her couch, she puts a blanket over him.

That last glass had half a sleeping pill in it.

Combined with the wine . . .

It's not entirely ethical. It's not ethical at all. But then, as George keeps saying, Turner Pharma isn't worried about ethics. And no harm will come to Colm.

She takes his room key and lets herself into his building. She moves quickly and quietly through the corridors. She's not overly worried. It's a Saturday night and most of the college's residents are out socialising and drinking. If anybody sees her, she'll say she's visiting somebody.

Even though there's nobody around, however, Dani can't shake the feeling somebody is watching her.

She looks up and down the empty corridor, then lets herself into Colm's rooms.

His computer is on. She goes through the same routine as last time, inputting the password for the DG file.

She's not expecting to find sensitive data on Colm's personal computer. Turner will be far too clever for that. But there may be something in one of the emails or saved documents that can add to their file of evidence or direct them elsewhere.

What she really needs access to will most likely be on Declan Graham's computer.

Dani and her team suspect that Turner knows full well what the most damaging side effect of their drug is. It will have been discussed in the Turner boardroom and on safe-line conference calls.

But nobody will have been stupid enough to write down the problem.

So, the real key is in the raw data of the trial's participants, which only St Edmund's has the central database for.

And if she can get that, the task force's scientists can start to analyse it against the health reports of those who've received Turner's drug and figure out what Turner is hiding.

It has to be something much bigger than the usual adverse reactions or their whistle-blower would never have come forward.

Cecelia Vargas would never have been killed.

That's what they're all thinking.

Dani compresses the entire DG file and saves it on to a USB. She'd like to read some of the Declan emails but not here. Not now, when time is of the essence.

When the file is saved, she takes the USB from the side of the computer. Then she goes into settings, opens data transfers and wipes the history, just like they've taught her to do in headquarters.

Dani leaves as anonymously as she arrived, only texting George when she's back in the courtyard and walking towards her own apartment building.

Got his personal computer emails. Next step, find a way to Declan's computer.

Just like I did ten years ago, she thinks, but doesn't write.

2014

Dani returns to college feeling both depressed and motivated.

There's no way she's going to take Mr Laurent's warning to stay away seriously.

Plan A is to find out if Declan Graham knows more than he's let on.

She hangs around the research school building, hoping to catch him when he finishes classes. Instinctively, she knows he won't make himself available to her for another appointment.

She misses her own lectures for the afternoon, but the day is warm, and sitting on the benches in the small park between the old college and the campus new builds is not an ordeal.

But the hours tick by and there's no sign of Declan. Dani needs to pee and her stomach is starting to groan with hunger. She checks her phone and sees it's 7 p.m. Either Declan is working late or he finished early. And she's not sure how to get hold of him.

She is planning to try again tomorrow when she spots one of Theo's classmates.

She approaches him and asks whether Declan had any classes today. He tells her Declan missed the day's lectures. He's been having meetings all day off-campus.

Dani bites down her frustration. She starts towards her own end of the college, thinking about the ambush attempt she'll make tomorrow.

Then she has a stroke of luck.

Declan is walking towards her, his phone to his ear, absorbed in conversation. He looks excited, animated; he doesn't see Dani until they're almost on top of each other.

'Professor Graham,' she says.

He looks at her, startled, the smile still on his face.

When he sees who it is, the smile falters, but he fixes it in place. He covers his phone.

'Dani,' he says. 'Sorry, I'm on a call.'

'I need to speak to you,' she says.

'It's not really a good time.'

Dani doesn't move.

Declan stares at her, bemused, slightly irritated, but then a look of patronly indulgence settles on his face.

'I'll call you back, Malachy,' he says into the phone.

He hangs up.

'What can I do for you?' he asks.

'There's still no word from Theo,' she says.

'I'm really disappointed to hear that,' he says. 'But I guess we just have to accept Theo doesn't want to talk to us. Give him time, Dani.'

'Can I ask you something?' she says.

'Of course.'

'Did something happen between you and Theo?'

There's a fraction of a moment where Declan hesitates.

'Something like what?'

'Did you have an argument?'

'Not that I recall. We debated some theory in class. But that was normal. I debate with all my students. Theo was one of the best.'

'What do you mean, he *was*?'

'Well, he's not my student right now.'

Declan is starting to look eager to get away.

'I really need to get on,' he says. 'I've work to catch up on. If there's nothing more . . .'

'Something changed between you and Theo,' she says.

'Excuse me?'

'I know he used to talk about you a lot and then he just stopped.'

'I don't know where you're going with this—'

'He used to challenge you in lectures and . . .'

'I expect my students to challenge me.'

'But did it get heated? Theo could be . . . He was always right. Did it get personal?'

'Excuse me? Personal how?'

'You tell me.'

Dani instantly wants to take it back. She's pushed it too far. Declan might be friendly at a superficial level to students, but she's still a student. And she can tell he's pissed off.

There's a moment of silence.

'I'm just trying to figure out what happened to him,' she says, breaking it.

'I am never, ever defensive with my students,' Declan says. 'When Theo argued with me, I encouraged it.'

'I just thought, maybe, if a line had been crossed, if he'd misunderstood an interaction . . . It might explain why he left.'

Declan takes a step towards her. His eyes are suddenly full of anger – so much so, Dani feels immediately threatened. She's suddenly aware there's nobody else around. It's teatime in the dining hall; most students are either there or in their rooms.

Something on her face must reveal how frightened she is because Declan seems to gather himself. He stares down at the ground then looks back up at Dani.

'I know you're upset,' he says. 'I know you miss him and you're searching for answers to why he left. But this is very unfair. I had an excellent relationship with Theo. There was never a cross word between us.'

Dani can't meet his eye. She doesn't know how to articulate her suspicions; she's not even sure what her suspicions are.

And she can tell Declan is completely infuriated by her accusation.

Dani wants to get away from him. And she's about to when she feels his hand on her arm.

'You can't go around saying things like this to anybody else, do you understand, Dani? It's unacceptable and I won't allow it.'

Dani looks at Declan's hand. It's tight on her arm. Then she looks at him.

Really looks at him. His eyes are boring into hers.

She realises in that moment: Declan isn't remotely worried about Theo. He doesn't give a toss about Theo.

He's only worried about Dani and the possibility of her telling people she thinks he had something to do with Theo leaving.

He's worried for himself.

And she knows, she just knows, with every fibre of her being, that this is a man who'll do anything to protect himself from harm. Wherever it comes from.

She pulls her arm away from his. He catches her eye again, surprised.

'Do you hear me, Dani?' he says.

Dani moves to his left. He steps the same way so she can't pass.

She starts to tremble. She swallows.

Her survival instinct kicks in.

'I hear you,' she says. 'Loud and clear.'

He removes himself from her path.

Dani walks away. She doesn't look back but she knows he's watching her.

She has to resist the urge to run.

He's hiding something. She suspected it before. Now she's convinced.

Dani knows Declan Graham won't talk to her again and yet, she can't shake the feeling that he's still holding a piece of the puzzle.

Which only leaves her with one option.

She takes the following day off lectures and spends it watching Declan's movements.

And the next.

By the end of the week, she's starting to get a feel for his daily routine, but she's also conscious she's running out of time. It's approaching May, the college will soon go into full exam prep mode, and by the start of June, it'll break up for summer. Dani will be going home, and more importantly, so will Declan.

She needs to get into his office and his computer before that happens.

She doesn't even know if there will be anything on his computer, but she's hoping it might be linked to his phone and that she can read his messages. He and Theo could have had a text exchange at some point and she wants to know exactly what was in it.

Does he know about Theo's plans to work for Amarita Medical, she wonders? She hadn't had the chance to ask him outright, not after she accused him of arguing with Theo. But for all she knows, Theo suggested it to Declan and Declan told him it was a terrible idea. Or Declan suggested Theo might go work there and Theo didn't want to. They might have fought about . . . well, anything. Dani can't stop speculating.

She's aware that when the professors leave their offices at night, most of them don't bother to lock their doors. The office floors are locked by building security, so there's no need.

From what she's seen so far, Declan departs most nights before seven and his secretary leaves a few minutes later. They're usually the last out of their building and the security guard goes upstairs shortly afterwards to lock up the floor.

Dani will have minutes to get into his office between the secretary leaving and the security guard arriving.

She'll most likely be locked in overnight. She doesn't care about that. She can hide in one of the offices, and first thing in the morning, make her escape before anyone realises.

But she has to be somewhere on the floor when his secretary leaves or she won't have a hope of getting into his office and being out of sight before the security guard arrives to lock up.

Dani's plan is to do it that night, Thursday. If she does it on Friday, she could end up being locked in all weekend.

So, this is her shot.

She's walking across the courtyard when she hears her name.

It's Professor Grace Byrne, her American history teacher.

Dani hesitates. She's timed this with minutes to spare.

'Hi Professor,' she says breezily.

Grace looks taken aback.

'I thought you were unwell,' she tells Dani.

Too late, Dani remembers she's been missing lectures all week. Her attempt at seeming natural and happy has now landed her in it.

'I was,' Dani says. 'I had a migraine. But it passed this morning. I just didn't want to risk it coming back. I'm going for a walk to get some fresh air.'

Grace doesn't say anything for a few moments. Dani can feel her neck and chest turning red.

'Well, I'm glad to see you're feeling better,' Grace says. 'But I have been worried about you, Dani. You haven't submitted your latest paper yet.'

Dani looks blank. What paper? She can't even remember one being set. Then she recalls it, a vague memory of Grace emailing everyone with the assignment.

'Oh, God,' Dani says. 'I'm so sorry. I have it sitting there. It just went straight out of my head.'

Grace doesn't look convinced.

'I know things have been a little off for you lately,' she says. 'And I'm here for you, if you'd like to discuss anything. But Dani, you still need to do the coursework. Unless you have a dispensation, and you need to ask for one of those.'

'I don't. Honestly. I'll get the paper to you tomorrow. And I'll be back in class on Monday.'

Grace nods, unconvinced.

Dani can feel time slipping away from her.

'I'd better go on this walk,' she says. 'Clear my head.'

She turns away before Grace can say anything more.

She knows her lecturer is watching her as she hurries across the courtyard. Probably wondering what on earth is going on with her previously excellent student.

Dani doesn't care. Education can wait. This can't.

Just before she leaves the courtyard, she sees Declan Graham entering his apartment building. So, he's clear.

She breaks into a jog and arrives as his secretary is leaving the school. Dani runs inside, nodding at the security guard as though she has every right to be there. He doesn't react and she guesses he thinks she's dropping off a last-minute paper.

She just hopes he doesn't realise he hasn't seen her come back out.

She takes the stairs so he won't see what floor she's going to on the lift display.

She pushes open the door to the second floor, out of breath, before realising she has screwed up. The building has a basement, so the second floor is actually the third floor. The floor she's landed on is undergoing construction work. There are sheets of plastic on the ground and half the doors have been removed from the offices, which are being renovated. Building equipment lies everywhere.

Dani pushes open the door to the stairwell and runs back down the flight of stairs, praying the door to the floor below isn't already locked.

At the next landing, she arrives out onto a small hallway. She's about to push open the door to the corridor when she hears the lift, right beside her, in motion.

The security guard is on his way up.

Dani bursts through the door to the corridor and runs along it at full pelt until she reaches Declan's office. She pushes down the handle to his outer office and nearly cries with relief when she discovers it's unlocked, as she imagined.

She's barely inside when she hears the door at the entrance to the corridor open again.

Dani, quieter this time, enters Declan's office.

She hurries behind his desk and crouches down into the leg space underneath.

The door to the outer office opens. She hears the security guard whistling tunelessly.

He opens the door to Declan's office. She imagines him looking in and she tries to make herself as small and silent as humanly possible. She's convinced he can hear her breathing.

But the whistling continues unperturbed, then she hears the door shut and he's gone.

Dani gives it a few minutes, guessing he's checking each office to make sure they are indeed empty.

When she thinks she's heard the fire door at the end of the corridor close, she emerges from under the desk.

She stands up, shaking out the stiffness in her legs from the awkward position she's just been in.

The college bell abruptly starts to ring; the piped-in sound makes her jump.

She waits it out and then looks around the office: at the seat she sat in the last time she was here, the filing cabinets, the crystal decanter and glasses.

There's nothing personal of Declan's here – only his computer, and that's sitting on the desk in front of her.

She touches the laptop. The screen comes to life.

It's password-protected.

Dani goes back out to the secretary's ante-office.

She looks at the spotlessly clean desk and the one Post-it stuck to the computer screen.

She goes back into Declan's office, pulls out his chair and uses his keyboard to type the password from the Post-it.

She's tense, right up to the second the computer screen reveals she's put in the right password.

Once Declan told her he'd be useless without his secretary, Dani had made the leap that the woman would always have her boss's computer password to hand.

First, Dani searches for messages.

Theo's phone is an iPhone and so is Declan's. And this is a Mac.

So, when Dani opens the messages app, she's expecting to see Theo's number somewhere in the left-hand sidebar.

She's seen Theo text Declan. She's seen Theo receive texts from Declan. He's one of those lecturers who has no problem sharing his mobile number. He's even set up a WhatsApp group for his class.

But there is no conversation between Declan and Theo.

There are other chats. Declan and his other students, some of his friends, family, colleagues. But no Theo.

He must have deleted the conversation.

Dani is both disappointed and buoyed. There's only one reason to delete a conversation and that's to hide something.

Dani opens Declan's emails.

She's expecting any communication here to have also been wiped but she still hopes she'll find something.

She searches for Theo's email address.

Dozens of emails appear on screen.

Dani frowns. It's easy to delete one text conversation. Maybe

Declan didn't feel he needed to get rid of multiple emails. And maybe that's because there's nothing in them.

But she can hope.

She checks the most recent email from Theo.

It was sent two weeks before he disappeared.

The subject title is empty.

She opens the email and her chest constricts as she reads the line Theo had written.

We need to talk. Malachy should know.

Just that. No sign-off, no best wishes.

Dani checks the second-to-last email from Theo.

It's a link to an article on research in Stanford. There's no text in the email and when Dani tries to open the link, it tells her the URL has expired.

The rest of the emails are coursework-related. Dani speed-reads through them, hoping to see something, anything that tells her Theo had fought with Declan, but his tone in all of them is polite, friendly, respectful.

She goes back to the top email. The one saying they had to talk and mentioning Malachy Walsh.

Declan never replied.

Dani sits back in the chair and drums her fingers on the desktop.

She puts her head in her hands and tries to think of her next move.

Desperate, Dani starts to search the office. She pulls open file drawers and flicks through papers that mean nothing to her. She gets on her hands and knees and checks under tables.

She stands up, shaking her head in despair.

She sits back down at the computer.

Idly, she plays with the mouse and then realises . . .

She hasn't checked for deleted emails.

Dani opens the trash folder in Declan's emails.

She types in Theo.

Nothing.

She scrolls through the emails there anyway, in case she sees something that will make this worthwhile.

Most of the deleted emails are junk, or unimportant emails from the college announcing dates, events and so on.

Then she sees one that makes her sit up straight.

It's an email from the provost's office and the subject title is HR review.

Dani opens it and reads.

Declan, a chara,

Apologies for the formal email but as promised, we want to put in writing that the complaint made against you has been dropped by the student involved. The college will be taking no action against the student, as per your request. We apologise again for the inconvenience and distress this matter has caused you and we wish to reaffirm how highly regarded you are at St Edmund's. Your temperament and quality of teaching have never been in doubt and we are sincerely sorry to have had to investigate this matter.

Best,

Malachy Walsh

Dani's blood runs cold.

Somebody had made a complaint against Declan – she checks the date – four months ago, and it had been quashed.

Had it been Theo? Or another student, who'd had a run-in with Declan?

She sits back in the chair, her mind whirring over all the possibilities.

His temperament. That implies anger. And anger can lead to anything.

Mr Friendly might not be that friendly when pushed, she thinks.

What if he threatened Theo? If he intimidated him in some way?

And because she's so lost in thought, Dani doesn't hear the fire door open down the corridor, she doesn't hear the footsteps along it and she doesn't realise she's about to be caught until the door to Declan's office opens and he's standing there, staring at her, his expression somewhere between shocked and bemused.

'What the fuck?' he says.

The head of college admissions, Mr Donaghy, is an older man who's seen it all, and if Dani wasn't so defensive, she'd realise that's working in her favour.

But she's not seeing anything, at least not straight. All she's aware of is the accusation in Declan's expression, the disappointment in Grace Byrne's (whom she's asked to sit in with her, after being told she can choose a faculty member) and Mr Donaghy's seeming determination to throw her out of St Edmund's. And even though she's been caught, essentially red-handed, Dani is convinced that everybody else is in the wrong, not her.

'I know how it looks,' she says.

'It looks very much like you broke into my office and were reading my private emails,' Declan says.

'I'm not denying that,' Dani snaps.

'Dani,' Grace says, her voice leaden with warning.

'How can you possibly defend yourself?' Declan says, his eyes wide.

'Declan,' Mr Donaghy says quietly. 'Why don't we ask Dani why she was in your office and what she was doing?'

Declan looks nervous, suddenly, and Dani feels smug. She knows from their brief altercation that he doesn't want her telling anybody her suspicions and now he's put her in a situation where she must.

'Theo Laurent is missing,' Dani says. 'He's been missing for weeks.'

This doesn't elicit the response she's expecting.

'Declan told us of your concerns,' Mr Donaghy says, and Dani realises she's been gazumped. 'And we've spoken to the police.'

'You have?' Dani says.

'Yes. They contacted us after you tried to make a missing person's report. They were concerned about you.'

Dani swallows her anger. Concerned about her but not about Theo.

'His father has reported him missing now,' she says. 'I was right to do what I did. They should have taken me seriously.'

'We've also spoken to Mr Laurent.'

Dani tenses.

'He told us he doesn't believe Theo has come to any harm but that you have made yourself such a nuisance to him and his family that he's been forced to report him missing.'

'That's bollocks.'

'Dani!' Grace sounds disappointed. 'You have to respect the fact that he's Theo's father.'

'Yes, and I know, he should know him better and all that rubbish, but none of this makes sense. I went to France, I met his aunt—'

'She went to France,' Declan snorts. 'All sounds sane and rational so far.'

'I am being fucking rational!' Dani yells.

Her outburst is met with shocked silence.

She takes a deep breath. Hesitates. Tries to pull herself together. Then she meets Declan's eye.

'I don't know,' Dani says. 'But . . . his aunt suggested that Professor Graham might have been inappropriate with Theo. And I don't think it was in the way she suggested, but I do think she might be on to something. I think Professor Graham did something, like, he fought with Theo or . . . I don't know. I don't think he was as nice as he's letting on. I think he knows what happened to Theo.'

The temperature in the room seems to change. Dani feels it and she also feels that it hasn't gone in her favour.

'This is ridiculous,' Declan says, looking at Mr Donaghy. 'I've gone out of my way to be friendly with my students. That's what I was advised. That's the ethos of the college, you all said. And now I'm supposed to deal with this? Completely unfounded accusations?'

'Did you do something to Theo? That night he vanished, did you have an argument with him or something?' Dani says, quieter.

'I most certainly did not! I never even saw Theo. I was in my room the whole night. I was nowhere near his block. What on earth gives you the right to just level smears at me like this? The chap ups and leaves and you think it's because of something I did? Like I'm some kind of, what . . . bully? Is it possible he might have just thought you were bloody nuts and wanted to get away from you?'

'Declan, that's not fair,' Grace interrupts.

'Well, it's not the first time you've been accused of something by a student, is it?' Dani snaps.

'What did you say?' Declan gawps at her.

'I . . . I saw your email. Another student made a complaint about you and it was dropped. Something to do with your temper?'

Declan makes a choked, indignant sound. Grace closes her eyes.

It's left to Mr Donaghy to respond to Dani.

'Professor Graham was accused by a student of unfairly grading him over the course of a term, which resulted in him failing his year. He claimed Professor Graham shouted at him when he was confronted about the grading. We examined the papers and found strongly in Declan's favour. And we were able to get witness statements from two other students who saw the altercation between the man who made the accusation and the professor. The student withdrew his complaint. He'd been under some pressure at home to do well. Professor Graham very kindly agreed to take no further action and the provost of the college himself has apologised to Professor Graham for having to undergo the review.'

Dani is trying to make sense of what she's hearing.

'I don't understand,' she says weakly.

'No, *we* don't understand,' Grace says. 'Dani, you've been missing lectures. I've spoken to your other professors. You're behind on your coursework. You've gone from being an honours student to somebody who may fail second year. And we know now it's because all of this is going on, but you realise why we are concerned? This isn't normal behaviour. Flying to France on a whim, stalking members of Theo's family, breaking into a professor's office . . .'

Mr Donaghy is looking at her kindly.

'You've obviously taken it very hard, your friend leaving as he did,' he says. 'But that can't excuse what you've done. This is an offence that warrants expulsion.'

Dani feels like her world is imploding.

Nothing makes sense. The thoughts she'd had about Declan Graham seem so ludicrous, all of a sudden. Like she's been having some kind of nightmare and she's just woken up.

Nobody says anything for a few moments.

Then . . .

'I don't want her expelled,' Declan says.

Dani's head snaps in his direction. She's confused.

He's not looking at her. He's looking at Mr Donaghy.

'I just want her to understand how serious this is. And I want to put a stop to it.'

'Can you do that?' Mr Donaghy says, turning to Dani. 'Are you willing to go see the college's counsellor and move on from this matter?'

'You're being offered an opportunity here,' Grace says.

Dani feels overwhelmed. They're all staring at her, waiting.

'The alternative is leaving St Edmund's,' Mr Donaghy says. 'And we all agree, you're a bright student who deserves the chance to prove that.'

Dani can't bring herself to speak.

She can't bear the thought of going home and telling her mother she's been thrown out of college. It was such a big deal, Dani managing to get a place here.

And she knows that Theo, wherever he is, would hate the thought of this happening to her.

She can feel tears springing in the corners of her eyes and she hates the way they're all looking at her now, with pity on their faces.

She's desperate to leave, to go back to her room, to be away from the shame and embarrassment she's feeling.

Dani gives a small nod.

'I'll go to the counsellor,' she chokes.

'Good,' Mr Donaghy says. 'And Declan, thank you for dealing with this with such equanimity. It's more than could have been expected from you, under the circumstances.'

'Yes, thank you,' Grace says.

'Well, I guess we've all learned something,' Declan says, his voice tight. 'I've learned to lock my bloody office from now on.'

Dani realises they're all waiting for her to say something.

'Thank you for giving me a second chance,' she says, her voice barely above a whisper. 'I'm sorry.'

She can't meet any of their eyes as she stands and leaves.

2024

Dani remembers Grace doing this, as she leads her tutorial class through the college grounds towards the courtyard. Grace could always sense an apathy or tiredness in the group and then she would say, *Right so, coats on, let's walk.*

Dani felt that today as she talked them through the timeline of wars between the nineteenth century's powerful nations.

So, she'd echoed Grace's words and actions. She'd told them to grab their coats and umbrellas – a soft rain is washing the day – and brought them outside.

They're all a little giddy, unused to just standing up and leaving a tutorial, not sure what Dani has planned for them.

They reach one of the oaks and stop and form a circle, as directed by Dani.

'Okay, we're all awake, right?'

Nods and grins.

Dani points at the tree behind her.

'Oak,' she says. 'Over two hundred years old, I'm guessing.'

'Are we doing the history of trees now?' one of her more smart-ass students says.

Dani laughs.

'A hard U-turn from politics,' she says. Then she shakes her head. 'We're sticking to the lesson of the day. While this tree was barely a seedling, the Napoleonic Wars had just begun. Not necessarily all to be blamed on Napoleon. He inherited a mess and spent most of his years in power trying to bring about peace. The conflicts hurt Europe, and for a time, there was much discussion about the futility of war among nations sat so closely together.'

'Which led to Britain directing its military strength at Africa and Asia,' a student says.

'Exactly,' Dani says. 'With the exception of her engagement in the Crimea in 1854 to 1856. So, when a century starts with a series of wars so damaging that the continent's leaders agree to try to find peace, what explains the end of that century and Europe being on the cusp of another one hundred years that this time would be dominated by world wars?'

Dani never gets an answer.

Stephen, her troublesome student who's missed the last few tutorials, comes into her eyeline and before she knows what's happening, he's standing in front of her.

'Who the fuck do you think you are?' he says.

Dani blinks, shocked. He's right in her face and it takes only a millisecond of her police training to see he's on something. His pupils are dilated and the veins in his forehead are throbbing.

'Excuse me?' she says, as calmly as she can muster.

'You fucking failed me again,' he snarls.

Dani's conscious of her other students watching in horror. She can see a few of the lads step forward a little, spurring each other on. They're tempted to tackle Stephen to impress the girls in the group, but he's so jacked up they realise they're going to be on the receiving end of a few digs if they step in.

'I didn't plagiarise the new essay,' Stephen says.

'No, you didn't plagiarise this one,' Dani agrees. 'But you don't get to pass just because the work is original. It also has to be up to standard. Stephen, this isn't the time or the place. We can discuss this in my office—'

'I want to talk about it now, bitch!'

The situation is escalating.

Dani knows she can deal with Stephen. Her Garda training has ensured she has the capacity to bring down somebody even twice her size in a way that causes the least damage to her.

She's just calculating how she'll explain that skill afterwards.

Stephen lunges at her.

Before she can kick into defence mode, Stephen is thrown backwards with force.

A man is on top of him, holding him on the ground as Stephen writhes furiously.

Dani turns to one of her students.

'Go get college security. Now!'

Two students run in the direction of the main building.

'Calm the fuck down,' Dani's protector shouts.

Dani's stomach flips.

The man holding Stephen in place turns and looks at her.

It's Declan Graham.

And the second he takes his eyes off Stephen, the lad punches him in the face.

Malachy Walsh makes an appearance in the medical station to make sure Declan is all right. Dani is there; there was nothing else she could do after Stephen punched Declan. She was just glad security arrived when they did and the situation didn't deteriorate any further.

The nurse reassures them nothing is broken and goes off to get some paper stitches for the cut that Declan is currently holding a pack of ice against.

'It's most unfortunate,' Malachy says. 'The lad comes from a good family, he has everything going for him. He did quite well in his leaving certificate.'

The provost shakes his head sadly.

Dani says nothing. She knows *good family* is translation for *comes from money*. She knows he probably did well in his leaving certificate because Mummy and Daddy paid through the nose for grinds to get him across the line. She also knows that Stephen was coked up to his eyeballs when he went for her and Declan, and that his sense of entitlement is too deep to ever unpack in one conversation.

'We'll have to expel him, obviously,' Malachy continues.

He's not looking at her, Dani realises. He's watching Declan, and then she understands – the provost is hoping Declan will tell him expulsion is a step too far. But Declan, the ice still firmly to his eye, doesn't say anything.

'A shame,' Malachy says. Then, almost as an afterthought, he turns to Dani.

'And you're okay?' he asks.

She nods.

'I believe he got upset because of a low marking on one of his papers?'

Dani is fully aware she should handle this carefully but something in the implied accusation makes her snap.

'I think he got upset because he's on drugs,' she says. 'And I don't think he took the drugs because I marked him down.'

'Oh, no, of course not,' Malachy says. 'I suppose it's the obvious thing to do, isn't it? Look for reasons when a good lad acts up. Sometimes, there's no reason.'

The provost fixes his features into an expression that manages to convey he has the weight of the world's young people on his shoulders and somehow, Dani has managed to add to his burden.

'Oh, by the way,' he says, his eyes narrowed, 'I recently learned you were a student here.'

Dani tips her head.

'You dropped out, I believe.'

Dani makes a conscious effort to slow her breathing.

'Family issues,' she says.

'I see,' Malachy says. 'I thought it might have had something to do with Theo Laurent.'

It's like a ghost has walked into the room.

Dani, despite being thrown by the remark, notices that Declan is staring at Malachy, confusion on his face.

'Theo Laurent?' she repeats, like an idiot.

'Yes. There was some problem with him, wasn't there? Wasn't he one of your students, Declan?'

'You know he was,' he says.

'What do you mean, there was a problem with him?' Dani says.

'Oh, I only mean everything that happened to him.'

Dani's breath catches.

'Did you know him?' she asks. 'Personally, I mean?'

'Not personally.'

Malachy turns to Declan.

'He had an issue with you, didn't he, Declan? Caused a few arguments?'

Declan looks dumbfounded. Dani stares at him.

'Not with me,' he says.

'Really? He came to my office that time. Spouting nonsense. Don't you remember?'

Declan doesn't respond.

'Spouting what nonsense?' Dani says, her stomach tight. 'What are you talking about?'

Malachy stares at her. Something passes on his face.

Dani feels a chill run down her spine.

His expression . . . it's like he's toying with her. Acting like this is just a casual old chat when really, it's loaded. And he knows it.

'Never mind,' he says. 'It's all in the past now. I didn't realise you'd had family issues on top of the Laurent boy. I'm sorry to hear it.'

Malachy turns back to Declan.

'Let me know how that eye heals up. I'll go deal with Stephen's family. Such a shame.'

He hesitates a second. Declan says nothing.

Malachy leaves.

Dani looks at Declan.

'What was that about?' she asks. 'Why did he bring up Theo?'

Declan is staring at the door through which the provost has departed. He looks as shocked as Dani feels.

'I have no idea,' he says. 'I remember what he was talking about, now. At the time, after that . . . incident with you in my office, Malachy came to me. The head of admissions let him know what was going on, so he knew Theo had left and that there'd been some problem with, well, you. He asked me if I'd heard from Theo. And then he told me that the day before Theo left, he'd turned up in Malachy's office.'

Dani's legs feel weak.

'For what?'

'To say he wasn't happy in the college. Malachy didn't say more than that. But it fitted with what I thought at the time: that Theo had gone off travelling.'

'What did he mean, spouting nonsense, though? That doesn't sound like Theo.'

'I don't know. I never understood why Theo went to Malachy. He'd spoken to me and I . . . I suppose I sounded quite disappointed. I mean, we both know he must have been unhappy. But why not come back to me and tell me what was really going on in his mind? I guess . . . I guess I took it personally. And maybe I didn't handle it as well as I should.'

Dani stares at him.

All this time, she'd known he was hiding something. Was this all it was? That he'd handled Theo in the wrong way?

'Why didn't you tell me?' she asks. 'Back then?'

'I know it was the biggest thing in the world for you at the time, but Dani, for the rest of us, he was just a student who took off. We didn't realise . . . well, it wasn't until afterwards that all that stuff meant more.'

'The time I broke into your office,' Dani says hesitantly, 'there was an email from Theo. He said he wanted to talk to you, that *Malachy should know*. Didn't you ask him then what he meant?'

Declan frowns.

'I never got that email,' he says. 'Or if I did, I don't remember what it was about.'

Dani is trying to put her thoughts in order when Declan speaks again.

'Look, whatever happened back then, don't let Malachy bother you now,' he says. 'He can be odd when it comes to the college. He obviously knows Theo was an issue for you and me, and he's trying to stir some discord. Get me to drop my complaint. That rubbish about Stephen being from a good family . . . Stephen had no right to attack you, and Malachy was wrong to try to put pressure on you. Sometimes, we just have to accept when someone is a prick.'

Dani is caught by surprise. She wasn't expecting him to say that.

'I knew Stephen was going to kick off at some point,' Dani replies. She's still distracted by what Malachy said. 'I should have been more prepared.'

'You can only do your job. And if Malachy thinks I'm going to go softly, softly on a lad who's just decked me, who could quite easily have decked you if I hadn't got in the way, just because he comes from a *good family* . . . he can fuck off.'

Declan spits the last words.

'There are students who work their arses off to get into this college,' he continues with his rant. 'And then there are the ones whose life path always included third level, who have it practically given to them. And in my experience, they rarely appreciate it. What's fought for is always more valued.'

Dani looks at this man who's just taken a punch for her and possibly saved her from worse. She listens to his words, sentiments she agrees with.

She thinks, who is this man? It can't be the same man I've had suspicions about all these years.

It's given her pause for thought.

What if he really was telling the truth about his interactions with Theo?

And what if it was something Theo and Malachy Walsh talked about that led Theo to do what he did?

Dani feels bad about what she's doing but she can't think of any other way to do it.

She's become genuinely fond of Colm and of Bridget, whom she's had a few drinks with by now, and yet, she's using them to her own end. First, stealing Colm's emails. And now, she's trying to get access to something Bridget might have.

The admin office is quiet. It's early evening and the staff are more settled into this term now.

One of Bridget's colleagues, Mohammad, is at the front desk but the other desks behind him are empty.

'You don't mind me waiting here for her?' Dani says.

'Not at all. I can ring her and tell her you're here?'

'Oh, no, please don't go to that trouble. She knows.'

'No problem.'

They sit in silence for a while. Dani is on one of the chairs near the front desk, flicking through a college brochure. Mohammad is typing away.

Dani hasn't any plans with Bridget for tonight. In fact, she knows that the other woman plans to go home as soon as she finishes up.

She's just really hoping she can change Bridget's mind.

Bridget had promised she'd try to call back into the office, once the weekly college heads of department meeting was finished. Dani is just starting to think Bridget has buggered off for the night when the door opens and she comes in.

'I'm so sorry!' she tells Dani. 'That shagging thing went on way over time. Thanks for covering for me, Mo.'

'Not a problem. I was going to get tea. You want some?'

'Feck that. Bar?'

She directs this at Dani.

'Are you sure?' Dani says. 'I don't want to eat into any more of your night.'

'I need this more than you,' Bridget says.

The college bar is busy, but mainly with students. The lecturers don't tend to drink there as much on Tuesday nights. As the week goes on, sure, they're happy to have a tipple or two after work, but the students have no such qualms.

Bridget and Dani are at a table by the window, not far from the one Dani sat at on her first night back in the college.

'It's a fucking nightmare,' Bridget says. 'Just endless reshuffling of timetables for lecturers on sabbaticals or going off to speak at conferences. Sometimes I think the staff here think they're more like boy-band members than bloody teachers. Sorry. Not you.'

'No offence taken. Apropos of nothing, are any of these conferences in sunny places?'

'You bet your arse they are. The head of physics is in Morocco next week. Morocco! And I have about eight months left before I get my annual two weeks in Santa Ponsa. FML, as my niece always says.'

Dani smiles.

'What did you need me for anyway?' Bridget asks. 'Your text sounded a bit . . .'

'Worried?'

Bridget nods.

'I had a bit of a run-in with a student,' Dani says. 'And then, I felt like I had a run-in with Malachy Walsh.'

'Oh dear. What happened?'

Dani gives her the potted version.

'I get the feeling the kid comes from money and his parents are probably donors or something,' Dani says. 'And look, it wasn't that bad. If they really contribute a lot to the college, I could drop it. I could probably get Declan to drop it, too. He ended up being involved.'

'But you shouldn't have to,' Bridget says.

'I know, but this is real life, right? I mean, colleges need money to run themselves. I'm not an idiot.'

Bridget shrugs.

'Tell me if I'm stepping on toes here,' Dani says, 'and you might not even be the right person to ask, but is there any way of seeing if Stephen's family are big donors? How can I get a look at the college's budget? Because if Malachy was laying it on with a trowel for no reason, he can shove off. But if the college is broke . . .'

'Broke?' Bridget snorts. 'This college isn't broke.'

Dani feigns surprise.

'I can send you our annual budget,' Bridget says. 'You can see for yourself. I'll even look up this little shit's parents.'

'Would you do that for me?' Dani asks.

'Why wouldn't I? It's not like you're going to go spreading it around. You work here, don't you? Why shouldn't you know how much the college is worth? It'll put your salary into perspective, believe me.'

Dani sits back, surprised. She'd expected to have to wrangle the information out of Bridget.

'Anyway,' Bridget adds, 'the annual accounts have to be published online, so you could have just looked it up yourself.'

Now Dani feels like an idiot.

Later, she sits in her apartment with the college's accounts open on her desktop.

Before she opens them, she does what she's done so many times before.

It's a habit now.

She opens the Cecelia Vargas video.

She watches her get in her car.

She watches the car leave the garage.

She knows Cecelia is driving to her death and she also knows she's missing something. She feels it every time she looks at the video.

She watches the video of the street outside the garage.

She rewinds and watches again.

What the fuck is it, she wonders?

Rain hits the window and she looks up sharply.

And down as quickly.

Just there.

Did she see something?

Dani stares at the screen, willing it to come to her.

Nothing does.

She sighs.

She closes the file and opens the accounts.

Bridget has already confirmed that Stephen's parents donate to the college but they're not the biggest donors. And Dani is starting to realise that donations to the college are not the biggest fund-raising activity by any stretch.

Dani has a fair head on her for numbers but she's not mathematically minded.

Even still, as she starts to drill down into the college's funding, her eyes grow wider.

When she's read through the last few years of accounts, Dani picks up her phone.

George answers after two rings.

'Let's talk.'

This time, they meet on the train to Dublin.

Dani sits in the last carriage and George gets on at the first station on the outskirts of the capital city. The carriage is empty; she chose it for a reason. It will fill up the closer they get to the city centre, but it's the middle of the day and for the moment, the commuters are barely a trickle.

He passes by her to take his seat and she smells his aftershave. Grey Vetiver. She inhales and realises with a jolt that it's a smell that's started to do something to her.

Her stomach tingles, but she quells it.

He's going through a messy divorce, she reminds herself.

She can see it in him. His unshaven face, the bags under his eyes, the general weariness that's creasing itself into his laughter lines.

And, oh fuck, she's still finds him attractive.

Stop it, she tells herself. He's not interested. And even if he showed the slightest bit of attraction to you, what would you do with it? You've kept back so much of your life. How could you ever tell him who you really are?

She puts herself in work mode.

'Before you ask, I haven't been able to get access to Graham's computer,' she says.

George drops heavily into the chair facing her.

'We're running out of time,' he says. 'Turner have sent over their top executives and the college is hosting a conference to discuss the findings to date. Next step is concluding the trial and presenting to the FDA. If we can't establish that they've corrupted their findings before that, the FDA is going to sign off on this drug. By the way, it's called Glatpezil. And you'll probably see it on shelves next spring.'

'I need more help, George. Even if I find a way in, it could take our scientists weeks, right, to establish what Turner is hiding? Don't we have *any* idea what this side effect is?'

'Jesus Christ, Dani, if we knew what it was, we wouldn't have sent you in there to retrieve the raw data!'

'But this whistle-blower,' Dani says. 'They must have heard something that can help us—'

'The whistle-blower doesn't come from the science end. They don't understand what Turner is hiding, they just know it's big.'

Dani exhales. That's the first time George has said anything about the whistle-blower outside of 'they exist'.

'So, how did they end up in the position of even knowing that information?'

George looks uncomfortable.

'They've had access to certain conversations. But they went to the task force knowing they couldn't discover anything more or stop Turner from doing what they're doing. That's our job. Dani, what did you want to meet me for? It wasn't to talk about the whistle-blower.'

'Cecelia's patients, the ones who died, can't we glean anything from their causes of death?'

'Two different causes recorded and absolutely nothing that can't be attributed to old age. And if we look for exhumations and further post-mortems, it's going to ring every alarm bell going for Turner. The point is to catch them in the act, not after they've cleaned up.'

'My only source so far believes the side effects of the drug are all within the normal range,' Dani says.

'This is the PhD student?' George says. 'Colm?'

'Yes. And I believe him. Whatever about the college and the Turner company, this guy is honest.'

George sits back.

'If you were Malachy Walsh or Declan Graham and you were being bribed to present statistics in a manner that helped a billion-dollar pharmaceutical company bring a new drug to market, would you let a PhD student know exactly what you were doing?'

Dani considers this.

'No,' she says. 'But the trial is a team effort. So how are the people helping to run it being kept in the dark?'

George says nothing. Dani grows more frustrated with each passing second.

'I need to know what you know,' she says. 'You're asking me to do my job with one hand tied behind my back.'

'I'm asking you to do the job you've been assigned to without asking so many questions; there's a difference.'

'I wouldn't ask the questions if I didn't think it would help me do my job.'

They stare at each other, at an impasse.

George relents first.

'Look, here's what we know. The trial team are all working with different groups of patients. If your PhD guy is monitoring say, fifty, sixty people's progress and somebody else is monitoring twenty and so on and so forth, how do any of them know what the total stats are at any given time? They're all in different hospitals, different countries . . . none of these people are talking to each other.'

'There are good people on that trial,' Dani says. 'Smart people, who want this drug to work and who don't want to be involved in something illegal. Why aren't they asking these questions? If they only see some of the data, isn't there somebody saying, hey, are we just supposed to trust this is all correct?'

George shakes his head.

'Why would they? Why would they question how St Edmund's is analysing the findings? And maybe the odd person does say that – and maybe they get bumped off the trial when they do – but look at it this way, Dani. Why would you assume something illegal or immoral was happening in a situation you're involved in? You wouldn't. And you have to remember, these people know and trust St Edmund's.'

The train has pulled into another station. A young couple enter their carriage, but seeing there's nobody at the far end, that's where they go. They want their privacy. Still, Dani lowers her voice.

'Are you sure Declan Graham knows what's happening with the data? What if there's somebody else in the college hiding the findings?'

'Like who?' he says. 'And we won't even know something is being hidden until we have proof. It makes sense for Declan Graham to be the man at the centre of all this. He's the lead researcher. Hey, here's an idea: how about you stop asking me questions and tell me what you've found.'

Dani leans forward.

'Ten years ago, St Edmund's was funded to the tune of approximately €300 million per annum,' she says. 'There was €50 million in state grants, €160 million in student fees, €40 million in research, €30 million in donations and endowments, and €20 million in investment returns. Last year, St Edmund's had an operating turnover of €450 million. What do you think has gone up the most of all those figures I just mentioned?'

George practically rolls his eyes.

'Research,' he says. 'I know how the college is funded, Dani. It's part of the reason we decided to investigate.'

'St Edmund's received €130 million last year in research funding, the bulk of that generated by their School of Medical Research.' Dani ploughs on. 'Do you know what their staff costs are?'

George rests his chin on his palm. He's waiting for her to make her point.

'Nearly €300 million. For a staff of 2,900 across the whole campus. Now, when you do the maths on that, George, and you take out the janitors and the cleaning ladies and the junior tutors and the security, et cetera, et cetera, you start to realise – there are a lot of people being paid very, very well to work in that college.'

'Obviously,' George says.

'The college started its first trials when Malachy Walsh took over as provost and he's a big advocate for them,' Dani says. 'And more importantly, his salary has gone up from €200,000 when he started, to over €1 million per annum for the last three years.'

George crosses his arms.

'So, he's doing well out of the college's research reputation,' he says. 'But are you saying you think Walsh is corrupting the trial? Because he's not a medical scientist. How would he know where to start?'

Dani looks away. She bites her lip.

'I know,' she says. 'But he *is* the boss. And he's not stupid. Not at all. Could it be the case that the trial is being corrupted in how it's presented, not in what the actual results are?'

'I don't understand what you're trying to do here,' George says. 'It's irrelevant, as far as your task is concerned, who made the decision to corrupt the findings.'

'It's relevant because I'm trying to get access to people and computers in the medical research building and if there's damning evidence that shows Malachy Walsh is involved, I might be looking in the wrong bloody place. What if the scientists are collecting the data with honest intentions and he's interfering with it?'

'How? Why? And none of it matters if we can't prove the results are different to what the medical reports say.'

Dani stares out the window for a few moments.

'This conference the college is giving,' she says. 'Who's going to be at it?'

'Turner execs in person, on Zoom, management from St Edmund's, visiting college professors, members of the medical community.'

'So, it's big enough.'

'It's not twelve people around a table, but it is by invite.'

'If I could get an invite?'

'Who's going to invite a history professor?'

'I've told Colm, the PhD guy, about my mother. He knows I'm interested in the drug. In its potential. I'm guessing he'll be there.'

'What do you get out of going? Like you say, they're not going to announce what they're hiding.'

'Sure,' Dani says. 'But they will be announcing the benefits of the drug. The success of the drug. And somebody is going to ask the obvious question. A question like I've just asked.'

'What are the side effects,' George says. 'To which they'll give an answer – none of note.'

'I don't think people in the field will buy a blanket *none*. I asked Colm about side effects and he listed lots of regular ones and dismissed them at the same time. But he wants this drug to work. I think members of the medical community outside St Edmund's might be a little more cynical. Even if it just stems from envy. They'll be more probing and you know what they say about lying?'

'Always do it with half a truth.'

'Exactly,' Dani says. 'Maybe that's what we need to be looking at. What side effects they *are* highlighting.'

'Elaborate for me.'

'Maybe it's the side effect they say is the smallest. Blood clots only happen in one in every thousand patients. Something like that. Or maybe it's the one they say they're anxious about, but that even with the drug at its highest dose, they've only found it triggering – I don't know – heart failure in three in every thousand. Colm has already told me they had a concern about the drug putting pressure on the heart, but the numbers were so small, it's not making any headlines. Is Turner going to try to bury what it's worried about or is it going to try a different tack? Say "well, we were concerned, but look, the numbers aren't that high".'

'Like Sterling Limited opioids,' George says, nodding.

'Exactly like that,' Dani agrees. 'They knew their painkillers were addictive, so they told people. But they lied and said they were only addictive for less than one per cent of patients. So, when doctors encountered a patient who became addicted, they assumed they'd been the unlucky statistic. All of the doctors, with all of the addicted patients.'

George mulls on this.

'There's no better way to distract people from a lie than by talking about the lie,' George says.

He cocks his head.

'That's smart,' he says.

She feels herself blushing. He's looking right at her and she realises she's struggling to look him in the eye.

This is new. And worrying.

Why is this feeling becoming so strong now? She's had a crush on George for ages and it's never interfered with her work.

Get a hold of yourself, Dani admonishes herself.

'So, I go to the conference,' she says. 'I listen to their presentation. Get hold of a copy of what they're handing out to the invitees—'

'They won't let anybody without a specific interest leave with any material.'

'Get hold of a copy . . . somehow. And then I keep trying to get into the lab computers, secure the actual medical records and then we let our scientists go at it.'

'And even though you've been there six weeks now, you reckon you can get all this done in a couple of weeks?'

Dani looks back out the window.

'It doesn't really sound like I have much choice,' she says.

★

The conference is being held in the O'Meara lecture hall in the main college building. Dani has only been inside previously for theatre performances. It's widely renowned as having the best acoustics of all the halls and visiting lecturers are always given the privilege of speaking in it.

Today, the stage has four seats set up just behind the podium. Declan Graham is at the seat nearest the podium, where Sharona Davies is currently standing. Malachy Walsh is in the far seat, trying and failing to hide his innate smugness. A man and a woman Dani doesn't recognise sit in the middle two seats.

She spots Ron Perry standing to one side of the stage. Again, she's struck by him. That feeling of unease. She's well aware that not all police are moral, upstanding citizens. Her own force is like any in the world. Put a group of humans together, there'll always be rotten apples among them. But there's something about a cop leaving the police and going on to work for bad people. It speaks especially to their nature. Were they ever good to begin with?

Even before George told her, she could sense Ron Perry was not somebody she wanted to have a run-in with. Now, she's doubly cautious.

The wall behind the speakers is a split screen. On one, a meeting room in Turner Pharmaceuticals HQ, with management and top staff all in place. The other screen has a graphic on it: a pink pill and its name. Glatpezil.

Dani flashed her pass at the door, a pass Colm bent over backwards to get for her. He's not seated with her; he's near the front, closer to the stage. She's slipped in the back. She's already flicked through the glossy document she was handed at the front door. It's numbered; she's expected to return it. But here in the back row, facing away from her neighbour, she's discreetly photographing every page.

Once everybody is settled into their seats, Sharona taps the podium microphone and politely coughs to get their attention. It's an easy room to call to order. No unruly students here. Just intrigued doctors and interested academics.

'Welcome everybody,' she says. 'My name is Sharona Davies and I'm the head of European Outreach for Turner Pharmaceuticals. I'm delighted to welcome so many esteemed colleagues here today, including, from Texas, members of the Turner family and our CEO, COO and top management at Turner.'

Sharona points to the first screen; polite waves of acknowledgement.

'And in our audience,' she continues, 'we have research experts from here at St Edmund's and right across the Irish third-level education field, alongside representatives of the medical profession from Ireland and Britain.'

Sharona leads them all in a polite, self-congratulatory round of applause.

Dani has finished photographing her booklet. She places it on her lap and smiles at her neighbour, a middle-aged man who has an air of conference-fatigue about him. He doesn't smile back.

'As you're all aware, this is our first conference to discuss the drug Glatpezil.'

She points at the enlarged pink tablet on the screen over her left shoulder.

'And as such, we are operating under the Chatham House Rule. We will release details of the drug to the media shortly, after it's been submitted to the FDA for approval. This event is to introduce to you, our select guests, the data we have established as we near the end of our Phase 3 clinical trial for Glatpezil.'

Sharona takes a sip of water from the glass in front of her.

'We are joined on the stage by Turner senior executives Mr John Dumas and Professor Cherry Foster-Adams, who join people I'm sure are familiar to you. The provost of St Edmund's, Malachy Walsh, who led the drive to bring clinical trialling to St Edmund's, and the head of the School of Medical Research, Professor Declan Graham.'

More applause, more smiles.

Dani sees a head turn in the audience. Colm is looking around for her. She catches his eye and gives a little wave. He nods, satisfied that she's got in.

'I'm going to hand over to Professor Graham now and he's going to give you a presentation on the ongoing, terrific work the guys here have been doing in conjunction with the scientists and doctors in Turner. Professor?'

Sharona gestures for him to approach. There's loud clapping as he takes to the podium.

A young woman at the side of the stage comes up and places a fresh glass of water on the podium, then adjusts the microphone a little higher for Declan as he stands in front of it. He thanks her, then faces the audience. His body language is relaxed and confident and Dani can appreciate why he's such a good asset for the college. Not all academics can hold a room's attention with their charm as well as their knowledge.

'Well, this is nerve-wracking,' Declan says. 'I have to say, I'm more used to mounds of paper and computer printouts and stats. Standing in front of such a prestigious group . . . forgive me if I start babbling. I'm babbling, aren't I?'

There are laughs at his self-deprecation. Nobody buys it, but the effort at humility is appreciated.

'I won't beat around the bush,' he says. 'You're all busy people and I'm sure there are going to be some questions after. So, let's get to it. I was delighted, several years ago, when we were asked by Turner to undertake and oversee the clinical trials for Glatpezil as the lead college. In this brave new world, we understand, as does Turner, that working alongside academia is the best, and the only way, to restore consumer confidence in the drugs sector.'

Declan takes a moment to nod at the execs on screen behind him. They smile and nod in return.

Dani arches her eyebrows.

'Alzheimer's is a disease that St Edmund's has always sought to specialise in,' Declan continues. 'And we are aware of the successful advances made in the fight against the disease by other Irish academic institutions. I want to acknowledge, in particular, the work of Mayfield College in Dublin and Carmine College in Cork, representatives of which are here today. They have allowed us access to some of their academics and partner hospitals in order to collect and monitor as much data as possible about Glatpezil.'

Clapping ensues.

'So,' Declan continues. 'We all know the various components involved in the current treatment of Alzheimer's, and we also know the limitations of the drugs attempting to target the individual strands of the brain-cell malfunctions. Turner, isn't it nine years ago now?'

Declan glances back at his panel; the two Turner execs nod. Declan looks back to the audience.

'Yes, nine years ago, Turner decided to take a ground-breaking approach to the treatment of this debilitating disease. And right on time. We know the incidences of Alzheimer's appear to be growing, even while the medical and scientific community are trying to make breakthroughs. In Ireland, almost 65,000 people are currently diagnosed with the illness. That's 65,000 people with countless family members and friends also affected.'

Dani winces. She's living proof of the numbers.

'Turner looked at all the various treatments currently in operation and asked what sounds like a simple question: what if we combined the various strategies into one single targeted approach? This drug would ensure a vigorous assault on the contributory causes of the disease, without undermining or aggravating other health issues in the patient. Sounds like a miracle, right?'

Dani notices the amount of heads nodding. There are people in the audience who'd probably devoted most of their lives to studying Alzheimer's. They'll be struggling to believe what they're hearing.

'And a miracle is what it is,' Declan says. 'From the follow-up period in trial two alone, we learned that not only does Glatpezil stall the advance of Alzheimer's, it does, in a small percentage of patients . . . reverse the effects of Alzheimer's.'

There are audible gasps of surprise in the audience.

Dani's stomach clenches.

Declan lets the audience catch their breaths, then he continues.

'As we moved into this third and final trial, this advance wasn't seen in all patients,' he clarifies. 'But in a significant number, and only where the disease was not at its most advanced stage, we saw memory recovery. In our 5,000 current participants, each on the drug for almost two years, 3,000 have seen *no* progression of their disease and of that number, 500 people have, in fact, regained some memory function. That's a sixty per cent success rate in stopping the march of the disease. Not ideal, but the Turner scientists have no intention of ceasing their efforts to improve this drug's performance.'

The audience is so astonished by this, murmurs of conversation start to ripple through the hall.

'It can't be true,' Dani hears her neighbour say.

Declan allows them a few moments, before tapping the microphone to get their attention.

'We ourselves were taken aback by not just the treatment, but the improvements we saw over the course of this trial,' he says, 'which is why we are hoping to bring the drug to the FDA for approval sooner rather than later. But, please, don't take my word on it. I'd ask you to do us the courtesy of watching this short video.'

Declan picks up a remote control and aims it at the screen behind him.

A grainy video comes to life, out of focus at first, but becoming clearer.

A woman appears on screen. She's wearing the classic white doctor coat, a name tag pinned on its front pocket. She's attractive; her demeanour reassuring and efficient.

She smiles into the camera.

'Hello. My name is Dorothy Tracey and I'm a doctor at St Paul's Dementia Unit in Dublin. Today, I'm going to show you two interviews undertaken with a patient of ours, Patrick Lonergan. Patrick started to experience the first signs of dementia in 2021, aged seventy-six. We admitted him to the Glatpezil trial in late 2022. The first interview was conducted in January 2023, when Patrick had been on the drug for four weeks, at a dose of ten milligrams, twice per day.'

The screen goes blank for a moment, then a man appears. He looks a little confused, a little frightened, but the person off camera is obviously working hard to put him at ease.

'Patrick,' a disembodied voice says, 'my name is Dorothy and I'm a doctor. I'm just going to ask you a few questions if that's okay? There's no need to worry about anything and it's fine if you don't know the answers.'

Patrick nods uncertainly.

'Can you tell me your name?'

'I'm Patrick.'

Dani tenses. He sounds so frail and so anxious. When the disease had really begun to take hold, Cora had been frightened to speak at all, not knowing what was right or wrong, terrified she'd reveal another part of herself to be lost.

'And where do you live?'

Patrick looks lost. Dorothy doesn't dwell.

'You're staying here in the hospital unit at the moment, aren't you?' Dorothy says.

A moment where Patrick tries to grasp what he should know.

'No. I live with my mammy and daddy.'

Dani closes her eyes.

The regression to childhood. Again, a familiar experience. There was a period when Cora thought Dani was her school friend and, in a way, it helped, because it meant Dani could get Cora to do things when the nurses made her nervous.

'Do you have any brothers or sisters, Patrick?'

Patrick shakes his head. Adamantly.

'And do you work, Patrick?'

'I . . . I do work, yes. With the . . . On the roads. I used to work on the roads.'

'That's right. You're retired now, aren't you, Patrick?'

'I think so. Yes.'

Patrick looks puzzled. Dorothy moves on.

'Are you married, Patrick?'

'They won't let me leave.'

'Who won't let you leave?'

Patrick points at something beyond Dorothy.

'I want to go home.'

Tears fill the older man's eyes. Dani can feel the sting behind her own.

The screen goes blank. When it comes to life again, a date appears on the bottom.

August 2024.

It's followed by a line of information. *Patient on Glatpezil 20 months.*

Patrick is on screen again. He looks entirely different to his last appearance. His hair is cut short and neat. He's shaved and wearing a shirt. But the main difference is in his eyes. He looks more alert. More aware of his surroundings.

'Hello, Patrick,' Dorothy says. 'You're okay for us to proceed with the interview?'

'Go ahead. Sorry if I get a bit muddled every now and then.'

'That's no problem. Can you tell me where you live, Patrick?'

'I'm a patient here at St Paul's Dementia Unit.'

'That's correct, Patrick. Are you married?'

'I am. Couldn't tell you how many years, but I'm fairly certain the judge would have let me out for murder by now, right?'

Patrick smiles and there's a chuckle from Dorothy.

'And you've been taking Glatpezil for twenty months now. How do you feel about the drug?'

This time, when Patrick's eyes water, it's with happiness.

'It's helping me.'

The screen fades to black.

You could hear a pin drop in the hall.

When the lights come back up, Declan is looking out at the stunned audience.

Within seconds, people start to clap. Then, they're standing. The applause is deafening.

Dani is staring at the screen still, her heart racing.

All she can think is, what if her mother had that drug?

The clapping goes on and on and Declan has to call for it to come to an end. On the other screen, the Turner family and executives are all smiling and back-slapping. Malachy Walsh is beaming so hard it looks like his face must hurt.

The crowd eventually sits back down, but the atmosphere in the room has completely changed. People are buzzing with excitement.

'Thank you,' Declan says. 'As you can see, we are exhilarated with the results. I must caution, Patrick is one of our best respondents, and in that regard it's probably not entirely fair to use that video. But even stalling progression in our patients is a win and an optimistic sign that the earlier the drug is used, the more likely it is to prevent the onset and advance of Alzheimer's.'

More clapping. People don't want to sit still any more. They want to be talking, circulating, asking questions, spreading the news.

A voice rises above the babble.

'This is . . . it's incredible,' a woman up front says. 'And I want to be the first to congratulate you on the success of Glatpezil, if it is passed by the FDA. But I'd like to ask some questions.'

Declan nods. The room grows more serious.

The woman is handed a microphone from an assistant at the end of the row of seats.

'Turner Pharma is not the first company to think of combining the treatment approach. But prior to now, the aggressiveness of this combination of drugs proved dangerous to patients' health. How have you managed to find the right balance between treating the disease and protecting the patient?'

Dani is barely breathing.

Because that's the big question, isn't it? They all know it.

Declan nods again, a reassuring gesture that he understands the question.

'Obviously, with a drug this effective, side effects were our big concern in all three clinical trials,' he says. 'A pre-Phase 1 trial in animals saw a few side effects that were immediately addressed. By the time we went to in-human trials, we were confident the side effects were minimal. Phase 3 saw our patients on the trial for the longest consecutive period, and this is where we expected any long-term effects to reveal themselves. As medical professionals will know, usually side effects make themselves apparent within hours or days. But sometimes a patient can take a drug for months before they show effects, and the longest period a patient has taken a drug without showing a side effect has stretched to six months.'

There are several people nodding in the audience. Declan takes another sip of water before continuing.

'And at about the six-month mark, we did notice some side effects becoming apparent that caused higher levels of concern. I won't dwell on the regular side effects that are associated with the drug. They are all within the normal range and all manageable. But at six months, we grew worried about a particular issue – the rise in patients' blood pressure. This was obviously of concern because of the age demographic of the patients. We saw quite a few spikes, and while some of this could be attributed to age itself and the growing awareness in the patients of how badly they'd been suffering from the disease, some of it we were able to isolate as being a direct result of Glatpezil.'

The woman asks for the microphone again. It's passed to her.

'In patients of that age, high blood pressure has the potential to cause heart attacks and death,' she says. 'Have you found a way to remove the threat?'

Declan nods sagely.

'The drug dosage, when altered, significantly addressed the BP issue. It also meant the results were not as desirable. However, Turner has discussed this with the FDA and we believe their label is going to carry a conditional warning for Glatpezil. Doctors will be advised to monitor the blood pressure of patients receiving the drug and, where they need to, treat any spikes with medication or prescribe blood pressure drugs alongside Glatpezil. Patients with underlying, serious blood pressure issues will have to be considered by a two-doctor panel before being prescribed and administered the drug.'

Dani notes the woman doesn't look entirely satisfied, but most of the audience seem pleased with the answer.

'We're happy to move properly to the Q&A section now,' Declan says. 'But it would be remiss of me not to mention, before we go to the panel, the contribution of the research staff here at St Edmund's, and the backing of the college itself, for our involvement in this trial, especially our provost, Malachy Walsh. The staff and students in the School of Medical Research have worked tirelessly to monitor the participants of this trial, including studying weekly medical reports, in-person interviews, experimentation with doses, meeting doctors country-wide as well as staying abreast of other advances in the treatment of the disease. If you'd be so kind as to join me in a round of applause in thanks for their endless devotion to eradicating this horrific disease.'

The audience clap enthusiastically.

Dani looks at the back of Colm's head. She can practically see his cheeks, he's smiling so widely.

And she looks back up at the graphic of the little pink pill.

Would she be happy to risk other health issues in Cora, just to have her back again?

Dani already knows the answer.

She'd do anything to have her mother back. Anything.

Dani feels sick. That's not what she's here for.

This isn't how she's supposed to feel.

She looks around the hall but her eyes are drawn to the stage.

Sharona Davies is staring at Dani.

And when Dani makes eye contact, Sharona keeps staring. Until she turns and looks at Ron.

Everybody in that room matters to Sharona. Dani is a nobody.

So why is the woman frowning at her presence?

All this time, Dani has been worried about Ron Perry.

But he's just a security man for Turner.

Sharona is, essentially, their salesperson.

Dani grabs her bag.

Sharona could be a problem for her. And Dani never even considered it.

Without looking back at the stage, she leaves the room quickly.

2014

After being caught in Declan Graham's office, Dani falls into a slump of despair.

She doesn't know what her next move is and she can feel her energy waning.

She phones Aimee at one point and asks her about Theo being in juvenile detention.

'Nobody told me that,' Aimee says, shocked.

'Is it possible his dad was responsible for it?' Dani asks. 'Could Mr Laurent have overreacted to something Theo did and had a friend, I don't know, charge him or something?'

Aimee is quiet for a few moments. When she speaks, she sounds uncertain.

'I understand why you'd suspect that,' she says. 'And you're correct in a manner. Alexandre is just petty enough to use his power in such a way. But you're forgetting that he's also obsessed with how our family appears. If Theo was detained for something, Alexandre would have ensured it was hushed up. Even from me, it seems.'

'He said something else. He said that Theo ran away. I don't know if he meant another time, or from the detention centre.'

Aimee grows quiet.

'Aimee?'

'That's not exactly true,' she says.

'What does that mean? Did he run away or not?'

'He ran from his father. He didn't run away.'

'How do you know?'

'Because he came to me. It was when my brother stopped his mother sending Theo to me during the holidays. He turned up at my door and he stayed here for a few days. Alexandre was furious when he found out. Accused Theo of, as you say, running away and me of harbouring him.'

'Was this when he was fifteen?'

'Yes. It was around that age. Theo didn't tell me why he'd left Paris. He didn't need to. I assumed it was my brother's fault. But he didn't mention anything about being in detention. And Dani, I know why Alexandre is trying to make this sound relevant and why you might think it is, but no, it is not the same. Theo didn't have form for running away. He came to me. And this time, he would have come to me, too. If he could have.'

The phone call ends with no more satisfaction for Dani. She might have learned more about one part of Theo's life but she's also learned that he did keep things from her. When she kept nothing from him.

And now she has the added pressure of seeing the college counsellor.

Dani can't tell the counsellor what's really upsetting her. She realises that if she continues to talk about Theo as though something has happened to him, she's going to end up in counselling forever.

So, she tells the counsellor she's heartbroken, and she's stressed about college work and how many lectures she's missed. She starts to study to catch up, hoping that if she turns in papers on time and to her usual standard, everyone will assume she's returned to normal and back off.

Her friends, on the back burner for the last few weeks, sense Dani is not herself and foist themselves upon her life with drinks and takeouts and study sessions.

When Dani submits a paper to Professor Byrne's class and gets ninety-three per cent, her own reaction surprises her. She's happy to get the mark but also sad because she realises that for the duration of writing that paper . . . She wasn't thinking about Theo.

It's like she's afraid to stop thinking about him every second of every day, and yet she knows she can't keep thinking about him every second of every day. It's exhausting.

She doesn't want to give up her search. She doesn't want to give up hoping. But her body is starting to give up for her and that's both upsetting and a relief.

She's so absorbed in catching up on her coursework that when Cora rings that Friday, Dani misses the first two calls. She texts her from the library and tells her she'll call back later.

Then some of her friends insist on taking her out. It's the weekend and Dani is staying on campus because she doesn't want to go home. She's still reeling from the argument she had with Cora.

She hasn't planned to socialise but her friends insist.

They head to the college bar and order double vodkas and shots of Baby Guinness.

Dani lets the alcohol do what it's supposed to. She's been careful not to drink too much since Theo left. She hasn't wanted to feel numb, she's wanted to be alert and thinking.

But now . . . now she enjoys the feeling it gives her, like more weight is being taken from her shoulders. She drinks enough to feel tipsy but not drunk. She's still conscious of having to do more work this weekend.

She's on her way back from the toilets when Sarah, the girl who has the room next to Dani's, thrusts Dani's phone into her hands.

'I was just bringing this into you,' Sarah says. 'You left it on the table and it keeps ringing.'

Dani's thoughts go to Theo almost immediately but when she looks at the phone screen, all the missed calls are from one number. Her mother.

She goes outside where it's less noisy and dials Cora.

'I'm sorry, sweetheart,' her mother says. 'I shouldn't have rung so many times, you must have been worried when you saw the missed calls. I just didn't want you to hear from anybody else.'

Dani hears the upset in Cora's voice.

'No, *I'm* sorry, Mam,' she says. 'I meant to ring you back earlier, but it went out of my head. What is it? What's wrong?'

'There was a fire. Our house went on fire.'

'Oh, my God.'

Dani is lost for words for a few seconds.

'What happened?' she says, when she gets her voice back.

'I'm so embarrassed, Dani. I put the cooker ring on to start getting the dinner ready and I completely forgot about it and went out . . . I'd left a window open in the kitchen and the fire brigade said a gust of wind must have caught a tea towel. Maureen from next door saw the smoke.'

'But you're all right,' Dani says. Cora has started crying and Dani wishes she was with her mother. It must have been so upsetting to see the house engulfed in flames.

'I'm fine,' Cora says. 'I'm in your Uncle Tom's.'

'Is Aunty Leanne taking care of you?'

'She is. They both are. I hate putting them out like this but I've no choice.'

Dani takes a breath.

'It's okay, Mam. You're fine, the house is insured. It's horrible, absolutely horrible, but at least you're okay. Was there much damage done?'

'The kitchen will need a refit and everything in the living room will have to be replaced. The whole place will need a repaint to get rid of that smoke.'

'That's all doable. I'll come home and bring some friends. Tom will probably know somebody.'

'I know, it will all be fine,' Cora says.

Dani can tell something else is wrong. Her mam is normally the reassuring one in these situations. Dani gets her ability to think practically from Cora. Even when her dad died, Cora made a point of noting the positives. His death had been instant, he hadn't felt any pain, he'd have been happy knowing he'd left both his girls taken care of . . .

'Is there something else?' Dani says. 'I feel like you're not telling me something, Mam.'

There's a few seconds of ragged breathing down the line. Then Dani hears her uncle in the background.

'Tell her, Cora.'

'Is that Tom? Tell me what? Mam?'

'I don't want you to get too worried about this, love. I know you have a lot on your plate. I didn't want to say anything to you until exams were over—'

'Mam!'

'I've been forgetting stuff lately. A lot.'

'What do you mean, forgetting stuff?'

'Dani, I've been to the doctor. I'm not well.'

'Not well how?' There's a physical pain in Dani's chest. Like somebody has put a hand in there and is squeezing.

Sarah has come out of the bar, looking for her. Dani must look like shit because Sarah comes over and puts a concerned arm around her.

'Are you really ill, Mam?' Dani asks. 'Is it cancer?'

'No, love. Of course not. I don't have cancer.'

'Mam, I'm panicking here.'

A breath.

'The doctors think I might have Alzheimer's, Dani. They're doing tests.'

It's like the world is spinning. Dani looks at Sarah, in complete puzzlement.

'You can't have Alzheimer's,' Dani exclaims. 'You're not even old!'

2024

Dani is walking down the tree-lined driveway of the college when a car arrives at the entrance and begins to drive up it.

She steps to the side of the road, only for the car to slow down as it approaches her. It comes to a halt and the driver winds down the window.

It's Declan Graham.

His eye is still black from the other day.

'Heading into town?' he asks.

'Yeah. I see that came up nicely.' She indicates his eye.

He touches it gingerly.

'Makes me look more interesting than I am,' he says.

She smiles, despite herself.

'Did I see you at the conference the other day?' he asks.

Dani tries not to react.

'I'm pals with Colm Ahern,' she says. 'He told me what you guys are doing and I said I'd go along to support him, but it's all completely over my head.'

'Honestly, Dani, some of it is over my head, too.' Declan laughs. 'Can I give you a lift?'

'No, you're fine. You're just coming in.'

'All right. If you're sure.'

He's about to wind up the window when Dani speaks again.

'Can I ask you something, though?'

Declan cocks his head. She can tell he's trying to be friendly towards her but there's a natural caution there.

'Sure,' he says.

'That stuff that Malachy said about Theo the other day. Back then, before Theo left, did you ever see Theo interact with Malachy? I mean, outside of that meeting they allegedly had.'

Declan frowns.

'I don't really want to rake over all that stuff again, Dani.'

'I know,' she says. 'I'm just curious. That's all.'

Declan doesn't look any happier but he's thinking.

'I don't . . . No, wait, there was something. I saw him and Malachy talking. Just once.'

'Talking? About what?'

'I don't know,' he says. 'The only reason it's in my mind is that it *was* unusual. The provost rarely talks to students. As you know.'

Dani nods.

'And it wasn't the same time that Malachy mentioned?'

'No. It was earlier that week. In the courtyard.'

'Did they look like they were arguing? Or discussing something amicably?'

'I really can't remember. They were just . . . talking.'

Declan shrugs like he's sorry he can't be more helpful. Then his expression changes.

'Why are you asking?' he says. 'You're not still . . .'

'Coming up with conspiracy theories?' Dani says. 'No. Not any more.'

'Good,' Declan says. 'Because we all know what happened to Theo, Dani. Sad as it is. I hope you've learned to let it go.'

Dani swallows.

Her whole life has revolved around it.

Letting it go is something she'll never do.

They're back in the same bar in town, even sitting at the same table. George is drinking water, Dani has a pot of tea in front of her.

'Have you said anything to anybody?' George says.

'About what?'

'Have you let anything slip about your background? About your real job?'

Dani stares at George blankly.

But she's worried. She's been worried ever since she caught Sharona staring at her.

'I'm not a fucking idiot,' she says. 'I know how to work undercover. What are you on about? You think I've picked a confidante and told them my deepest secrets just to kill the time?'

George shakes his head.

'This isn't a joke,' he says. 'The college went back to our contacts in Glasgow and Cork. They were asking about you.'

Dani pales.

'You're in Edmund's two months,' George says. 'There's no reason they'd be checking up on you again. No reason we can think of. Unless somebody suspects your references. You're absolutely positive you didn't tell anybody from the college you'd joined the Guards? You didn't run into somebody on a night out over the years, or post something on Facebook . . .'

'I didn't keep in touch with any of my college friends,' she says. 'Let alone lecturers. I went through hell when I left, George. And when I joined up, I certainly wasn't announcing it on social media. I was barely on social media.'

Dani tries to quell the rising panic. She hasn't given anything away. Not that she can think of.

'When you say the college is asking about me,' she says, 'who in the college?'

'I don't know,' George says. 'High up.'

Dani concentrates.

Then she realises what it is.

'I think I know what it's about,' she says.

George tilts his head, waiting.

'I had a run-in with a student. And Declan Graham intervened and took a punch in the process. The kid comes from money and Malachy Walsh wanted us to let it go, give the kid a slap on the wrist sort of thing. But Declan insisted he be expelled.'

George's mouth has fallen open.

'Go back,' he says. 'Declan Graham, one of the people we're investigating, took a punch for you— What? Dani, what the fuck?'

'I know. You had to have been there. But Malachy Walsh was a bit pissed off and he made a few remarks to me afterwards. I got the impression he isn't keen on me.'

'Shit, Dani.'

'It's not an issue, though, is it? I mean, we haven't suddenly lost our contacts in the other universities. He's not being told I'm not qualified to do the job I'm there for.'

'Of course not. But it's still a problem. He shouldn't be noticing you at all. And I don't just mean the provost. Why is Declan Graham jumping in to defend you from anything?'

'He didn't seek me out. He was just passing when it happened. It was bad timing. Or good, depending on how you look at it. He was assaulted and we both took the same stance afterwards. Now we're friends.'

'You're not friends.'

'Of course we're not friends. I'm being facetious. He just thinks I think he's a nice guy now. So, if he's on his guard against anybody, it's not going to be me.'

'I still don't like this.'

'Well, we are where we are.'

'I hate that phrase.'

George picks up his water but puts it back down before it touches his lips.

'Blood pressure,' he says.

'Yes. They're admitting high blood pressure is a problem, but within the realm of acceptable statistics.'

'But they might be massaging those stats.'

'I don't know,' Dani says truthfully. 'They could still be hiding the real problem.'

'So, now you and he are buddies, can you get access to his computer?'

Dani doesn't blink.

'I can try,' she says. 'But again, it will take time.'

'That medical conference was Turner's first salvo, Dani. They're telling the market they're coming. Which means they're confident the FDA is going to approve shortly. Turner has sent the preliminary findings. Everybody's confident this drug has no life-threatening side effects that can't be managed.'

Dani looks down at her tea. It's gone cold. Shadows have formed in its milky surface.

'I'm on it,' she tells George.

'I know. Declan Graham is your best friend. Whoopity-doo.'

Dani doesn't reply.

'You're not . . .' George trails off. She looks up at him.

'What?' she asks.

'You've not got feelings for him or something?'

'What? Why would you say that?'

'I don't know. It felt like, when I asked you to go in there, you had a problem with Graham. And I know your boyfriend studied under him before all that . . . well, what happened. I figured you blamed him. But now, you're different when you speak about him.'

Dani swallows.

She has to play this carefully because George knows some of what happened but not all. He doesn't know about her stalking Declan or being caught in his office or the accusations she made against him.

Hide a lie with the truth.

'I thought Declan knew more back then,' she says. 'About Theo. But when I learned the truth . . . he'd had nothing to do with it. But I mouthed off a few times and yeah, I was embarrassed about dealing with him again. I told you all this, when we talked about the task. But I'm in there now and the only interactions I'm having with him are to try to get closer to that trial. He hasn't held a grudge and nor have I. This investigation is separate.'

George is studying her. She feels like he's not buying it. And she's worried because she doesn't have much more to say.

Why is he acting like this?

And then, looking at him, it hits her.

He's not asking whether she's developing feelings for Declan because he's concerned about her mission.

He's asking because he wants to know.

For him.

Dani's breath catches.

Surely not?

Does George even think of her like that?

'What?' he says.

'What?' she replies.

'You're smiling.'

'No, I'm not.'

'You absolutely are.'

Dani laughs.

'I'm smiling at you,' she says. 'What, you think I'm going to shag Graham and sneak on to his computer later that night? Not my style, George.'

He doesn't say anything for a few moments.

'Good.'

She smiles again.

'I'm much more devious,' she says.

'Good,' he says.

'I'm still embarrassed about passing out that night in yours,' Colm says. He hands her a string of fairy lights.

They're in one of the lecturer lounges in the main hall. Dani has volunteered to help decorate it for December, hoping word travels back that she's super helpful and enthused about college life.

And that it's enough to keep Malachy Walsh off her back and her firmly watching his.

Colm has offered to help.

'You've nothing to be embarrassed about, like I said at the time,' she says. 'I plied you with booze. My own head was banging the next day. I was a disgrace.'

'Yeah, but you're only a girl. Your body weight can't handle alcohol.'

'I'll have you know I'm nearly ten stone.'

'Yep. Lightweight.'

'Piss off.'

Dani trails the string of lights around one of the windows, roping it around the curtain pole.

'And thank you,' she says. 'For getting me into that Turner conference. It was fascinating. I mean that.'

Colm looks up from the box of decorations he's rummaging through.

'That was my pleasure. I know how much this drug means to you. Hey, this place is starting to look really good. You're like an interior designer.'

Dani looks around at the decorations she thinks she's thrown up haphazardly.

'You think?'

'You wanna take a pic for Insta? I'll pose with some tinsel around my neck.'

'I don't have Instagram.'

'That's right. I forgot.'

Dani narrows her eyes at him.

'You've looked me up. Are you stalking me, Colm Ahern?'

He's blushing.

Dani laughs.

'How are things going?' she says casually. 'With Glatpezil, I mean. Is it . . .'

She stops playing with the fairy lights and looks at Colm.

'Is it going on the market soon?'

'It's almost there,' he says. 'But even after it gets approval from the FDA, it will be a few months before it can be retailed in the States, let alone in Europe. We imagine, given how successful it's going to be, anybody who's financially able to will head to the US once it goes to market. It will still need to be prescribed because of our concerns; you can't just buy it in bulk over the counter. Not yet, anyway. But people will easily get it through private healthcare over there.'

Dani looks away.

'I'm sorry,' Colm says. 'I'm sorry we didn't achieve this earlier. That it's not available for your mam.'

Dani shrugs. She hesitates.

'I had a weird incident with Declan last week,' Dani says.

'He told me about that student who went for you. What a dick.'

'It could have been a lot worse if Declan hadn't been there.'

'Probably best you don't say that to him too much. They're going to have to widen the college doors if his head gets any bigger.'

There's only jest in Colm's words. Dani can tell he genuinely does see Declan as a hero.

'Well, I saw him yesterday but I would like to thank him properly,' she says. 'Buy him a drink, maybe. Does he hit the college bar much? I saw him there that first night you and I went for a drink, but I haven't seen him socialising much outside that.'

'He works crazy hours. We all do, obviously, but nobody as much as him. He's rarely out of his office. I'm sure you can tempt him out when he's back, though. He'll be in the mood for celebrating.'

'Back from where?'

'He went to the States today.'

Dani tenses but tries to keep her voice casual.

'Really?' she says. 'What's he over there for?'

'He's part of the group presenting the trial's current findings to the FDA,' Colm says.

'Wow.' Dani joins Colm on the floor and starts taking some decorations out of the box.

'I'll call into him when he's back and try to lure him to the bar,' she says. 'Is he still in his old office or have they given him a fancy new one now he's the boss?'

'I'm pretty sure the office he's in is the one he's always been in. Apparently, the old head of school had a large one that Declan insisted was split into four desks for tutors. I don't think he feels the need to impress people with the size of his office.'

Dani forces a laugh.

'Who's overseeing the trial while he's away?' she asks. 'In case anything goes wrong at the last minute, I mean?'

'I am.' Colm shrugs. 'In as much as it takes to just keep sending off the weekly reports. We're just bringing it home now.'

Colm stands and walks over to the fireplace on the far side of the lounge. Dani watches as he places red ribbons on its mantle.

Colm has access to Declan's computer, she thinks.

He has access to whatever Declan's been keeping on that computer during the third trial.

This is the break she's been waiting for.

'Random question,' she says. 'But did you say you had a late tutorial this evening?'

Colm nods.

'And as an even more random follow-up, does your shower have hot water? Mine seems to be bust.'

'I have hot water and I even have shampoo,' Colm says. 'You're welcome to both.'

He tosses her his keys and turns back to the mantlepiece.

'Thanks. I'll leave the place spotless. You won't even know I've been there.'

Dani wastes no time once inside Colm's apartment.

She's hoping against hope that Colm doesn't have Declan's office keys on his person. She can't believe he'd bother to, but a surface glance at the counters and tabletops in his apartment tells her he's not left them out, either.

She starts with his desk, pulling out drawers and running her hands along the back of each one.

Nothing.

She looks through his kitchen cabinets and drawers and comes up fruitless. There aren't any keys, let alone the one she's looking for.

Dani doesn't want to go through Colm's personal items, but she has to search his bedroom.

She looks through his bedside locker, then his wardrobe.

She finds a set of keys, but they look like they're for a front door and that's confirmed by the key-ring fob – 'Home'. Colm's parents' house, she assumes.

There's no office key.

She's sitting on the edge of the bed and thinking about giving up when she spots her last chance.

Colm has left a coat hanging on the back of the bedroom door.

Dani stands and walks towards it, too afraid to get her hopes up. She checks the pocket nearest her first. Nothing.

Then she checks the other pocket.

And takes out the key to Declan Graham's office.

The layout of the office floors in the School of Medical Research is all too familiar. And Dani knows, too, that security will wait for the last office to empty before they lock up the building.

She's not nervous as she passes by the security man at the main door. She's wearing her lecturer's ID and he won't question her calling into one of her colleagues, even if it is after teaching hours.

She uses the lift and gets out on Declan's floor. There are one or two offices still in use, their occupants at their desks, lights on. Dani walks past each one quickly, not making eye contact. If anybody asks, she's just calling in to see Declan. But she doesn't want anybody to ask.

When she gets to his office, she tries the door. It's locked. As she knew it would be. He'd said it after that time he'd caught her. It was a lesson for him to start locking his office.

She takes the key from her pocket and inserts it quietly and quickly.

It won't turn. Dani presses harder.

Why won't the bloody thing open?

She stands still for a moment, her heart pounding, trying to figure out where she's gone wrong.

It dawns on her.

This was never Declan's office. This was just the office he was using while his was being renovated.

Dani has never been in Declan's actual office. Does she even know where it is?

Then she remembers. The first time she broke in, she came out on the wrong floor, the one that was being renovated. She doesn't know which one of those offices is Declan's, but she figures it has to be on that floor.

Dani goes up in the lift.

The floor she lands on is empty. She walks along, wondering why on earth these lecturers don't put their names on plaques outside the doors. Each door bears only a number.

The only thing Dani can think of is to try every door.

Most of the doors on this floor open as she turns the handle.

The first one that doesn't, she slips the key into.

It doesn't budge. Not that one then.

She's almost at the end of the corridor when she finds it.

The key turns easily in the lock and then Dani is in.

She looks around. Declan's office has an anteroom for his secretary, just like last time. But this time, there's no Post-it on the bottom of her screen with his password. He clearly learned that lesson, too.

Dani walks into his room. She pauses for a second to take in her surroundings. All of the offices on this floor were renovated at one time, made modern. But Declan's office is a carbon copy of the offices in the main college building where the most senior professors reside. Right down to the oak bookshelves and desk, and ornate chandelier. He's even had a fireplace installed.

Dani walks over to the desk. The computer is not just asleep, it's shut down.

She powers it up and sits behind the desk while she waits.

Declan has several photographs on his desk – most of them are him with friends on holidays. There are two of him receiving awards for his work.

She spins in the chair and looks around. The wall behind her is covered in accolades.

Just in case one visited his office and forgot how brilliant he is.

The computer screen flashes awake and Dani stares at the password prompt.

She tries the various things she knows about his life. His date of birth, where he's from, when he started lecturing, when he graduated.

She's studied Declan plenty but obviously not enough.

No success.

She stands and walks to the fireplace and looks at the photographs he's placed there.

There's a recurring theme.

Holidays with his friends. Him building houses with a charity team in Kenya.

In most of the holiday photos, they're on bikes.

And they seem to visit one location, a lot. The side of a mountain, idyllic slopes behind them.

Dani peers at the background.

The Alps.

And cycling.

She walks back to the desk and looks at those photographs.

More cycling. More Alps.

She takes out her phone and texts George.

Cycling destination, the Alps.

While she waits, she opens Declan's drawers.

There's nothing of note in the first few.

And then . . . she sees a couple of vials.

There are pink tablets inside.

Dani's heart is racing.

She picks up one of the vials.

There's no label but she knows it's Glatpezil. She stares at the tablets through the plastic casing for a few moments. Each one is ten milligrams.

Then, before she can talk herself out of it, she puts the vial in her pocket. Then the second one. She knows what she's doing is wrong but she can't help herself.

Her phone buzzes and she jumps. It's George's reply.

How good is the cyclist?

She considers this.

Probably just below a pro.

She watches the three dots as George types.

Alpe d'Huez.

She reads the reply, then types it into Declan's computer, all small letters, no gaps.

Nothing. Then she types it again, this time with 2024 at the end. She's in.

Dani holds her breath as she scans the desktop. Her eyes are drawn to a folder on the bottom right.

Weekly reports.

It can't be this easy.

Can it?

Dani clicks the mouse to open it.

She's so involved in what she's doing, she doesn't hear the door opening.

But she looks up when Colm says:

'You took his key.'

Fuck, is all Dani can think.

How the hell has she allowed herself to be caught twice?

'Colm, wait!'

Dani chases after Colm as he marches back towards his apartment building.

He asked her to explain herself in Declan's office.

She didn't know where to begin. She couldn't even think of a convincing lie.

'You need to leave,' he'd said. 'And I need to report this.'

Dani couldn't meet his eye as they descended in the lift together. It's only now, outside, that she realises she can't let him go to the provost.

'Please!' she cries.

There's enough plaintive desperation in her voice for him to turn and look at her.

'I need to tell you what I was doing,' she says.

'No need,' he snaps. 'I know what you were doing.'

Dani panics.

George was right.

She'd already given herself away, she just hadn't realised.

'You're a spy, aren't you?' Colm says.

It takes Dani a few seconds to work out what he means.

Then she almost laughs.

'Oh, God,' she says. 'You think I'm from another pharmaceutical company.'

'What else could you be? Why the hell would you want to break into Declan's computer? Well, I can tell you, whatever you think you're going to find, you won't. All we're doing is collecting the trial data. The drug's components are outside our purview. I don't know why I'm even bothering to talk to you. You can explain yourself to the police.'

'Colm, please, you need to listen to me. It's still me, Dani. I'm your friend. You're my friend. Can't you give me one chance to explain?'

'How the hell can you explain industrial espionage?'

Colm is glaring at her but, as she watches, his expression changes from anger to hurt.

'Did you seek me out?' he asks. 'That day in the dining hall, did you already know who I was?'

Dani bites her lip.

Whatever the best way forward here, she knows instinctively it's not to lie any further.

'Yes,' she says.

Colm starts to laugh, a harsh sound.

'The drinks, the dinners, the hanging out . . . you were using me.'

'No, I—'

'You were! I hope your bosses are happy with you, Dani. What a bloody good job you've done. Who are you with anyway? Which company hired you? Shit. We've been told to look out for you lot but I didn't think they'd go to such lengths.'

'They didn't. Or if they have, that's not me. Colm, I'm not from a rival company.'

'And I didn't just catch you in Declan's office? Save it. I'm calling the Guards.'

Colm takes his phone out of his pocket.

Dani weighs up her options.

The cops won't be a problem for her. But Colm will also tell Malachy and Declan.

Is it better they think she's from a rival company than learn what she's actually there for? Are they less likely to cover their tracks if her cover isn't completely blown?

Will this affect Grace, given she was responsible for Dani being hired?

Then Dani realises there's another way.

Tell him everything and bring Colm in as an ally.

She'd already floated it to George. It's not completely out there.

Does she know him well enough to do that?

'Wait,' she cries. 'I need to tell you something.'

He hesitates.

He has enough lingering affection for her to do that, she realises. And in that moment, her decision is made.

'Everything I told you about my mother is true,' she says. 'She's in Rose Hill Residential Centre right now and she's had Alzheimer's for ten years. I want Glatpezil to work. I swear to you, I do. And I'm telling the truth, I don't work for another pharmaceutical company.'

'So, what, Dani?' Colm says, his voice full of despair. 'What is this about? Why are you using me?'

Dani takes a deep breath.

'Because *I'm* a police officer,' she says. 'I'm undercover, investigating the clinical trials. But I want you to be right about Glatpezil so badly, it's tearing me apart.'

2014

The doctor is a no-nonsense, matter-of-fact sort of man and Dani isn't sure if that makes things harder or easier. He ushered them into his office brusquely. There was no preparation for what was to come, no hand-holding or soft-soaping.

Just the devastating truth of Cora's diagnosis.

'Forgetfulness in itself wouldn't have been a sign,' the doctor says. 'But the other things you'd mentioned – apathy, listlessness, not able to find the right words, unable to solve problems, the repetition, the mood swings – all of these ring alarms for dementia specialists.'

Dani gawps at her mother.

How long has she been hiding this?

Cora doesn't make eye contact back and it makes Dani irrationally angry.

Dani looks back at the doctor.

'Dementia. Is that the same as Alzheimer's?'

'Dementia is the general term. Alzheimer's is a specific strand of brain disease. More common in women. Early-onset is rare but, unfortunately, increasing.'

'Are there ways to stop it?' Dani asks. Then, in the face of the doctor's frown: 'Or even ways to slow it down?'

'There are a range of treatments to try to keep the worst at bay,' he says. 'Cognitive training, various forms of physical exercise, diet, antioxidants. But we can't reverse it and we can't stop it. I'm afraid this is something you're going to have to live with. Treatments are advancing every day but . . . not fast enough.'

Dani stares at the doctor, lost for words.

'How long?' Cora says.

'He can hardly tell you when it will kick in properly, Mam,' Dani intervenes. 'He doesn't know how well the measures to slow it down will work.' She looks back at the doctor. 'Is there a way of knowing when she'll . . . when she'll stop remembering things altogether?'

'No,' Cora says. 'How long do I have to live?'

'Mam.' Dani's breath catches in her throat. 'You're not dying.'

'Early-onset tends to carry a life expectancy of about eight years,' the doctor says. 'But some people can live as long as twenty.'

Dani looks at him incredulously.

'She can die from this?'

The doctor's face softens, for the first time since they sat down.

'Alzheimer's itself doesn't tend to kill you,' the doctor says. 'It's often that the patient does something dangerous. Wanders off alone or has an accident. If not, it tends to be organ shutdown. Heart, liver, kidneys.'

They sit in the car outside the hospital, not talking. Cora drove them there, making black humour jokes on the way about whether it was safe for her to be behind the wheel and if she could claim forgetfulness if she knocked somebody over.

Dani didn't laugh at any of the jokes.

She hadn't been able to believe her mother's doctors had got it right. She had to hear it for herself.

Now the doctor has confirmed the diagnosis, Dani still can't really believe it's happening.

'I didn't want to worry you,' Cora says. 'All the stuff with Theo—'

'How long were you hiding it?' Dani asks. 'This didn't just come on in the last few weeks, Mam. You've clearly being having those symptoms for a while.'

When Cora doesn't respond, Dani looks at her.

'I'm not angry. I just want to know.'

'It's hard to say when it started.' Cora sighs. 'Who hasn't walked into a room and forgotten why they're there? The mood swings, feeling depressed or not being in the humour for something, I put all that down to your dad's accident. I mean, when did that stop being a normal grief reaction and start being this? I don't know, love. I just know that in the last few months, I've found myself struggling to remember things. And people have been saying it to me. I turned up at Tom's for a dinner on the wrong night, then on the right night, I forgot to turn up at all. I've been writing stuff down and leaving it all over the place. Putting reminders in my phone. I thought it was the menopause at one point.'

Dani rubs roughly at her eyes. She feels like crying but she won't, not in front of her mother. This is worse news for Cora. Dani can't make it about her.

'I'm sorry, Mam,' she says.

'You've nothing to be sorry for, love. Nobody made this happen. It's just one of those things.'

'I'm sorry I didn't notice. I'm sorry I wasn't there for you. I was so caught up in my own drama . . .'

Dani swallows hard. She's just thought of Theo and this time, it wasn't a sad or worried or anxious feeling that accompanied his face.

It was anger. She's been consumed with Theo for weeks.

And all the while, Cora has been going through this alone.

'Your life is not drama,' Cora says. 'You're worried—'

'No,' Dani snaps. 'Not any more. He's gone, Mam.'

'But you still think something happened to him.'

'I don't care,' Dani almost cries. 'I can't prove whether something did or didn't, but there's no reason for anything to have happened to him, and I keep thinking about that night he left. He went during the night, Mam. If he'd left that morning, I'd have woken. So, at some point, he got up and decided to leave without telling me, without leaving a note, a text, anything. That was his choice. Whether something happened to him or not, he left me with that. And I . . . I hate him for that. That wasn't fair.'

'No,' Cora says gently. 'It wasn't. But this isn't his fault, sweetheart. This disease was already in me, whether I told you or not. I would have wanted to protect you for as long as possible and I would have kept doing it were it not for the fire. So, please, don't be angry at him. Whatever happened, he loved you very much when you were together. And maybe . . . maybe he felt he had no other choice but to go. Maybe he thought it was better that way.'

Cora turns and looks out her window. She's crying and doesn't want Dani to see.

Dani fights back her own tears by blinking rapidly.

Right now, all she can think about is her mother.

And what's ahead of them.

'It's slow,' she says. 'This thing. It's not like cancer. It goes on for years. They might find a cure.'

'Of course, they might,' Cora says.

Dani watches her mother's side profile.

Cora has always been strong for Dani.

And now Dani will have to be strong for her mother.

'I've been thinking,' Cora says. 'I should say . . . I've been remembering. Ha! Ironic.'

'Remembering what?'

'A conversation Theo and I had one night.'

When Dani doesn't respond, Cora faces her.

'He said he wanted to make the world a better place.'

Dani snorts. It sounds like a strangled sob.

'And I said, I know you do, love. But then he said something strange.'

'Strange like what?'

'That he didn't know if he was in the right place to do that. I thought that was weird. He obviously loved that college when he started there. I saw that in him, the first night you brought him home. So, something must have changed.'

'Yeah. Clearly. When did he say that to you?'

Cora starts to laugh. Dani is startled.

Then the laugh turns into a sob.

'I can't remember,' she says.

2024

Even though it's cold and dark, Colm refuses to go inside any of the buildings with Dani. It's almost like he thinks that if she gets him indoors and warm, he'll fall for whatever bullshit she's planning to spin him.

So, they're walking around campus, aimlessly, Colm refusing to make eye contact, Dani doing her best to make him understand.

And the whole time, she's conscious of the vials of tablets in her pocket. The ones she stole from Declan's desk.

The saviour drug.

'A multi-jurisdictional task force was set up to monitor a number of pharmaceuticals,' Dani says. 'It started in the US, where most of them are based, but the companies started to notice the increased scrutiny of their operations and of their clinical trials in particular. It became apparent to them that the only way to avoid US monitoring was to bring in European academic institutions to bolster research, with the added bonus of having a lot of the clinical trials run outside the US.'

'Global research and cooperation is not breaking the law,' Colm says. 'Academics and universities have always worked across borders. It's not like the big diseases are contained. When Covid hit, it took a lot of international research and skills to find a vaccine.'

Dani nods.

'You're right, of course, but that was a specialised, necessary

257

response. Colm, you're too smart to think that medicine isn't just about money for these companies. Whatever lofty goals researchers might have to cure illnesses—'

'Lofty? You think wanting to bring an end to Alzheimer's is lofty? When I came here to intern ten years ago, when I decided to dedicate my life to this, I didn't do it because I was deluded or had notions of grandiosity. I did it because I knew this university was going to be part of a movement to change the world for the better. I did it because I wanted that to be my job. It was an ethical thing to do. Not lofty.'

Colm's voice is dripping with indignation.

'Okay, that's the wrong word,' Dani says. 'But, come on. You and people like you come from a different place to the big pharma companies. Otherwise, medicine would be free, right?'

'Medicine can't be free, no matter how much we'd all like that to be the case. It takes years of work and millions in funding to bring an idea from conception to realisation. Capitalism isn't a dirty word when it works.'

'I never said it was. And I have no objection to Turner or any pharmaceutical company spending money on a drug like Glatpezil and charging for it as long as that drug's conception is lawful and moral.'

'Moral? You've lied to me for months, Dani. Are you even qualified to teach here? You've got a lecture hall full of twenty-year-olds relying on you to teach them their course. Are you trying to fuck up their careers as well as mine?'

Dani can't help but be stung.

'It's not like that,' she says. 'I studied the same course here for two years and I'm fully across the module I'm teaching these kids.

I'm only due to be here for a term or two, and not one of them is falling behind. We'd never put those kids at risk.'

'Why did they pick you? Why not a medical researcher?'

'If we'd had access to an officer who had a background in medical research, we'd have used them. But we can't put a civilian in undercover.'

Colm stops. They've done two circuits of the main building now and only for the pace they're keeping, Dani would be freezing. As it is, her fingers feel like ice and no amount of squeezing them or blowing on them is warming them up.

'And what do you think we're up to?' Colm asks. 'Because I'm all over this trial, Dani. Do you think I'm corrupt? Do you think I'm in this for the money?'

'No,' Dani says, shaking her head. 'I know that you're not. But you're just a cog, Colm. We're almost certain − in fact, we are certain − that Turner wants the results of this trial manipulated in order to hide something from the FDA.'

'Like what?'

'We don't know what side effect they're burying. That's what I'm here to help find out.'

'So, what? You're just going to keep shooting until you hit something? Doesn't exactly sound targeted. It sounds like you're just out to get Turner, any way you can. Why even look at Turner? Why not another pharmaceutical or another drug?'

'I can't tell you why we're focusing on Turner, but I can tell you that they are more dangerous than you can possibly imagine.'

And as she says it, Dani has a flash of memory.

Something she saw recently.

Cecelia.

Could she have . . . Is she right?

She blinks rapidly. She wants to get back to her apartment this instant, but this is just as important.

Colm is shaking his head adamantly.

'There are no side effects outside the normal range,' he says. 'I've been monitoring my group for months. Every stress test, every cognitive test, every minor illness, from colds to headaches to kidney infections. This drug doesn't make people sick. It helps them. And I would have thought that you of all people would appreciate that.'

And there it is again. Something niggling at the back of Dani's brain. Something Colm has just said.

But she can't put her finger on it.

And she's angry. Defensive, but also angry.

'I would appreciate it if I thought it was safe.' Dani has raised her voice to match his. She knows that's the wrong tack. She takes a deep breath.

'I'm not your enemy,' she tells Colm. 'If there's a flaw in this drug, wouldn't you want that fixed before the general population starts taking it?'

'I'm not a fucking criminal. Of course, I'd want it fixed. But I've just told you—'

'*Your* group, Colm.'

'What?'

'You've been monitoring *your* group. You have, what, twenty, thirty, fifty people? And somebody else has another fifty, and so on and so on. Do you see all their results?'

Colm looks confused.

'No. We don't examine other groups' results. We don't want to contaminate our own set of statistics.'

'So how is the total trial's performance assessed?'

'Everything is submitted to a central database. It's the computer that cross-checks. Not humans.'

'Really? No humans?'

'Well, the information is checked, obviously.'

'And who has access to the central database with all the primary data on it?'

Colm narrows his eyes. He's just realised where she's going.

'No,' Colm says, shaking his head. 'Declan is more passionate about this drug than any of us. He's honest. He would never—'

Colm could probably protest all night, but Dani just waits.

He stares at her, still shaking his head, but she can see the seed of doubt has been sown.

'At the conference,' she says, 'he mentioned high blood pressure is an issue with some of the trial's participants. Have you seen that?'

'Sure. But all within the normal range of people in that age group. And there were only one or two people in my group who suffered with it.'

'Again, in your group,' Dani says. 'How do you know what the rest of the groups looked like? What if one of your colleagues had ten people in his group suffering with it? Would they ask all of you if you had the same? Or would they check with their supervisor if this was an ongoing issue?'

'They'd check with their supervisor,' Colm says. He's starting to sound weaker. Dani can tell he still wants to fight the accusation but he's too intelligent not to give her position some consideration.

'And who would their supervisor check in with?' Dani prompts.

Colm hesitates.

'Declan Graham,' he says.

Dani lets that sit.

'I can't believe it,' Colm says. 'I just . . . this doesn't make sense. None of it does.'

Dani lets him absorb everything for a few seconds. When she speaks again, her voice is gentle.

'We don't undertake this kind of operation on a whim, Colm. You have no idea what it took to get me in here. The preparation it entailed. We wouldn't have started this – and let me tell you, there are officers from all over the United States and Europe watching this case – if we didn't think Turner wasn't in the process of doing something that could result in people dying.'

Colm seems to sway for a moment. Dani puts her hand on his arm. He leaves it there for a moment before shrugging it off.

She can tell he's still hurt by her lying to him.

But she knows he's already starting to believe her and doubt everything he knows.

'If this is true,' he says, 'I can't have my name associated with this drug. I don't even mean for my career. In general. I don't want to be associated with it.'

Dani nods.

'What can I do?' he asks her.

And now he reaches out and grabs her arm, his voice full of desperation.

'What can I do?' he repeats.

'You can help me,' Dani says. 'I need access to Declan's computer. I need to see what he's seeing in the individual groups before that information is massaged. Will you help me with that?'

Colm considers what she's said.

'Will Declan get into trouble?'

'If he's manipulating results for Turner, yes. He's going to get into a lot of trouble.'

Colm gulps.

'But he's a good man,' he says.

'We'll see,' Dani answers.

'Could I get in trouble? I'm stealing information. Could Turner come after me?'

'Not if they don't know it was you.'

Colm shakes his head.

'They made us all sign papers when we joined the trial. NDAs, confidentiality agreements. And there's an exit document you have to sign as well. If I leave, I'll have to put my name on one, and if it ever comes out that I leaked data, they could sue me. They'd ruin me.'

'I'll protect you,' Dani says.

Colm looks uncertain.

Dani feels for him. He looks lost. Frightened.

She hopes she's just told him the truth. That she can protect him.

Back at her apartment, Dani pulls up the Cecelia video as soon as she's in the door.

She watches it. The woman walking to her car. Getting in. Driving out of the car park.

She stares at the car, around the car park at the other cars, at the couple of CCTV cameras that showed nothing suspicious.

She knows she's seen something. She knows she's been seeing something since Cecelia came on her radar – but if she's honest with herself, she's discounted it because others have looked at the nurse's death and found nothing.

But everyone in the task force arrived at the same conclusion.

When Cecelia Vargas reported her concerns about Glatpezil to the medical board, she signed her own death warrant.

She drove her car into work that day. She left it in the car park.

Somebody messed with Cecelia's car that day.

'Where are you, you fucker?' Dani mouths quietly.

She tries looking away and looking back, just as she did previously.

She's about to give up for the night when it hits her.

Dani shuts the file and opens another one. This is the street outside the car park. Pedestrians pass by shops and offices.

But it's not the pedestrians that Dani is looking at.

She has no idea what's guiding her thought process. But she's happy to go with it. The subconscious mind is a funny thing.

She's staring at a shop window and the reflection in it.

In that millisecond, Dani realises what she's looking at.

The slant of the shoulders, that shape of the head . . .

She picks up her phone and dials. Even though it's late, George answers immediately.

'I've found something,' Dani says.

'What is it?' he asks. He can hear the tremor in her voice and his own is unable to contain his excitement.

'I'm about to send you a camera still. From the day Cecelia Vargas died.'

'From the car park video?' he says, confused. 'We went over and over that.'

'I know. So did I. Are you in the office?'

'Yes.'

'That list of cars I sent you, have the regs been checked yet?'

'Wait a sec.'

She can hear him pulling up a file.

'In the process,' he says. 'Some of them are problematic. The ones where you didn't get a whole reg.'

'Sure. Tell me something, do you have the car details for the two Turner employers who are over in Ireland at the moment?'

'Of course we do.'

'Either of them driving one of those models of car?'

George falls quiet for a few moments.

'Ron Perry is driving a rented Audi.'

'I have him,' Dani says. 'He was clever, but I'm looking at his reflection in a shop window en route to that parking garage. The day Cecelia died. I assume he didn't want to drive in and have his car reg recorded. So, he must have parked nearby. This is why he looked familiar to me. I think I saw this before, but I didn't *see* it. Does that make sense?'

'Jesus. Send me the still.'

'Sending it,' Dani says. 'Can we check all the surrounding CCTV for his car?'

There's a sharp intake of breath down the phone as George looks at what she's seen.

'Sure,' he says. 'Dani . . . if he did this, he's in St Edmund's right now. Where you are. And he's really fucking dangerous.'

'I know.'

'So . . . be careful.'

'I will be,' she says.

'No, I mean it. I don't . . . I don't want anything to happen to you.'

Dani closes her eyes for a moment and thinks about how much that means to her.

'I'll be careful,' she says.

She hangs up.

She's not really worried about herself.

She's worried about Colm.

If Turner was willing to kill Cecelia Vargas for just raising concerns . . . What will they do to somebody who steals their trial data and hands it over to the police?

Dani is finding it hard to concentrate on anything while she waits for Colm to make up his mind.

Almost a whole day has passed and she's spent every hour expecting college security to turn up and turf her out, her real identity revealed. She's praying he'll find something for her, but too afraid to hope he will. And she's hyperconscious of the loyalty he so obviously feels for Declan and the work he's been doing up to now.

She weighs that against the worry she feels for him if he actually does help her.

She wants to warn him, but he's told her to give him space and he hasn't replied to the one text message she sent: *Please be careful, whatever you do.*

The tablets she stole are now hidden in her apartment. Dani doesn't know what to do with them.

She knows what she wants to do. She wants to start giving them to her mother every day.

But she can't.

Those tablets could kill Cora.

Would that be any worse?

Last night, Dani dreamt about Theo.

She's tried to suppress her memories of him.

She knows what happened to him, but there's always been this niggling doubt.

And it's grown louder and louder since she arrived in St Edmund's and began this investigation.

To distract herself and make it feel like she's doing something, she's sent an email to Detective Sonia Wall, the woman she'd first dealt with when she tried to report Theo missing.

Dani tried to keep it light and casual. She told her she'd been inspired to join the police force by what happened and then apologised for being so lacking in understanding of the limitations the detective faced at the time.

She'd laboured over how to frame the next few sentences. She wanted to sound interested, but not obsessively curious.

I've never really been able to forget Theo and I suppose it's the unanswered questions that stay with you — I know that now from my own cases. Would you mind terribly if I asked you a little bit about that time? You've probably forgotten most of the details, but small things have plagued me. For example, I know you talked to Theo's professor, Declan Graham, but I'm wondering if you ever talked to the college provost, Malachy Walsh? I learned recently that Theo spoke to him before he left, and part of me wonders if Malachy knew more about what Theo was planning to do than he's ever let on.

Dani supposes the reason she's thinking about Theo so much, apart from the obvious, is that Colm reminds her of him. His passion for medical advances, his love of the department, his awe of Declan Graham.

But she also saw the look of disappointment and fear in his face when he realised he might be working with people who don't feel the same.

Had Theo encountered something similar?

Did he go to Malachy and express his concerns?

Did Malachy say something to Theo that scared him away?

Did he do something to him?

Declan was then and still is the college's star lecturer, who was about to lead the college into a new phase of trialling with MNCs. If there was a threat to him, Dani can only speculate how far the new head of the college might have been willing to go.

And what if Malachy himself had something to hide . . . what if he still has?

At 7 p.m. that night, she decides to walk into town. She needs a drink and she can't face putting on a smile and sitting in the college bar.

As she walks, it feels like she's treading in the footsteps of ghosts.

She recalls this very trip, in the run-up to the Christmas before Theo left.

When we get to town, you're not allowed to come into any shops with me, she'd told him.

Why can't I go into shops with you?

Because I want to buy you a present?

What? You mean you haven't bought it already?

You mean you have bought mine?

I bought you your present in October.

Well, we're not all as prepared as you! What did you think we were going into town for?

To drink proper wine. Not that shit they serve in the bar.

You can have proper wine, and I'll shop.

Can I have a peek at what you get me?

That will ruin the surprise.

Is it going to be underwear?

Do you want pants?

He'd cupped her face with his hands then and tilted it until she was gazing up at him.

I mean underwear on you, he'd said.

He'd pulled her hand and they'd run, laughing, into the edge of the woods. And because they couldn't keep their hands off each other, even in the freezing cold, he'd laid his coat on the ground and covered her with his body while they made love.

Dani reaches the road at the edge of the wood and has to pause. She grabs the stone wall for support, swaying a little. The memory was potent; she could smell Theo's neck and his Gucci aftershave, taste his lips.

A car drives past, jolting her from her memories.

In years past, the car would have slowed and offered her a lift. A woman on her own in the countryside. But this one just drives on.

Dani's relieved. She can't do small talk.

She starts to walk again.

She's almost reached the high street when she hears a voice calling out her name.

She turns and sees a blonde woman approaching. Dani is so distracted, it takes her a moment to realise it's Sharona.

Dani swallows hard. She looks around to check if Ron Perry is with her, but Sharona is alone.

'I thought it was you,' Sharona says.

'Hi,' Dani says.

'Are you going for a drink?'

It takes Dani a second to fabricate a lie.

'No, just picking up some stuff in the shops.'

'Oh. Do you want me to drop you back?'

I want you to fuck off, Dani thinks but doesn't say.

'I'm fine,' she says. 'I like the stroll.'

'Right.'

Dani is expecting Sharona to move on, but she seems fixed in place.

'I saw you at the conference,' she says.

Dani can feel her stomach knot.

'Yeah,' she says. 'I'm just interested in what the college is doing.'

Sharona tilts her head questioningly.

'That's not really true, is it?'

Dani's grateful it's evening and the shadows of the lamplight are hiding her blushes.

'Excuse me?' she says.

Has she messed it up so bad that this woman suspects her?

Has Colm told her something?

'Your mom has Alzheimer's, doesn't she?' Sharona says.

Dani baulks.

'How do you know that?' she says.

Have they done background on her?

How much do they already know?

'Colm told me,' Sharona says. 'When he asked for your pass?'

Sharona is looking at her quizzically and Dani suddenly realises her emotions must be playing on her face.

'Oh,' she says. 'I see.'

'I'm sorry, maybe I shouldn't have said anything. I didn't think.'

Sharona sounds so apologetic, Dani's aware she needs to say something before she comes off like a total bitch.

'No, that's fine,' she says. 'I just hadn't realised Colm had asked you for the pass. My mother's disease isn't a secret.'

'How long has she had it?'

'Ten years.'

'Damn.'

'Yeah.'

'My grandmother had it,' Sharona says. 'She raised me. It's one of the reasons I started working for Turner when they began developing Glatpezil. I want so badly for there to be a cure. She's gone now but I wouldn't want anybody else to go through what my family did.'

Dani tries to reply but she can only nod. Sure, she thinks. Turner is a latter-day saint.

'I'll let you go about your business,' Sharona says.

She hesitates.

'Take care of yourself,' she says, then walks away.

Dani shivers. Was that a warning?

But, as she watches Sharona retreat, Dani is hit with a thought.

She'll have to wait to check if she's right because her phone has started to buzz with an incoming call.

She takes it from her bag, expecting to see George's 'no number' come up.

But it's Colm.

★

They meet in his apartment because he's suddenly conscious of being seen with Dani.

He's awkward with her. She can tell his natural reaction is to offer her a drink, but he thinks that's too like they're still friends. So, Dani takes the initiative and opens the bottle of wine that's still in her bag. She'd called a taxi as soon as he rang, but she'd had time to pop into the small supermarket before it came.

'You look like you need a drink,' she says, as she takes out the glasses.

He nods.

His expression is unreadable and she hopes to God he's not going to drop a bombshell on her.

She pours two healthy measures of wine and hands him a glass.

She takes a large sip of hers while she waits for him to tell her why he's summoned her.

They don't sit down. Instead, they hover at the breakfast island.

He's as nervous as she is, Dani realises.

'I spent a long time thinking about what you said,' Colm says eventually. 'I couldn't sleep last night. I kept tossing and turning, thinking you're wrong. The police are wrong. This is a witch-hunt. Some rival firm has planted something. Anything that could explain away why the trial is being investigated.'

He stares into the red wine in his glass, lost in thought.

Dani watches. And waits.

'And then I thought, the only way for me to be sure is to look at Declan's files. To breach the trust he put in me when he left.'

Dani is holding her breath now.

Colm looks up at her.

'So, I went to his office this afternoon and I started reading the individual group data. Weeks and months of recordings from different groups in different hospitals and collected in different universities. All uploaded to the system. I did that for hours. And you know what I found? Nothing. I found nothing out of the ordinary. Every report that came in was uploaded as it was and held in the database in its correct form. And I know I didn't read all of them, but of the ones I did, chosen at random, I can tell you that for a fact. The records are not being changed after St Edmund's receive them.'

Dani feels like the ground is giving way beneath her.

They'd been so sure, the whole team.

So how can this be?

She looks up at Colm. He's still standing, his fingers twiddling with the stem of the wine glass.

He meets her eye.

'And then I looked at the data compilation system and how it operates,' he says. 'Declan has access to the administration of the programme. The senior Turner executives do too, but Declan is the one analysing and reporting the findings. Technically, the college paid for the system, so administration in St Edmund's can access it, too. For obvious reasons, they're all shut out. The information is commercially sensitive. But one person can still get in and make alterations to how the system works.'

'Who?' Dani asks.

'Malachy Walsh. The provost. I have no idea why he's allowed to access it. He doesn't need to see it and, arguably, he shouldn't. That was breach number one.'

'Breach number one? What's breach number two?'

Colm takes a deep breath.

'I'm not an IT expert. But I know the sort of information processing system we're using to collate these results. And I checked the format to make sure everything was operating correctly.'

Dani stands up straighter. Colm looks even more anxious now.

'That's when I found something,' Colm says.

'What did you find?' Dani asks, her voice barely louder than a whisper.

He stares at her.

'I want to tell you,' he says. 'But first, I need you to be honest with me. Are you doing this because you want to expose Turner? Or are you doing it because of what happened to Theo?'

Dani starts.

'What do you mean?'

'A couple of weeks ago, Declan told me what really happened to your boyfriend. And how you'd blamed Declan and the college and his family before the truth came out.'

Dani blinks rapidly.

'You know they're not responsible, right?' Colm says. 'You're not doing this because you want to see them punished or . . . I don't know. Is this revenge?'

'No,' Dani says. 'Absolutely not. This has nothing to do with Theo. I swear to you. I didn't even want to take on this job; I didn't want to come back here. For obvious reasons. But when they told me what the drug was . . . This is about my mother, Colm. I'm doing this for her and for all the families that will suffer if this drug hits the market.'

She meets his eye directly.

He nods slowly.

'I'm sorry,' he says. 'I had to ask. And I'm sorry about what happened to your boyfriend.'

Dani shakes her head. It's gone. In the past.

'What did you find?' she asks.

Colm takes a breath.

2014

All of Dani's fellow students are pretty much living in the library at this point, as they prepare for their summer exams.

Dani has already assumed she'll need to retake the papers later in the year. She can't imagine anything other than a fail is on the cards.

She hasn't made the same mistake this time, though. She's not kept it all to herself like she did with Theo.

When she returned to St Edmund's after being at home, she called Grace Byrne's office and told her about her mother's diagnosis.

Grace has been full of sympathy and support. She's told Dani all they expect is that she try her best in the summer exams and if she has to resit later in the year, her lecturers will give her as much out-of-hours tutoring as they can over the summer months.

Dani isn't sure she deserves the kindness being offered but she's happy to take it.

She does most of her studying in her room.

Theo liked to study in the library. He liked the smell of old books. She can picture him so clearly sitting at his favourite desk, the lamplight on, an old copy of a medical journal in front of him. His smile when he looked up and saw her.

She's in her room when there's a knock on the door.

She opens it and is surprised to see Declan Graham standing there.

The expression on his face alarms Dani.

'What is it?' she says.

'The police phoned,' he says. 'They didn't call you because . . . well, because of your age. I was his lecturer, but you're the closest Theo had to family here in Ireland. It's going to take a day for his father to get over. Dani, you need to come identify—'

Dani doesn't hear the rest. Her knees give way and she's on the floor before she even realises what's happening.

There's a couple of seconds where she's just looking at Declan's knees before he crouches down and tips her face up so she's looking directly into his eyes.

'Breathe,' he says. 'Just breathe.'

And that's about all she can do.

The police send a car for Dani and Declan accompanies her.

They don't say anything throughout the drive. She's aware of his right leg tapping, his knee bobbing up and down, and she assumes that's a nervous thing.

For her part, she's just concentrating on not vomiting.

The car heads towards Dublin and ascends into the Dublin mountains. They travel along Military Road. Dani knows it well. Her father used to take them on drives through the mountains on the weekends, ending up in the famous Johnnie Fox's pub, where they'd have the chowder and smoked salmon, the smell of turf in their noses and her father enjoying the one Guinness he allowed himself when he was driving.

They arrive at the lake sometime in the late afternoon. There's another Garda car in situ and an unmarked police car parked beside it.

A woman gets out of the unmarked car and Dani recognises her. It takes her a few moments to remember her name.

Detective Wall. Sonia. That's it. The officer to whom Dani first reported Theo missing.

Dani is out the door before Declan has even unbuckled, and Detective Wall approaches her.

'Dani, thanks so much for doing this. I just want to reiterate what I told Professor Graham on the phone. I'm sorry we didn't take your concerns more seriously. But, I don't think there's much we could have done. Once somebody makes up their mind . . .'

She walks Dani over to a series of rocks near the lake.

Dani's knees almost give way.

Tucked in behind the rocks is a rucksack and a hoodie. A plastic sheet has been erected to cover them from the elements, even though the summer evening is still and warm.

She reaches for the bag but Detective Wall stays her hand.

'We're going to take them back to the station and examine them. We just need you to confirm that they're Theo's.'

'They're Theo's,' Dani sobs. 'Where is he?'

And then she follows the detective's gaze, out over the lake.

Dani stands up.

'You haven't found his body?' she says.

'We might never find his body, Dani.'

'You think he killed himself,' Dani says then, her voice leaden with sadness.

'It's not uncommon for an individual to leave their belongings like this,' Detective Wall says. 'His wallet is in the bag. And to come all the way up here . . .'

'But if they were just lying there, why weren't they found before now?'

'We don't know when he did it, Dani,' Detective Wall says.

And then she averts her gaze and Dani realises the detective feels guilty.

She thinks Theo was alive when Dani reported him missing. And if they'd acted, they might have found him before he killed himself.

Dani looks out at the lake. She's conscious of Declan standing nearby.

He looks devastated.

Dani feels numb. She can't believe Theo would take his own life. She just can't.

She walks towards him.

'They're his belongings,' she says, when she's standing beside him.

'I'm sorry,' he says. 'I'm so, so sorry.'

Declan's voice is choked with emotion and she sees now that he's crying.

'I should have done something to prevent this,' he says. 'I should have seen . . . I've never had a student who took their own life before.'

Dani drags her eyes back to the water.

'They'll never find him out there,' she says, echoing the detective.

'They'll find him,' Declan says. 'I know they will. We'll get him back.'

Dani doesn't know why it's that moment the switch flicks but she can't help it when it does.

'He killed himself,' she says. 'He was happy with me. I know he was. So, if he was unhappy, it had to have been because of St Edmund's. Or your course. Or something. He wanted to leave. He was going to get a job. That's how much he hated the place. And he couldn't tell me, but you should have known. You're right. You should have done something to prevent it. It's your fault.'

Dani walks away.

Even in the moment of anger, she knows she's in the wrong, but she's too overcome to retract what she's said or apologise.

The last thing she sees before she gets back into the police car is Declan's completely stunned expression.

Later that night, her phone rings. Dani is lying in bed, staring at her ceiling and remembering all the times she looked at the ceiling when she and Theo lay in bed together. When he was on top of her and her legs were cupped around his back and he was as much a part of her as she was of him.

When he was alive.

She answers the phone without even checking who it is.

'Miss MacLochlainn, it's Theo's father.'

Dani sits up.

'Mr Laurent,' she says.

'I want to thank you for what you did today.'

'I . . . It was nothing.'

'It was not nothing. I made plans as quickly as possible to travel to Ireland but . . . I realised that even when I saw his belongings, I might not recognise them. You did not need to do this, especially after how I spoke to you. And yet you did it anyway. And you saved me a painful trip, for which I am grateful.'

Dani swallows the hard lump in her throat.

There are a few moments of silence.

'I have been angry at Theo for being so stubborn and strong-willed,' Mr Laurent says. 'But he was my son. You were correct, it was my duty to find him.'

Dani's breaths are shallow. She doesn't want to cry.

'When . . . when you said he was in juvenile detention years ago, what was it for?' she asks. 'Is there more about Theo that might . . . help me understand? Had he tried to hurt himself before this? Or hurt somebody else?'

Another silence. Dani waits, with bated breath. She can't decide if she'd feel any better if she'd known this was coming, if she'd had some clue that all wasn't well in Theo's mind.

'I don't think what he did then had anything to do with what has happened,' Mr Laurent says. 'Theo discovered one of his teachers was abusing two of the kids in his year and he attacked him. Physically. The school said he had anger issues. And I presumed he did. That he was just like me. I was disappointed in him. There are cleverer ways to deal with such an issue. We clashed on many things and that is the first time I told him, aloud, that I was ashamed of him. I wish now I had not. I wish I had seen it for what it was and told him I was proud of him for standing up for somebody other than himself.'

Mr Laurent's voice fills with emotion.

Dani is stunned.

Theo attacked somebody? She'd never heard Theo so much as raise his voice at anybody.

And yet, it makes sense. If he thought that he was righting a wrong . . .

'I must go,' Mr Laurent says. 'But thank you, again, for your assistance today. It won't be forgotten. And . . . I am sorry Theo put you through this. The police have asked where his belongings are to go. If you so wish, you may have them.'

He hangs up.

★

Forty-eight hours later, Dani gets Theo's belongings. She's stayed in St Edmund's because she still hasn't told her mother what's happened. She doesn't think Cora could handle the extra stress of it right now.

So she's alone when Detective Wall drops off the bag and his hoodie.

The police have sent divers into the lake but it's large and deep and Detective Wall is already intimating that these expensive searches rarely go on that long and aren't always successful.

The first thing Dani does when she's closed the door to her room is take Theo's hoodie from the brown paper bag and smell it. She's hoping it will still hold his scent, that she'll be able to inhale him again.

But the material only smells of ozone and something chemical. There's nothing left of its owner.

Then she opens the rucksack.

The main body of the bag is filled with a couple of T-shirts, a sweater, two pairs of rolled jeans and some underwear. One of Theo's textbooks is also there – a book on cell research. In the back pocket, she finds his wallet.

Dani stares into the bag for a moment, the question that's been bugging her finally finding form.

Where's Theo's laptop and phone?

They weren't in his room.

They're not in this bag.

She phones Detective Wall.

'Hi Dani.' The detective sighs.

Her voice sounds echoey, like she's on a speakerphone.

'I'm driving,' she says, confirming it. 'Is it urgent or can it wait until I'm back at the station?'

'It's just a quick question,' Dani says.

'Go on.'

'Have you found Theo's laptop and phone? Were they kept in evidence or something?'

There's a beat of silence on the phone.

'No, we haven't found them.'

Dani takes a sharp breath.

'Isn't that odd?' she says. 'Why are they missing?'

'His bag was probably up by the lake for a few days. Somebody could have taken them.'

'But not his wallet?'

'It's unusual, yes, but there was no money in the wallet, just cards, and most people are wary about scamming cards.'

Dani has no response to that. She thanks the detective and hangs up.

After a while of mulling on that puzzle, Dani takes out Theo's other belongings. Even though she knows the police will have done this very thing, she searches the jeans pockets. She doesn't even find lint.

The thing that's confusing her is that this is the rucksack Theo used to go back and forth from her room to his all the time. He'd throw a T-shirt or book in, usually his laptop . . . She remembers him having this rucksack the very last night he stayed over.

Was it already packed with these belongings? Or did he go back to his own room before he left?

And then she comes right back to — and where's his laptop?

She picks up the textbook and idly flips through the pages. She's hoping to see a note and knows that is also something the police would have looked for.

There's no note. Just underlined and highlighted paragraphs and scribbling in the margins.

The book is thick, with hundreds of pages. She will think afterwards that it was luck that made her land on the page she did. Luck, or something beyond her knowledge guiding her.

As she's looking at Theo's writing and thoughts on one of the pages, something catches her eye. Theo has highlighted a paragraph and written beside it *St Edmund's???* with several question marks. Dani frowns. She reads the paragraph. It's a short explanation about the lack of research into a particular cell malfunction that leads to anaemia.

She checks the first few pages of the book. It's an American publication; there's no mention of St Edmund's.

Dani flicks through the next few pages until she finds another highlighted paragraph. This again is about cell research deficiency and Theo has written *St Edmund's* and underlined the name.

Dani reads the whole page. It makes no sense to her.

She picks up her computer and opens the intra-college web page. She goes to news and scans back a few weeks.

Then she sees it. There's an article, published shortly after Theo vanished, about the School of Medical Research. In it, it describes how St Edmund's has agreed to work with an American pharmaceutical company to research the cell deficiency mentioned in Theo's textbook.

Malachy Walsh, the college's provost, is quoted:

This is ground-breaking work which St Edmund's will be to the fore of, and it's our privilege and honour to be working with such a great team of international, experienced researchers in Amarita Medical. As provost of this college, I'm delighted to be leading it into a new era of academia-led cooperation with multinationals.

Amarita Medical.

Dani's blood runs cold. That's what Theo told Louis, Mr Laurent's fixer, he wanted to ask him about.

And Louis said Amarita Medical was a small company about to go bankrupt.

Dani's fingers fly over the keyboard as she types Amarita Medical and St Edmund's into the search bar.

An article appears. It's from a medical journal and announces a large research funding deal recently agreed between the pharma group and the Irish university. Dani reads the article, which quotes a lot of the college news statement. Then she sees there are comments beneath it. She reads those too. One of them jars with her.

One she won't think about for another ten years, not until she's sent to investigate St Edmund's for this very reason.

One doctor from Maine has written:

This has disaster written all over it. Haven't we learned anything from the opioid crisis? Academic institutions' research and analysis of these drugs should be at an objective remove from pharmaceuticals. If we have universities lending trials veracity, having been paid to do so, at what point do we start discounting the reliability of academics also? This is the bosses buying the unions all over.

Dani switches her search to images.

The first photo catches her eye.

It contains two men she doesn't recognise and one she does. She reads the caption: *Executives from Amarita Medical meeting Malachy Walsh of St Edmund's.*

The provost is smiling widely.

Dani frowns.

Is this why Theo wanted to go work for the company? Because he knew the college would be entering a research partnership with them?

Did he have a crisis of conscience, realising he was happy to follow the money route, as opposed to research?

And is that what he meant when he told Cora he wanted to make the world a better place?

Unnoticed, the textbook has started to slip from the bed, and when it hits the ground, she jumps.

'Jesus!'

Dani picks it up by the back cover.

When she puts it on her lap to close it, that's when she sees the handwriting scrawled within the margins of the last page.

It's Theo's and it says . . .

I'm sorry, Dani.

Dani's eyes blur. She can't believe what she's seeing.

Then she reads it again and this time, the tears fall freely.

It's only three words.

But it's obvious what it is.

They might not have found Theo's body.

But she's just found the suicide note he left for her.

The college choir performances have always been renowned. The choir is so well regarded, it's considered a huge achievement for students to be accepted as a member.

Dani has never been able to hold a tune, but she does enjoy listening to those who can, especially choral music, and never more so than at Christmas.

The event is being held in the college chapel, and is only for staff, giving it an air of exclusivity.

Dani and Bridget sit together in a side pew.

From her vantage point, Dani can see Declan, freshly returned from his US trip, sitting near the front of the chapel. Sharona is beside him. Malachy Walsh sits on her other side.

Dani scans the crowd looking for Ron Perry. She can't see him anywhere and she hasn't seen him at all since she came to the conclusion he was involved in Cecelia's death.

The choir open with 'Carol of the Bells', and she feels goosebumps as the vocalists reach their crescendo. Bridget nudges her, beaming. She's delighted to be there, as is Dani, though all Dani can really think about is when the call or text will come.

And come it does, during 'O Holy Night'.

Dani reads the message and puts her phone away. She doesn't react for a few seconds, then she leans across to Bridget and whispers that she has the beginnings of a migraine.

'I'll walk you back,' Bridget says. 'Get you sorted.'

Dani shakes her head.

'You shouldn't miss this. I'm going to take some Nurofen and lie in a dark room. See you tomorrow.'

Bridget hugs her and Dani slips out of the pew, grateful that they're on the edge of the chapel.

Before she exits, she glances over.

For a second, she thinks Malachy Walsh is watching her. But almost as soon as she's thought it, she sees his gaze is fixed on the choir.

The bar in town is full of festive cheer and patrons. Dani has to squeeze through the crowd until she spots him.

Colm is seated in a snug in the back. He's shredding a beer mat and already has an empty pint glass in front of him, with another pint about to make it two. Dani watches him for a moment before he spots her. He looks like a man with the weight of the world on his shoulders and she's filled with guilt.

She takes a deep breath and joins him.

'You got it?' she said.

He nods.

'Did anybody see you come in?' he asks. 'I mean anybody from the college?'

'No. Most of the staff are at the private concert. And students wouldn't think anything if they saw us together, anyway.'

'Maybe. But I don't want anybody knowing about this. You've promised.'

'I know.'

'This could ruin my career. It won't matter that it's the right thing to do. All that will matter is that I handed over confidential information.'

'I swear, Colm. Your identity will be protected.'

Colm takes a long slug of his pint.

'It probably doesn't matter,' he says. 'Declan will know I was the only one with access to his computer.'

'That doesn't necessarily mean anything. And there's legislation to protect whistle-blowers; you can't be penalised.'

Colm shrugs.

He reaches into his pocket and takes out a USB.

He looks at it for a few seconds, hesitating, then hands it to her.

She holds it in the palm of her hand. It feels hot against her skin.

'In every trial group,' he says, 'there are patients with high blood pressure side effects. But after the data is fed into the computer programme, the overall figures for the trial are smaller.'

'How was it corrupted?'

'The system was altered to only recognise blood pressure readings over a certain level. Not the clinical level, which it was set up to do originally. So only the highest readings were flagged. That's irrelevant in people of those age groups. Ten or twenty points higher than normal is enough to precipitate heart failure.'

Dani clenches the USB in her fist.

'How long will it take your team to cross-check the original health reports with the statistics in the database?' he asks.

'A week or so, I imagine. We'll subpoena the medical records for all the patients from their own doctors. They'll be obliged to give them to us because the patients will have signed off on their records being shared for trial purposes and the trial is under investigation. No doctor-patient privilege.'

Colm starts ripping up another beer mat.

'Are you really going to leave?' she asks.

She's hoping he'll say yes. It's safer that way.

He nods.

'I can't stay here. I'm not a good liar. If I'm asked if I did this, I'll end up admitting it.'

Dani sighs heavily.

'I'm sorry, Colm. What will you do?'

'Go to the States. There's an internship there I've got my eye on. I can finish my doctorate. I'm hoping that I'll be well ensconced before what happened here is revealed. They might accept it as a good thing that I walked away from the trial before it finished.'

He starts to get out of his seat.

'Are you going already?' Dani asks, surprised.

'There's not much more to say, is there?'

'I . . . I don't want us to part like this. You were a good friend to me, Colm. I wasn't to you, so much, and I hope you'll forgive me for that. But I was only doing my job.'

'So was I,' Colm says.

He starts to walk away. Dani hangs her head. She's still staring at the table when he returns. She lets him embrace her, his arms tight around her upper body.

'I'm sorry,' he says. 'I wish it hadn't had to be this way.'

'Me too,' Dani says. 'You remind me . . . you reminded me of Theo. I'm glad, at least, that we got the chance to say goodbye.'

Colm kisses the top of her head and leaves.

Dani waits until she spots a passing waitress and orders two glasses of red.

Minutes later, George sits down in front of her.

He's clean-shaven and wearing a fresh shirt.

And that aftershave she likes.

To everybody around them, they probably look like they're on a date.

'We have to stop meeting like this,' she says.

'Do you have it?' he replies.

Dani pushes his glass of wine closer to him. 'No small talk then?'

George says nothing.

He looks more anxious than she feels.

Dani hands him the USB stick, still grasped in her right hand. She's been afraid to let it go.

'The original trial data before it was collated,' she says.

George takes it. His relief is palpable.

'Will it be enough?' she asks.

'If there are inconsistencies in here, it should be enough for the FDA to put a halt on the drug until Turner can get a new trial going. If they get one going.'

'What about holding them accountable?'

'We'll still need something on paper that shows the top Turner execs knew St Edmund's was altering the trial results with their permission. Direction, in fact.'

'Will you get it?'

'We have people working on it. It's the one part of the investigation our initial whistle-blower can help with. But what you've done here, it's huge, Dani. It won't go unnoticed.'

Dani nods.

'Is your contact okay?' George asks.

'You tell me. Have you nailed him? Ron Perry, I mean? I'd really like him to be picked up sooner rather than later.'

George looks grave.

'They got his car, parked, on a camera two kilometres from Cecelia's car park. And we have him on an earlier CCTV walking in the right direction. But it proves nothing, except that you're right to suspect him. We have a bigger problem, though.'

'What?'

'He's gone to ground.'

'How?' Dani asks. 'Has he gone back to the States?'

'Not through an Irish airport,' George says. 'We're looking, don't worry. It just bothers me that we can't find him. He would only hide if he knew we were looking for him, and I can't understand how he could know that.'

Dani tries to quell the uncomfortable feeling in the pit of her stomach.

Ron Perry at large is not something she can live with.

They sit in silence for a few moments as Dani contemplates what will happen next.

Then she remembers something.

'The initial whistle-blower,' Dani says. 'I know who it is.'

George stiffens.

'It's Sharona Davies, isn't it? She's the one who came to the task force.'

'Not my place to say, Dani.'

'Her grandmother had Alzheimer's. She made a point of telling me. I think she wanted this drug to work. I guess she's as disappointed as I am.'

George shrugs.

Dani accepts the lack of a no as a yes.

She hopes Sharona is safe. If Ron Perry knows something is wrong, God knows who Turner suspects.

'We can take you out now,' George says.

Dani fidgets in her seat.

She's trying to look nonplussed, while feeling anything but.

'Does it have to be immediate?' she asks.

George narrows his eyes.

'Why?' he asks.

'We said at the start that we'd make sure the kids I was lecturing wouldn't suffer because of our operation.'

'Don't lecturers leave mid-course all the time?'

'Rarely mid-term,' Dani says. 'It's just a couple of weeks until the Christmas exams. If I could see that through, then over Christmas we could use the same exit plan. Family emergency, blah blah. It's hardly going to make a huge difference, is it? It's going to take a while for all this to run its course, anyway.'

George rests his chin on his hand as he ponders her proposal.

'It might buy us a little more time,' he says. 'We don't want St Edmund's getting suspicious and covering up what's been going on before we can issue arrest warrants.'

Dani nods, trying not to give away what she's thinking.

She'd known, when George asked her to go into the college, that she'd be opening a can of worms.

She can admit it to herself now.

Theo might have taken his own life, but she's always suspected, ever since that day she found the notes in his medical book, that his decision was driven by guilt. That he'd learned something about his course or the company he'd considered working for that made him suspect something bad was happening.

She doesn't know if it's just a coincidence that he studied in the same department she's now investigating, but she's desperate to know if what's happening in the present has anything to do with the past.

She catches George smiling at her.

'What?' she says.

'You always do that,' he says.

'Do what?'

'Bite the inside of your cheek when you're thinking.'

'Do I?'

Dani runs her tongue around her mouth. The inside of her cheek is mildly irritated.

She hadn't even realised she was doing it.

George starts to laugh.

'Stop laughing at me,' she says.

'Okay,' he says.

He stops, but his smile remains. Dani starts to feel awkward under his gaze.

'Why are you still looking at me?'

Now he looks a little embarrassed.

'I'm always looking at you,' he says.

'Yes, but normally in a judgemental slash slightly disappointed way.'

'Bollocks.'

'Bollocks to you.'

She lowers her eyes. She's aware her cheeks are blushing.

Not again. George is her boss. She has to be able to sit with him and not feel this awkward.

'I'm not supposed to do this,' he says. 'Though, fuck it, it happens all the time.'

Dani frowns.

'What happens all the time?'

'When all this is over,' he says, 'would you consider coming out with me for a drink?'

Dani's heart skips a beat.

'We're always drinking,' Dani says, nodding at their glasses.

She goes for humour because that's what she does. It's what they do. She and George.

'You know what I mean,' he says. 'A drink, drink.'

She's lost for words. A first.

'If I've made you uncomfortable,' he says, 'just tell me to fuck off. We've known each other long enough.'

Dani hesitates.

'You haven't,' she says. 'But . . . I thought you were still dealing with everything after the divorce?'

He sighs.

'She's going to make this as uncomfortable as she can for as long as humanly possible. I thought I'd never come to terms with that, but it's funny how your brain starts to kick into survival mode before you're aware it's even doing that.'

'I think I know what you mean.'

George watches her for a few moments.

'Yes. I imagine you do. She broke my heart, Dani. She broke it by having an affair. And I've dealt with that. I wanted the divorce and she didn't. She regrets what she did and wants us to go back. But we can't. I don't feel the same any more. And I'd really like to take you for a drink. If I'm honest, I've wanted to take you for a drink for a long time, but I wouldn't have gone there. Not as a married man. I guess some of us do and some of us, well, don't.'

Dani feels a warmth start to spread through her. She smiles. Then she grows serious.

'How would it look?' she asks. 'Not that it would stop me, but you are my boss. You know what they're like.'

George half smiles.

'Yeah. I guess it's as good a time as any to tell you that when we close this case, you will be up for a promotion. And when I say up for, you'll get it. A little bird told me.'

'So, you're dangling a promotion in front of me to make me go out with you?'

'No . . . I, I mean . . .'

He trails off. She had him there for a moment.

'I don't give a fuck what the bosses say, George. If I want to go for a drink with you, I will. If I don't, I won't. It's our business.'

'Jesus! You put the heart across me there.'

He smiles again. Properly this time.

But she can't quite meet it.

She would like to go for a drink with George. But she has unfinished business in St Edmund's and she doesn't want him to know about it.

She'd rather they start this, whatever it is, honestly.

'Can we wait a little bit?' she asks. 'This job . . . it's taken a little bit out of me. With my mam going through what she is, and being back in that college, thinking about what happened with Theo . . . I feel a little wiped.'

'I get it,' he says. 'So, it's a not yet but not a no?'

She laughs.

'In a nutshell. You think about how to clear it with HR. I'll get my head in order.'

They gaze at each other, a little shyly.

George looks away this time. He takes a long sip of his wine.

In for a penny, Dani thinks.

'Speaking of the job, those background files I asked for, the stuff on Declan,' she says. 'Was a decision made?'

George looks up at her sharply.

'You don't need that now, do you?'

'I wouldn't mind having a look at Malachy Walsh's file too,' she says. 'Come on, George. I've got us what we need. But I'm a detective. I'd like to know who made this decision. I no longer think we're right about Declan. I think Malachy is worth looking at.'

George frowns.

'I don't have Malachy Walsh's file,' he says. 'But you can have a look at Graham's.'

He reaches into his laptop case and takes out a folder.

Dani's eyes widen.

'You brought it?'

George gets out of his seat. He stands beside her and leans towards her ear.

'I know you, Dani MacLochlainn.'

For the second time, Dani is speechless.

'And just so you know,' George continues. 'I'm going to make sure Malachy Walsh is hammered. Whether for this or for what he did to Grace Byrne. As for Graham . . . you might be right. This guy has been squeaky clean his whole life.'

George pats her shoulder and leaves.

Dani stares at Declan's file.

She knows he has. And she doesn't know if he's involved in what's just happened with Turner.

But there's a little part of her that can't quieten the suspicion that history might be repeating itself at St Edmund's.

2014

For two days, Dani barely leaves her room.

She can no longer avoid the horrific truth that Theo took his own life.

On the third day, she goes through the whys.

If Theo had made a bad decision about his future or where he'd work, who can she ask?

He'd contacted the Fox, but never met him.

Who else might he have spoken to?

The only thing she's learned for certain is that Theo had a whole life that she wasn't privy to. Thoughts in his head that he didn't share with her.

When she's not obsessing about why he did what he did, she's trying desperately to cram all the knowledge needed to pass her end-of-year exams. She's struggling in some of her more boring courses. The Industrial Revolution leaves her cold and architectural history is beyond her. She knows she's going to fail those papers, which will mean an overall fail. But she doesn't want that to be something else Cora is worried about. The doctors are saying stress doesn't help the condition.

She's walking to the library one day when she sees a familiar car pull into the college grounds. It's Detective Sonia Wall's.

She watches from afar as the car drives in the direction of the School of Medical Research.

Dani is still watching when she realises there's somebody in the back of the car.

Declan Graham.

Dani walks towards the road and waits. Minutes later, Sonia's car returns.

The detective sees Dani and pulls over.

She lowers her window.

She looks on her guard, Dani thinks.

'Hi Dani,' she says. 'I know what you're going to ask but I'm afraid I've no update. We haven't found a body, and unfortunately, the search and recovery operation was suspended for funding reasons.'

Dani doesn't bother to correct the misuse of the word suspend. Suspended gives hope it might be resumed. Dani knows it won't be.

'Is his father going to organise a private search?' she asks, a final hope.

'I believe he considered it but, well, apparently he talked to a friend of the family. A bishop. And it was reconsidered.'

'What? What does that mean?'

'I'm going to hazard a guess it has a lot to do with the Catholic Church and suicide. Theo's best left unfound.'

Dani grimaces. The detective has a similar expression on her face.

'Um, what were you talking to Professor Graham about?' Dani asks, trying to regain focus.

The guard is back up.

'We were just getting his statement,' Sonia answers curtly.

'His statement for what?'

'The coroner will have to record a verdict on Theo at some point. Even without a body, it will most likely be deemed misadventure.

We need statements from everybody who saw him on his last day here and might have seen him the following morning. Don't worry, we've already got your version of events on record.'

'Did anybody see him?' Dani asks.

Sonia shakes her head.

'Nobody saw him during the night or the next morning,' she says.

'What did Professor Graham say?' Dani asks.

'I don't want to go into that with you,' the detective says. 'But he didn't see him.'

Dani is about to press for more when her phone rings. She has it in her hand, like she does most of the time these days.

She sees her Uncle Tom's number and frowns.

'Do you mind?' she says.

'Fire ahead.'

Dani can see the policewoman is eager to get away but is too polite to shoot off.

Dani answers the call.

'Tom?' she says.

There's a sharp intake of breath on the other end of the line.

'Dani, love,' he says. 'I wasn't sure whether to call you or to drive out, but I didn't know where to find you if I came out—'

Dani can feel the blood draining from her face. She's starting to get a feel for these types of calls. She knows something bad has happened.

'What is it?' she says.

'You need to come home.'

'Is it my mam?'

Sonia is getting out of the car.

'Has something happened to her? Tom, tell me, please. I don't want to wait.'

'She's okay, now,' he says. 'But you have to come home.'

'Did she have an accident again? Did she hurt herself? What happened?'

Dani is crying now, the shock and worry intermingling. The detective is standing beside her, in emergency response mode.

'She's in hospital,' Tom says. 'Just come home. I'll get you there.'

'No, I'm going right to the hospital. Which one?'

Dani feels like she's going to vomit, but that can wait. Right now, she just has to act.

Sonia drives her.

She offers to come inside but Tom's wife, Dani's Aunt Leanne, is waiting outside.

'You take care of yourself,' the detective says. 'You have my number.'

Dani nods and practically jumps out of the car.

Dani has always thought of Leanne as the most glamorous person in the world. Her aunt always has her dyed blonde hair perfectly coiffed and usually wears the nicest tailored blouses and skirts.

Today, though, her hair is pulled into a messy ponytail and she's wearing a rumpled hoodie and sweatpants. She looks like she's been up all night, and she has.

She hugs Dani tightly.

'Jesus, love,' she says. 'You're going through a time of it.'

'I'm fine,' Dani lies through her teeth. 'Can I see her?'

'Of course you can. She's very embarrassed, though. You might be angry with her, love. God knows I am. But we can't let that show. Not today. She had no idea what she was doing.'

'What?' Dani asks. 'What did she do?'

Leanne looks desperately upset.

'They were *my* sleeping tablets,' Leanne says. 'I got them a few months ago for insomnia and just left them there after taking one or two. God, Dani. If I'd known how dangerous they were—'

Dani doesn't hear any more. She runs inside.

Cora is lying in bed in a private room. They don't have private health insurance, but Leanne works as a secretary for a surgeon and he pulled in a few favours.

Cora's staring out the window and doesn't notice Dani until her daughter sits in front of her.

Cora immediately pulls herself up into a sitting position. She just as quickly tries to rearrange her features from abject misery to her usual no-nonsense look.

'Mam, don't,' Dani says. She grabs Cora's hand, then pulls her in for a hug. Her mother feels thinner than Dani can remember.

Cora's sigh is a whole-body shudder.

'I'm sorry, sweetheart,' she says, her voice half a sob. 'I'm an idiot. I can't bear that I've put you through this.'

Dani releases her mother. Cora sits back and faces her.

'You're not putting me through anything,' Dani says, her voice small.

Cora sobs properly. When she speaks again, Dani can barely hear her through the tears.

'But I am. When they told me what I'd done, I actually thought . . . I wish they'd bloody killed me. Those tablets. I wish they'd done the job even if it had been an accident. The thought of not being myself when I die, Dani . . . it's breaking me.'

Dani is crying, too.

They embrace again, both their hearts aching with the unfairness of it all.

When they part, Cora searches Dani's face. Dani knows what she's looking for. Anger, disappointment, shame.

Dani feels only relief.

But she also can't hide the pain she's been feeling all week.

'What is it, love?' Cora says, reading her mind.

'Mam, something happened, something I need to tell you about,' Dani replies.

Cora nods, encouraging.

Dani tries to speak but she realises she's struggling to catch her breath.

She draws one in, but it doesn't hit her lungs. Another. And another.

Cora's sitting up now, her legs coming out of the bed.

'Dani, what's wrong? Breathe, sweetheart, breathe.'

Dani can't. She tries to get the words out.

'They found . . . they found—'

More gasping.

'Oh, God, Dani, I'll get help . . .'

'Theo's dead.'

Cora gasps now.

Dani is starting to feel light-headed.

She wants to breathe, she wants to tell her mother she's fine.

But there's a pain in her chest and it's so bad, she thinks she's going to die.

She finds herself slipping off the bed.

And then, everything is darkness.

It was a panic attack.

And Dani was lucky enough to have it in a hospital.

Later, Tom and Leanne take her home and make her strong tea.

Leanne holds her hand and Tom sits across from them, watching Dani with concern.

'I thought the worst thing that could happen to your little family was my brother dying,' he says. 'I can't believe what the two of you have gone through these past few months. It's not fair.'

Dani says nothing. The tea has made her feel calm, and the fresh flowers on the coffee table are erasing the stench of hospital disinfectant that clings to her skin.

'We'll get you back to college,' Tom says. 'But you should stay here tonight. We'll put some good food in you. Christ knows you could do with a bit of minding.'

'I'm not going back,' Dani says.

Tom and Leanne exchange a shocked look.

'We're going to take care of your mam, pet,' Tom says. 'You don't need to be worrying about that.'

Dani believes him. Tom stepped up when her father died and she knows he'll continue to do that.

But she knows what she's doing.

'I'm not saying I'm never going back. I'm saying I need to take a break. Too much has happened. The house needs to be renovated and the insurance money arrives soon. Mam is going to need proper care. And I'm failing this year, anyway. I'm going out of my mind with stress. That panic attack, it really scared me. I'm going to talk to my lecturers and ask if I can resit the year.'

'Resit it when?' Leanne asks, her voice wary. 'Dani, your mam's diagnosis, it's . . . it's not going to get better.'

'I know,' Dani says.

Tom and Leanne are looking at each other again, their expressions full of worry.

'I'm studying history,' Dani adds. 'The course is not going to change. But I can't have my head stuck in the past when the present is in such a bloody state.'

Tom opens his mouth to protest some more, but Leanne stays him with a look.

'I think that's a very mature, selfless reaction,' she says. 'This has been a rough year for you and sitting it again isn't the worst idea. Take the summer off and then in the autumn, the house will be fixed up, your mam will be on whatever medication she needs to be on, and we'll have everything in place for you to go back to college.'

Dani nods.

She's happy to go along with Leanne's plan for now.

What she doesn't say is that she's not going to go back. Not to that course and certainly not to St Edmund's.

Dani is tired of feeling so powerless. She's tired of having so many questions and no answers.

Whatever she does in the future, she wants to make sure it's a job that allows her to be in control.

2024

When Dani gets back to her apartment, she doesn't automatically open Declan's file.

She realises, for the first time in a long time in this place, that she feels happy.

It's not just getting hold of Turner's trial results.

George's proposal of a drink — a proper drink — is playing on her mind.

She remembers the first time she met George, in the mess hall in police training college. He'd seen her sitting alone and came over to join her. She'd been wary. Plenty of women joined the force in 2016, it wasn't that unusual, but the numbers were still skewed in favour of men.

In the mess hall that day, Dani had felt like a very female minnow in a very male pond.

George, though, had been a gentleman. He'd asked her about her reasons for joining, how she was finding the course, if she was happy with her sleeping quarters and so on. She couldn't detect any undercurrent and when they'd finished chatting pleasantly, he just wished her well and left. There was no final, *fancy-a-date* bomb lobbed.

The next time she saw him, it was when he was assigned to mentor her group of recruits. She realised then the reason for the caring outreach. And as time went on, she grew to like him, a lot.

Especially when he told her her grades surpassed everybody's in that recruiting year and his superiors wanted to talk to her about a niche post on the force.

Did she fancy him then?

Maybe. Of course, she wasn't exactly in the frame of mind for fancying anybody. Two years after Theo's disappearance, she'd managed to move on in many respects, but not all. A lot of that had to do with the increasing care Cora needed. But, as time went on, Dani's brain had kicked into survival mode and she'd started to live again. To bury the past and all its pain.

Dani pours herself a peppermint tea and sits on the sofa with Declan's file in her hand. She grins, still thinking about George and where a drink with him could end up going.

She's about to open the file when her phone pings with an email. She reads it and is immediately engaged.

It's from Detective Sonia Wall:

Dear Dani, it's good to hear from you and I'm delighted to hear you joined the force. You were always determined, I'll give you that.

I'm sorry for the late reply but I've been off sick for a couple of days. Would you believe I never got Covid when it was a thing and this week I got bloody Covid.

Anyway, your question. Look, you know by now we don't talk to interested parties in a case about other parties' statements. But, given this is old history and you're one of us now: we did talk to Malachy Walsh at the time. I don't even need to look it up, I remember it well. It was a matter of courtesy because he was in charge of the college. He told us Theo had been in to see him prior to his disappearance. He said Theo was acting erratically and making claims about the college being

involved with unethical companies. Theo didn't go into details but
Malachy did say he was concerned for Theo's mental health.

I pressed him, as you know we have to do. But I had no cause to
investigate the college for any wrongdoing.

I hope, to this day, I was correct on that. You'll understand now,
it's almost impossible to find out why somebody takes their own life, but
I sincerely hope Theo wasn't driven to it by something we overlooked.

The detective carries on with some pleasantries and wishes Dani
well for the future.

Dani can hear her heart beating, it's so loud.

Does this mean that Theo had learned something about the college's research agreement with Amarita Medical?

Could it be true . . . was St Edmund's running corrupt trials even
as far back as ten years ago?

She stares at the email.

Malachy Walsh. He just keeps cropping up.

Almost as a distraction, she starts to read Declan's file. There's no
criminal record, obviously.

The task force have a list of all the times he met with Turner and
other pharmaceuticals over the years.

And they have been watching him for years.

Dani flicks through the pages until she reaches the earliest
recorded entry. It was made in 2017 and it mentions that Declan
was involved in a Amarita Medical research project in 2015, one
that later came up in an investigation by the Drug Enforcement
Administration in the States. The research led to the creation of
a drug that was added to the list of dangerous prescription drugs
fuelling the opioid crisis.

Dani's hands grip the file tightly.

St Edmund's was mentioned as being involved in early trials but wasn't part of the active investigation, despite Malachy Walsh having pushed to be involved in the trial.

Questions were raised, however, about the possibility of the college manipulating research.

Dani reads a note made by a task force officer under the entry:

It's possible that the college was in receipt of bribes in the form of cash payments from pharma companies from as early as 2013. There's no record of St Edmund's senior management or board auditing the School of Medical Research's interactions with these pharma companies or stress-testing the findings of its own research department. However, there are no obvious links to the current head of research at St Edmund's, Declan Walsh, financial or otherwise.

Dani's hands are clammy as she turns the page. There's some brief background on Declan's private life and financials. Generally clean-living, law-abiding.

If he was ever taking bribes, he had to have been very clever, Dani thinks.

But if he wasn't, that really only leaves one person who might have been.

Of course, it might not even be that much money. She suspects the more important thing to Malachy Walsh is his ego and, these days, having his name all over something like Glatpezil would hold more appeal for him than mere cash incentives.

Theo always liked Declan, she remembers.

She shouldn't have doubted that.

So why had she been so biased against the man?

Dani turns to the next page of the file.

Her heart stops.

There's a record of Declan being questioned in relation to the disappearance/suspected suicide of a St Edmund's student. It's the one and only time he'd been brought into a police station and whoever compiled the report must have decided it was worth adding the statement.

Dani reads the short entry.

By the time she's finished, she's ready to throw up, but she can't believe what she's read so she scans it again.

And then she's standing, the loose pages in the file falling from her hand until she's left holding just one:

I saw Theo Laurent in a lecture that morning, but I left the college shortly afterwards, returning to my home in Dublin. I wanted to visit my elderly father, who's ill, and decided to stay in the capital overnight. I didn't notice Theo was missing until he'd been absent for several lectures. I haven't heard from him since. He was an excellent student.

Dani's hands are shaking.

There's no mention of Theo having told Declan he was 'going travelling'.

But more to the point . . .

In 2014, when she'd confronted him after being caught breaking into his computer, Declan had told Dani that he'd been in his room on the night Theo disappeared.

He never said he'd gone to Dublin.
So, he was either lying to the police or to her.
And Dani imagines he was lying to the police.
She closes her eyes and lets the memories wash over her.
She'd been right.

2014

Dani is outside her house talking to the kitchen fitters when a car pulls up at the kerb.

She's so engaged in what the head of the fitting crew is telling her, she doesn't realise for a few moments that the car belongs to Declan Graham and he's getting out.

'We can measure for the units today, love, but it's best if that room has another lick of paint before we start putting them on the walls,' the tradesman says. 'You don't want to be painting around the new wood. God love ye. Doesn't look like that kitchen was even that old before the fire started.'

The tradesman steps back on the pavement, aware they have company.

Dani turns and sees Declan.

'Oh,' she says, surprised.

'Sorry,' he says. 'I'm catching you at a bad time.'

'No, we were just talking about a refit.'

'I'll leave you to it, love,' the tradesman says. 'We'll get started.'

Dani nods.

'I heard about the fire,' Declan says.

'Yeah. The insurance came through so, it'll all be sorted.'

'That's admirable,' he says.

'The insurance paying?'

'You keeping your head together with all this going on.'

Dani doesn't know what to say. She doesn't feel very together.

'Why are you here?' she asks.

Declan looks awkward for a moment or two.

'Just to check up on you,' he says. 'To make sure you're hanging in there.'

'Oh. Thank you. I'm fine.'

'I saw a coffee shop up the road. Do you fancy one?'

Dani shrugs. She has to wait for the kitchen guys to finish before she heads back to Tom and Leanne's.

'Why not?' she says.

The coffee shop is full of mid-morning parents and toddlers, but Dani and Declan manage to get a table by the window.

Dani hasn't been sleeping very well and the coffee is appreciated. Declan orders a green tea and she resists the urge to smile. Any time she went into a coffee shop with Theo, if he heard anybody ordering anything that wasn't coffee, he'd take it as a personal insult.

Even if the coffee is Irish coffee, they should order the coffee.

Ireland doesn't actually grow coffee beans. We import them.

And then do horrific things to them. In France, if I was served this shit, I'd refuse to pay.

If you don't like the coffee, have a tea.

Christ above!

'You've been through a lot,' Declan says.

Dani sighs. No point denying it.

She doesn't say she thinks the worst is yet to come.

'You're a strong girl,' Declan says. 'Not many twenty-year-olds would be able to step up and renovate their home after something like that happening.'

'I'm not renovating it. I'm just directing a load of tradesmen to renovate it.'

Declan smiles.

'As somebody who feels intimidated around anybody who can do manual labour, let me tell you, I'm in awe of your foreman skills.'

'Theo used to say something similar. He grew up with people always doing things for him and he couldn't even use a hammer. I guess, when my dad died, I saw my mam step up and it just seemed like something you have to do. Theo kept saying he was going to try to fix my curtain pole for me but I knew I'd do a better job of it . . .'

Dani trails off.

Declan's face has clouded with emotion.

'I can't stop thinking about him walking into that lake,' Declan says. 'I wish I could have done something differently.'

Dani sips more coffee. She needs something to focus on. She doesn't want to think about Theo walking into the lake.

Sometimes, she doesn't want to think about him at all.

'You know when I came to you and you told me Theo had said he was going travelling,' she says.

'He did,' Declan starts to protest. 'That's what he told me.'

'I'm not saying he didn't. I guess that was his way of trying to make sure people didn't look for him. No, what I was going to ask is, did Theo ever tell you he was thinking of going to work for a company called Amarita Medical?'

Declan frowns.

'Going to work for them? When did he say that?'

'He mentioned it to a friend of his father's. That he was thinking of working with them.'

'Oh. I don't think that's what he meant. The college is going to be running a trial with them—'

'A trial?'

'Yes. We're going to oversee the testing of a new drug they've just received funding for,' Declan says. 'I asked him if he wanted to be on the trial. I presume that's what he meant by working with them. But I asked him to keep it to himself because we hadn't confirmed it at that point. Why did he bring it up with his father's friend?'

'I don't know. I'm just trying to figure out what was in his head.'

Declan's face flushes with emotion. He stares out the window for a few seconds.

'If he had concerns, he should have raised them with me,' he says.

'Sorry,' Dani says. 'I don't mean to sound like I'm accusing you of anything. I'm just looking for answers. He . . . he left me a note.'

Declan looks shocked.

'What note?' he asks.

'It just said, *I'm sorry, Dani.*'

'Really? Where was it?'

'On the back page of the textbook that was in his rucksack.'

Declan looks at her pityingly.

'That wasn't fair,' he says.

Dani shrugs. She might never have found it at all, so in that respect, she does agree with Declan.

But something was better than nothing.

'Well, I'd best get back to the college,' he says. 'Summer exams have started.'

Dani's stomach twists. She thinks of all her friends sitting in halls, looking at the empty desk where she would have sat.

They've all been in contact. And most of her lecturers. Grace called to her uncle's house with flowers and a promise to help Dani reapply next year.

Declan gets out of his seat.

'Good luck, Dani,' he says.

He's about to leave when it dawns on her.

'How did you know where I live?' she asks.

'It's in your college file,' he says. 'I looked you up. Listen, you call me if you need anything, okay?'

He smiles encouragingly, pats her on the back and then he's gone.

Dani stares at him through the window, watching as he walks back down the street.

A couple of days after the fire, she'd called into the admin office and had them change her correspondence address to her uncle's. The secretary had done it onscreen in front of her. Dani had explained that their house would be unliveable for six months so she'd be staying in Tom's when she wasn't on campus.

So, why did Declan go straight to her mother's house?

Had he looked her up previously?

There are butterflies in Dani's stomach.

It's nothing, she tells herself.

Her old paranoia kicking in.

Her breathing quickens a little but she slows it down.

Stay in control, she remembers.

She takes out her phone.

She opens up the Garda Síochána website and follows the link to new recruits.

There's a request link for an application form.

Dani hits it.

2024

Dani relies on Bridget to find out where Malachy Walsh is this evening.

She's already called to the office of the provost, only to be told his next free appointment is in three days' time.

Not satisfied with the wait, Dani decides to try to find him outside of hours.

Bridget, tapping into her extensive secretary network, is able to discover Malachy's plans. He's wining and dining donors for the college in a restaurant in Rathlow.

She doesn't ask why Dani wants to know or is in such a rush. She assumes they'll discuss it over a cuppa the next day.

Dani arrives at the restaurant, a renowned Italian in the centre of town, and takes a seat at the bar just inside the door. She can't see Malachy but she can hear him and his table. It sounds like a raucous night.

The head barman, a sleazy, oily-haired man in his fifties, keeps asking Dani if she'd like to eat at the bar. Dani is driving him crazy, nursing her sparkling water. When she realises she's going to be there for a while, she orders some bread and olives and he seems to relax a little.

It's almost midnight when Malachy's table starts to leave. He escorts them all to the door. He's had a few drinks and doesn't notice Dani watching from the bar as he helps one of the female donors with her coat.

'The taxis will take you to the hotel,' Dani hears him say. 'Or I'm heading back to the college if anybody fancies a nightcap.'

His guests politely decline.

Dani pays her bill and follows them outside. She waits while Malachy puts the others in taxis. There's one last taxi remaining and he heads towards it.

'Malachy?'

Dani calls his name. He turns, a smile on his face, but when he sees Dani, he frowns.

'Miss MacLochlainn,' he says. 'What are you doing here?'

'I was out with friends. Are you heading back to the college? Can I share a cab with you?'

He nods, unable to think of a reason why she shouldn't share his taxi.

Malachy opens the door for her and she gets in.

They sit for a couple of minutes in silence.

Dani is conscious of how short the trip is. She can't guarantee Malachy will stay and talk to her when they arrive back in St Edmund's so she knows she can't waste any more time. She'll just have to get to what she needs as quickly as possible.

'It never stops, does it?' Dani says.

'Excuse me?'

'Working for the college. I'm guessing they were donors?'

'Yes,' he says.

'You're doing an excellent job. This project with Turner is a triumph by the looks of things.'

There's barely any light in the taxi now they've left the town and are on the country road. So, Dani can't really see Malachy's face, but she senses him stiffening.

'It certainly is,' he says. 'I didn't realise you were so interested in how the college is funded.'

It's strange, Dani thinks, how quickly he's become defensive.

And there she is, just an ordinary junior professor making small talk.

It's almost like he has something to hide.

'I've always been interested in the School of Medical Research and its activities,' she says. 'As you know, it's where Theo Laurent was a student.'

The clouds part overhead and some moonlight hits the taxi. She can see Malachy's face, fleetingly.

He looks nervous.

'Last week, when that student attacked Declan, you mentioned Theo,' she says. 'I didn't realise until then that you knew him.'

'Of course I did. He's not the only student in my tenure to have taken his own life, but Theo's family were quite . . . well, you know how wealthy his father was.'

'His father didn't want him in the college, though.'

Malachy doesn't reply.

'So, that's what you remember most,' Dani says. 'The fact he came from money.'

'No. What I remember most is the fact he was never found. It struck me as tragic that a young man from such a privileged background could have met such a sorry end.'

Dani's chest hurts.

But she has to keep going.

'When he came to you that time, what did he say?'

Malachy is silent. Dani tries not to let her frustration show.

'It's been ten years,' she says. 'If there's nothing to hide, I don't know why you won't tell me what Theo was worried about.'

'Who said there's anything to hide?'

'Theo was incredibly intelligent. He was passionate about what he did. And I'm starting to wonder if he feared something was amiss with the college entering into partnership with pharmaceuticals. I'm not saying he was right, but I do think he may have been confused.' Dani takes a breath. 'I just want to know so I can put him to rest. I still think about him, sometimes. I feel like I failed him.'

Dani thinks Malachy isn't going to tell her anything but then he sighs.

'You're correct,' he says. 'Theo came to me with what I can only describe as well-intentioned but misplaced allegations about the research school's future strategy. I tried to reassure him but clearly, I failed, too.'

Dani nods. She's working overtime to look like she's on the same page as Malachy.

'I don't understand why he got so mixed up,' she says. 'Was he reading stuff that was anti what the college was doing? What made him so paranoid? Was it just the project with Amarita Medical? That was the first one, wasn't it? Or did he have a chip on his shoulder about pharmaceuticals in general? I mean, that was his chosen study career. It doesn't make sense.'

'It doesn't,' Malachy says. 'I explained to the lad that he'd end up working in one of these companies, if he was lucky. Academics don't make drugs. They go work for the people who can make them. Declan tried to explain that to him as well. I believe Declan tried to bring him in on that first trial. As you say, Theo was a brilliant student. It's such a waste.'

They've entered the grounds of the college. Dani is in turmoil.

Declan tried to bring Theo in on a trial, which she already knew. But what exactly had he asked Theo to do?

'The sad thing is, in taking his own life, he deprived the world of any contribution he could have made,' Malachy says. He reaches over and pats Dani's knee. 'I'm so sorry you had to suffer through that when you were so young.'

Malachy lets his hand rest on Dani's knee for just a fraction of a second too long.

She swallows back the bile that's risen in the back of her throat.

She thinks of Grace Byrne and the sacrifice she made to help Dani get into this college.

Continuing to endure this creepy little man.

'May I ask you something?' she says.

Malachy smiles. The taxi interior is better lit now; the lamps from the college's driveway are doing their job.

She hasn't pulled her knee away or reacted badly and Dani knows exactly what's going on in his mind. She needs him to keep thinking like that until they're out of the taxi.

'Of course,' he says.

'I know you tried to help Theo when he came to you, but did you tell Declan or any of his lecturers afterwards the full extent of his concerns? I'm not saying you could have done any more, I just wonder if they knew and they also tried to help.'

Malachy frowns.

'Of course. I told Declan everything Theo said. He was very concerned, obviously. He also said he'd speak to Theo. But I don't know if he ever got the chance. The day after I spoke to Declan, Theo left.'

Tears prickle at the corners of Dani's eyes.

The taxi has pulled up outside the main building.

'Thank you for telling me all that,' Dani says.

'You should have come to me sooner,' Malachy replies. 'I'm happy to have been able to help.'

He leans forward and taps his card for the driver.

'Do you fancy a nightcap?' he asks Dani.

'That's so lovely of you,' she says. 'But I have a headache. I think it's having everything dredged up again.'

She can see the disappointment in his eyes, but he's trying to look compassionate. He might get another chance with her and he doesn't want to blow it.

Dani's skin is crawling. The man is almost thirty years older than her.

He probably doesn't even think of it as an abuse of his power. Two consenting adults and all that bullshit.

She jumps out of the cab. She hears him calling goodnight as she walks quickly towards the entrance to her apartment.

Everything is clear now.

Theo might have taken his own life, but she's starting to suspect Declan Graham drove him to it.

Dani's in the middle of a lecture when the message comes.

She's deviated from the topic of the day – the politics of European royal marriages – to discuss her own second-year Christmas exams at St Edmund's.

'I think first year lulled us all into a false sense of security,' she tells her students. 'Because I certainly remember thinking, the Christmas exams won't be that hard. Not as hard as the summer ones, anyway.

And then I spent my whole Christmas break convinced I'd failed them.'

She leaves out all the fun she had with Theo that Christmas, who'd spent it at home with her in Dublin. He'd spoiled Dani and Cora rotten.

'Had you failed?' a student asks.

'I passed by the skin of my teeth. But you don't want a repeat of my Christmas break and all that stress.'

'Could you give us an easier exam?' another student asks. It's followed by laughter.

'I wish I could,' Dani says. 'But the paper's already been set and, boy, it's a tough one. Apropos of nothing, shall we get back to the Habsburgs? The Habsburgs being a very interesting, very complex family, and one I think we should concentrate on in the run-up to Christmas?'

The students are all smiling now, happy with the hint of at least one of the exam questions. Dani isn't giving any spoilers, really. She's concentrated on the Austrian dynasty for much of the term under Grace's direction. There was always going to be an exam question on them.

The lecture hall door opens and Dani is surprised to see Bridget. She gestures for Dani to come out.

'Excuse me,' Dani tells her students.

She leaves the hall and joins Bridget outside in the corridor.

'Sorry, Dani, it's your friend,' Bridget says.

Dani frowns.

'Your mobile is off,' Bridget adds, by way of explanation. 'So he rang the college directly. Said you were expecting a call from him?'

'Oh, right,' Dani says.

'I hope it's nothing urgent. You said your mam is in a care home so I worried . . .'

'I'm sure it's fine,' Dani says.

Dani hates lying to Bridget.

But she's also excited. There's only one reason George would be desperate to get through to her. There must be good news about the case.

George's car is warm from the drive down from Dublin but it's not warm enough to stop the cold feeling that's running through Dani.

'I don't understand,' she says. 'What do you mean, the trial data isn't corrupted?'

George stares straight ahead, his grip hard on the steering wheel even though he's parked.

They're just outside the college gates, in a lay-by off the main country road to Rathlow.

'Exactly what I said,' he says. 'The team have gone through the original medical reports and they match the collated data that's being presented by the Turner execs to the FDA. They're not hiding any dangerous blood pressure statistics.'

Dani is lost for words. She looks out her side of the windscreen, trying to make sense of what George is telling her.

'But that can't be right,' she says. 'Colm said himself the programme had been adulterated—'

'Well, he was wrong.'

'No,' Dani protests. 'Something must have happened. Declan changed the programme back or altered the original data or—'

'Dani, it's over. There's no way anybody could have consistently altered five thousand original weekly medical reports. We have word that the FDA is going to approve Glatpezil in the new year. The task force has nothing to prove Turner has committed a crime.'

Dani groans with frustration.

'We can't be wrong,' she says. 'The whistle-blower . . . Sharona, she didn't come to us for no reason. And my source didn't make up what he saw.'

'It's irrelevant,' George snaps. 'None of it is relevant if we can't prove St Edmund's and Turner are misleading the FDA with those trial results.'

Dani shakes her head. She has nothing more to say but she can't believe what's happening.

They sit in the car in silence.

Dani wants to cry. And part of it is because she can hear the disappointment in George's voice and she realises how happy it had made her, him being proud of her.

'It was a long shot,' George says, after a few moments. 'We needed more time to establish what Turner was up to. Maybe they're hiding something else, but that data we have, there's no inaccuracies in it when it comes to blood pressure readings. You need to leave the college, Dani.'

A sick feeling has registered in Dani's stomach.

All she can think is that the data can't be wrong.

Unless . . .

She can't even believe she's thinking it.

'I can't leave yet,' she says.

'Dani, I'm telling you, the case is closed. We don't want you in there any longer. The task force doesn't have the resources to waste on this. We need to look elsewhere. There are rumours about a company in Germany. Interpol want us to focus on that.'

Dani says nothing. George looks at her.

'Are you listening to me?' he says. 'Go back, pack a bag, ring in sick and go home. The students will be fine. You were due to pull out in a few days anyway.'

He keeps staring at her so Dani forces herself to nod.

'Okay,' she says.

George lets out a breath.

'Good,' he says. 'Go on. Better you just walk back in.'

He looks away from her again.

She's let them down, Dani thinks. She's let him down. He can't look at her. All that effort to establish a background for her and get her inside the college and she's delivered nothing.

And now she thinks she knows why.

The next few hours are a blur. Dani dials Colm's number over and over. It rings out a few times before it stops ringing altogether.

Then she takes out the vials of Glatpezil she'd stolen from Declan's office.

If she's been wrong about everything, maybe she's wrong about these drugs.

Maybe she could give them to her mother.

Dani paces her apartment, staring at them.

It's madness, pure madness.

Eventually, she goes to the admin office and throws herself on Bridget's mercy again.

'Are you okay?' Bridget asks when Dani arrives in. Dani, who's consciously tried to make herself look okay, acts surprised.

'Why wouldn't I be okay?' she asks.

Bridget cocks her head to one side.

'That phone call you got. You look very pale. Was it bad news?'

'Oh, I think I'm just coming down with something,' Dani says. 'Everything is fine at home.'

'Thank God for that. What do you need, anyway?'

'You know I was friendly with Colm Ahern? He's left the college and it felt kind of sudden. I've tried to call him but I can't get through. I'm just wondering if everything is okay.'

Bridget frowns.

'He didn't leave that suddenly,' she says. 'He handed his notice in last month.'

The room is spinning. Dani steadies herself on the edge of Bridget's desk.

'Last month?' she manages to say. 'He never said he was planning to go.'

'Now that surprises me,' Bridget says. 'He was a chatty lad. Are you all right? You really don't look well.'

'I might need a lie-down,' Dani says. 'Did he leave a forwarding address? I'd like to send him a good luck card or something.'

'I'm sorry, honey, I'm not allowed to give it out. I know you were friends and all . . .'

'I understand.'

Dani feels like she's swaying on the spot.

Last month.

Colm knew weeks ago he was leaving.

It wasn't a spontaneous decision.

'I don't think he meant to hurt you,' Bridget says. 'I imagine he was just caught up in the excitement. It's a huge opportunity.'

The blood is rushing in Dani's ears.

She knows what's coming even before Bridget says the next words. She realises how much she's been played.

'Working for Turner Pharmaceuticals while finishing his PhD . . . That's going to look good on any CV,' Bridget says.

The last time she was in this office, she was terrified of being caught.

This time, she's waiting for Declan. She sits on the student side of the desk, tapping her fingers on the wooden surface, staring up at all his accolades on the wall.

Her eyes are drawn to the photos on the mantlepiece above the fireplace. Him smiling, happy, away with friends on his cycling trips.

Dani looks around the office, seeing the couch and coffee table and crystal decanter. She remembers Colm telling her Declan didn't have the ego to move into the old head of department's corner office.

Dani snorts. Declan had recreated that office here.

The college is barely awake, but Dani knows he'll be here soon. She told his secretary she was happy to wait.

Her phone buzzes with a text message. It's from George, no longer bothering to text from the anonymous number.

You're due upstairs at 3.

He means in HQ.

Dani deletes the message.

The door behind her opens and she turns her head.

Declan has entered his office, a stack of paperwork in his hands.

'Dani?' he says, frowning.

'Good morning,' she replies.

He walks around to his side of the desk and places the paperwork on it.

328

'Sorry,' he says. 'You told my secretary it was urgent but she should have told you I've a meeting soon.'

Dani studies his face. There's nothing in it to give anything away.

'I hear the presentation to the FDA went well,' she says.

He smiles broadly.

'Ah, yes. Looks like Glatpezil is getting the go-ahead. It's such an achievement for medical science. And for the sufferers of Alzheimer's. You must be delighted. Your mother has it, am I right?'

Dani flinches.

'Yes,' she says. 'But she's too far gone to benefit from the drug.'

'Oh. I'm sorry. But there's always hope. Turner is already looking at how the science can be accelerated. If she can just hang in there.'

Dani digs her nails into her palms.

'So, they were happy you had the blood pressure issue under control?' Dani says.

Declan smiles again.

'We took that far more seriously than we needed to,' Declan says. 'We were just being cautious. The last thing you want to do is be associated with a drug that has life-threatening side effects. The pharmaceuticals have learned their lessons. That's why they came to us.'

It's all Dani can do not to scream.

Something flashes through her mind. Some thread of information she feels she missed. It's just on the edge of her thoughts . . .

That time she spoke with Colm.

There are no side effects outside the normal range. I've been monitoring my group for months. Every stress test, every cognitive test, every minor illness, from colds to headaches to kidney infections. This drug doesn't make people sick. It helps them. And I would have thought that you of all people would appreciate that.

She lets the puzzle sit there, on the periphery of her thoughts. If she ignores it, maybe it will resolve itself.

'I hear Colm has a terrific new job,' she says.

'He has,' Declan says. His smile fades a bit. 'I think he should have waited until the trial was officially complete, but Turner was so impressed with him.'

Declan looks stern.

God, he can act.

'And I suppose his timeline was brought forward,' she says.

'Really?' Declan looks confused. 'How so? Nothing to do with you, I hope? You didn't drive him away?'

He laughs. And then he stops.

They stare at each other.

Dani's mind flashes to the moment – her spilling her water to get Colm's attention that first night in the dining hall.

Not realising, never realising . . . he was already watching her.

How had they figured it out? Had it been Declan? Had he been monitoring her since she'd left college? Known that she'd joined the police?

Perhaps that had been her mistake. Assuming he'd forget about her the way she'd tried to forget about him. When George asked her if she'd kept in touch with anybody from St Edmund's, she'd told the truth. No. She'd actively avoided people, truth be told. But she couldn't have imagined anybody would have been monitoring her.

She should have told George everything. She should never have put this job at risk.

'What happened?' Dani says. 'When you asked Theo to join the Amarita Medical trial? What did you ask him to do?'

Declan's face is blank.

'Colm was here ten years ago,' Dani says. 'Had you already identified him as being somebody who'd do what you'd ask? Somebody you could trust?'

'I have no idea what you're talking about,' he says. 'I asked Theo to join that trial but he never even responded. He took his own life, remember?'

Dani can't stand it any more.

She can't win this dance with him. He's two steps ahead, all the time. And she feels ill just sitting with him.

She gets out of her chair.

'I don't know what you did to make Theo . . . to make him do what he did,' she says. 'And maybe I never will. But you'll slip up eventually, Declan. You know what all these corrupt pharmaceuticals have in common? They always get found out.'

'Dani, I don't know where this is coming from. I thought we were friends.'

Dani can't take her eyes off him.

He's a psychopath, she realises.

'I never told you my mother had Alzheimer's,' she says.

She turns and walks to his door. She's almost there when she hears him. He says it so low, it's barely audible, but she still catches it.

'No. Her nurse Sini did.'

Dani spins on her heel.

She's about to walk back in, to grab him or punch him or something, when the atmosphere in the room changes and she feels somebody beside her.

It's Ron Perry.

He smirks as he squeezes past her in the doorway.

'Everything okay here, Professor Graham?' he says.

'Oh yes.' Declan nods. 'Just a little disagreement. *Professor* MacLochlainn here was just leaving.'

Dani bites her tongue so hard, it almost bleeds.

She glares at Declan then turns and looks at Ron.

She wants to tell him she's bringing him in for questioning. She wants to tell him she knows what he did to Cecelia Vargas.

But she can't say anything. They know where her mother is.

They know everything.

She has to check Cora is okay.

And then she has to regroup and plan.

Because she's not letting them get away with this.

And maybe it's Theo or God or just the universe, but standing there in Declan's office, glaring at him and Ron Perry . . .

She's just realised exactly what Colm said that now makes sense to her.

The first thing Dani does when she gets to her apartment is phone the care home. Sini answers. Cora is fine, everything is okay, she reassures Dani.

Dani asks her to keep her posted and then fires a text message to George begging him to send a squad car out to the home.

He rings her, repeatedly, but she doesn't answer. Eventually, he replies with a text message. *I will, but you need to answer your phone.*

Dani doesn't. She's on her computer in her apartment, desperately researching.

The memory that was triggered in Declan's office.

We took the blood pressure issue too seriously.

But they dismissed other problems.

Colm had already told her what they'd dismissed as being within normal range.

And she remembers that very first visit to her mother's doctor.

Alzheimer's itself doesn't tend to kill you. It's often that the patient does something dangerous. Wanders off alone or has an accident. If not, it tends to be organ shutdown. Heart, liver, kidneys.

A knock on the door makes Dani jump.

She opens it, her heart racing. George phoned five minutes ago and he's obviously aware she's not in HQ but he's hardly here already.

It's Grace Byrne.

She looks upset.

'What is it?' Dani asks. She ushers her in.

Grace starts talking straight away.

'Malachy Walsh wants me to meet him to discuss your tenure. He said he didn't think you're the right fit. It's rare that he inserts himself like this. I think he knows something is up.'

'I'm so sorry,' Dani says. 'I swear, I never wanted to put you in this position.'

'I'll do what I can to delay things,' Grace says. 'But I think you had better leave. Quickly.'

Dani leans forward and hugs her.

'I will repay you,' Dani says. 'I promise. Can you do me another favour?'

Grace nods.

'Bridget in Admin has been really good to me. Let her know I'll be in touch when I can.'

'I will. Take care, Dani.'

Grace has just left when Dani's phone starts to ring again. This time, she answers it.

'Where the fuck are you, MacLochlainn?' George says.

'I'm still in St Edmund's,' Dani says.

'You are meant to be here!' George snaps. 'I told you to leave. The case is closed.'

'Is the task force still operational?' Dani says. 'We still have those medical records, right?'

There's silence for a few moments.

'Why do you ask?' George says.

'The data compilation we were given was fake, George. And I think I know what they're hiding. They told me. I just didn't hear it. I need to get the real file.'

'What the hell are you talking about? *Your* contact gave us this file.'

'My cover was already blown,' Dani says. 'They were on to me, from the start.'

She listens to George's groan.

'But this is good,' she says.

'Good? Are you in the middle of a nervous breakdown? How is this good?'

'It means we're right. They are hiding something. I need your help. Can you have Declan Graham brought in for questioning tonight?'

'Dani . . .'

George sounds at a loss. Dani hopes and prays that he'll stay with her. That he'll trust her. That whatever fondness he'd developed for her, even if that's now in the bin, means something.

'What did he do to you?' George asks. 'This Graham fucker?

What has he done that makes you want him so bad? And I don't mean the trial. There's something else, isn't there?'

Dani hesitates.

'If you're not going to be honest with me, I'm not playing this game,' he adds.

Dani takes a deep breath. She didn't want to have this conversation on the phone.

'Before Theo died . . . Declan Graham asked him to join St Edmund's first research trial. I didn't realise the importance of that back then. I suspected something was wrong but I couldn't prove it. And I went off the rails after he died. I did some crazy stuff. But since I've been back, I've started to think it's all connected. I think Declan might have applied pressure to Theo and Theo realised there was something illegal happening and . . . and that's what made him take his own life. I think Declan has been doing this for years and I was the first person to suspect him of being up to something.'

There's silence for a moment. Then:

'Jesus fucking Christ! Jesus Christ! Are you fucking crazy? What possessed you? Why didn't you tell me this? He must have kept tabs on you. He must have known you signed up. Dani, you fucking . . . you fucked it!'

Dani lets George's anger wash over her. She waits.

When he stops yelling and cursing, she speaks again.

'You knew Theo studied here, George. I didn't keep it from you. And I didn't know all this for sure. Please, can you bring Declan in? I just need a few hours. You can make something up, surely?'

George breathes heavily for a few moments.

'A few hours, MacLochlainn,' he says. 'And I won't be able to protect you from the fallout of this. No more than you'll be able to protect me when they have me by the bollocks for recommending you. You should have disclosed everything. What you did, it's not fair. It put us at risk.'

'I know that, George. I know that now.'

'Shit, Dani. I don't know what to say. I'm . . . This is really disappointing. I gotta go.'

He hangs up.

Dani holds the phone in her hand.

There goes their chance at being together.

She can't dwell on it.

She knows what she has to do. And it has to be tonight.

Luck isn't on Dani's side.

George has organised for Declan to be out of the picture, but the second she walks into the School of Medical Research, the security guard asks her who she's there to see.

He's a new guy, not the guy she's seen there the last couple of times she's been in the building.

'Just popping into Professor Graham's office,' she says, making sure to hold out her staff badge.

'He's not here,' the security guard says. 'He left early.'

'No problem. I'll just get the file I need.'

The security guard looks at her doubtfully.

'I don't think I can let you go up there without him,' he says.

Dani fishes a key out of her pocket.

'I have his key,' she says. 'He trusts me.'

The security guard hesitates. He's young, he's eager, but Dani sounds completely confident and it's thrown him.

Plus, her office key doesn't look that different to the keys for the doors in this block.

'Look, between you and me,' she says, 'Declan is digging me out of a tight spot. I only started here this year and I've fucked up on my student record-keeping. He's helping me with it. You know what it's like being the newbie. One mistake and your trial becomes an execution. I need to get the file he left for me and drop it off tonight or I'm . . .'

Dani runs a finger across her throat. The security guard still looks hesitant, but sympathy is creeping in.

'I guess, if you have his key,' he says.

Dani beams.

'Thank you,' she says. 'And thank you for being alert. I have a few students who'd love to have a root around in my office now the exam papers are set.'

He smiles, more relaxed.

Dani walks away casually.

The second she's in the lift, her palms start to sweat.

She runs into her next bit of bad luck when she reaches Declan's office.

The door is locked. She'd suspected it would be but was hoping that the fact he'd beaten her so completely might have made him less cautious.

She wishes she'd been able to keep the key from the last time she broke in but Colm had that back off her within seconds of finding her.

She can't fail now.

Dani looks down the corridor for something that might help.

And sees her solution.

A moment later, Dani is back in front of Declan's office door, a fire extinguisher in her hand.

She looks at her phone. It's two minutes to the hour.

Dani waits.

When the first bell tolls, she gives it a second. On the second bell toll, she smashes the door lock.

It takes four smashes before the lock breaks in the door.

She's in.

Dani doesn't waste any time. She steps over the debris and gets in behind Declan's desk.

She's praying she's due a bit of luck.

One out of three wouldn't be bad.

She looks at Declan's keyboard and types in the password she used last time.

Declan's screen comes to life.

Dani could cry with relief.

She stares at the desktop and tries not to get too excited.

She's had one bit of success. She might not have another.

She goes into the folder at the bottom of the screen and opens it.

The first file stops her in her tracks.

It has her name on it.

And another word.

Dani bitch.

That wasn't there before.

And it gives her hope. She was right.

They have become cocky.

She clicks twice on the file. It opens and hundreds of documents cascade down the screen. The compiled trial data, or so she and her team were supposed to think.

But it had already been falsified.

Dani's heart skips a beat. The lengths they went to. She's actually quite impressed.

She closes the folder and scans through the rest of the files until she finds one that jumps out at her.

It's named simply *Alpha*.

The original.

Could they be that clichéd?

She opens it.

It also contains hundreds of files.

She might be wrong. This could be just another hoax, another pile of data that's been messed with to cause her trouble.

But instinctively, she feels it isn't. The database is somewhere on this computer. She just didn't have the chance to find it before.

Dani opens up the Firefox server and types in her own email provider. She logs in and attaches the file on the desktop to an email.

It tells her it will take ten minutes to load.

Dani can't stay sitting. She gets up and starts to pace. She looks at Declan's accolades again, the ones she looked at this morning.

When he was convinced he had one over on her.

This time, she hears the lift coming.

She tenses. She's not going to be caught a third time. If the security guard heard the door smashing – or even if he didn't and he's just come up to tell her she needs to leave – he's going to see the mess she made breaking in. She'll be turfed out before she can finish uploading the file.

And he's the least of her worries.

Ron Perry is still out there somewhere.

Turner's fixer.

He won't hesitate to fix her.

She decides to stop him in his tracks.

She leaves the office, stepping out into the corridor.

It's not the security guard approaching.

It's George.

Before she can say anything, he takes in the broken door.

'Care to explain?' he says.

'Who's with Declan?' she asks.

'He refused to speak to us until his solicitor arrived.'

'He knows I organised that,' Dani says.

'Yes, he does. But that doesn't mean anything. He's protecting himself.'

'Not for long,' Dani says.

She leads him into the office. He steps gingerly over the debris.

'None of this is legal,' he tells her.

'How we got it the first time wasn't legal.'

'Accessing falsified data is one thing. Breaking and entering to seize it is quite another.'

Dani ignores him and checks the computer. Six minutes.

'How did you know I was here?' she says.

'I've been watching you all evening,' he says. 'I knew you'd do something, I just didn't realise it would be this stupid.'

'How did you get past the security guard?'

'I told him somebody was breaking into a car outside.'

Dani half laughs.

'Well, that's not going to keep him busy for long. I presume nobody is?'

'No, but I did give a student fifty euros to hang around my car looking suspicious.'

'Genius,' she says. 'Students will do anything for cash. Five minutes and I can send you this trial data. What we get after that is anybody's guess. What about Perry?'

'He's outside the station, watching us, waiting for Graham to be released. And we're watching him, but he doesn't realise it. Which leads me to believe they're confident there's nothing here for you to find, Dani.'

Dani shakes her head.

'I worry about that too,' she says. 'But you know what I think? I think they reckon they've won. As far as they're concerned, we've no idea what we're looking for. So why bother hiding any more?'

George studies her.

'And what do you think they're hiding? Something has obviously crossed your mind.'

'Colm said something that stuck in my brain. He said one of the side effects of Glatpezil was kidney infections, which can lead to kidney disease. When my mother was diagnosed, the doctor said Alzheimer's sufferers often die from organ failure. Kidney disease can lead to renal failure. It's one of the things that kills older people naturally.'

George weighs this up, considering.

'So, if you have an older patient on Glatpezil and it's successfully treating their Alzheimer's, but they happen to have kidney failure . . .' he says. 'It might be seen as completely separate because of their age.'

'Exactly.'

George takes a seat.

Dani doesn't look at him but she can tell he's excited.

'One of Cecelia's patients died from organ failure,' he says. 'It was the heart, but he'd had a kidney infection in the run-up.'

Dani nods, and George nods in return.

She has a lot to prove and he's happy to let her try to prove it.

'I looked at Theo's file,' George says. 'No body.'

'No body.'

'But there wasn't any doubt he took his own life?'

Dani hesitates.

'I doubted it,' she says. 'At first, I thought there was no way he'd hurt himself. But then, when his belongings were found . . . and I thought he'd left a note . . . It just made sense. That made more sense than him leaving and being out there and not telling anybody. I learned to accept it. But I guess becoming a detective and knowing to always ask questions . . . There was something too staged about it. I should have thought about that more. His bag and hoodie being left out, but no laptop and no phone. His clothes all pulled down in his wardrobe. Like somebody had been searching for something.'

George hesitates.

'Have you considered he might not have killed himself? That he might—'

'Have been killed? Has it crossed my mind? Yes. But who? It's one thing to falsify a medical trial. To kill?'

'Cecelia Vargas.'

'I know, but that was Ron Perry. He wasn't around back then. Unless the company the college was working with had a similar guy . . . I don't know.'

Dani is standing in front of the mantelpiece looking at Declan's photographs. Him cycling with his friends. Building houses for charity.

I hate you, she thinks.

'But I can't understand how his body never turned up,' she says. 'We both know victims' remains usually surface. Even after years.'

'But a murder victim's remains don't always,' George says. 'Not if they're cleverly hidden.'

And then, a ghost of an idea arrives in her head.

'You're right, though,' George says. 'If Graham killed him and put him in that lake, I think his body would have floated up eventually. We've had droughts, everything, since then. It seems risky, even if he had him loaded with weights or whatever.'

Dani is staring at the photograph.

And then she takes a step back.

A chill runs through her.

She looks at the fireplace. The artificial fireplace that was built when the office was being renovated.

She looks back at the photograph on the mantle again.

Declan taking part in the charity builds in Kenya.

Declan, the builder.

'Oh, my God,' she says.

'What?' George asks.

Dani doesn't reply.

Her face must give it away though because George stands.

'What?' he says. 'There are three minutes left on this, so if something is up, you need to speak now.'

'I never felt anything different. You're supposed to sense it or something, aren't you?'

'What are you talking about?'

343

'Give me the fire extinguisher. Or do I need something bigger? A sledgehammer? What would break through brick?'

'Break through brick? Dani, you're making no sense.'

Dani grabs the fire extinguisher herself.

'He knows how to build,' she says. 'And this fireplace, it's fake. There are no chimneys in this building. And it was renovated around the time . . .'

She stands back, then she swings the fire extinguisher with all her might.

It smashes the wall over the fireplace, making an almighty noise.

Shards of plaster fly towards her.

'What are you doing?' George yells.

Dani doesn't answer him. She has to know. She just has to.

She raises the fire extinguisher again.

'Dani. Please, talk to me. This is . . .'

George trails off. He's looking at the computer.

'It's just about there. I'm going to email it to myself. Dani, put the fire extinguisher down.'

She doesn't.

The fire extinguisher is going through too easy.

It's just a drywall, Dani realises.

George stops talking for a few moments and Dani concentrates on what she's doing.

She's broken through.

She senses George beside her.

She still hasn't answered him but it doesn't matter because he sees she's on a mission and even if he doesn't understand, he knows it's important.

She's aware of a new noise, shouting behind her. The security guard from downstairs has arrived.

'What the hell are you doing? I'm calling the police! Stop!'

'We are the police,' George says. 'I've sent it. Dani, I've sent it.'

She's no longer listening.

She starts to pull the chunks of plasterboard away with her hands. She cuts herself. She doesn't even feel it.

It's coming away. George is helping. The security guard has left. To call the police, no doubt.

And then she sees it.

The plastic covering.

The body ensconced within it.

The shape of a laptop, wrapped with the remains.

George swears.

Dani falls to her knees.

And weeps.

He was here all along.

They made her believe he killed himself.

But he never left the college.

Theo never left her.

2014

Theo slips out of Dani's room.

On the other side of the door, he doesn't hesitate. He starts down the corridor.

Moments later, he's in the courtyard.

He has no choice, Theo tells himself.

He's done everything he can within the college to raise his concerns.

Malachy Walsh was defensive and then hostile from the second Theo mentioned Declan's name.

'Sorry, run that past me again,' he'd said. 'You're accusing Declan Graham of being willing to take bribes to skew the findings of a clinical trial?'

'That's what I think he wants to happen. He didn't say it exactly, but he was drunk and he hinted that we could make the trial work well for everybody. He said we'd all make money, that it would look good on my CV.'

'And what proof do you have?'

'I don't have proof but if you look into it . . .'

'You want me to go to one of our most brilliant professors, a man you yourself describe as your mentor, and accuse him of abandoning all professional standards and ethical conduct because you, what, have a theory?'

'I know what he meant. It might have been between the lines but he was intimating corruption. He's going to give Amarita Medical the results they want. He said that it would start a lucrative partnership for the college.'

'There's no law that says what we're doing shouldn't be lucrative for *everybody involved, but that doesn't mean anything illegal is happening. Of course we want to give them what they want. They want the drug to succeed. But we won't fake results. It will be a legitimate trial that proves the drug's success. That's all he meant. And I was the one who suggested the college undertake the partnership. Do you believe I'm corrupt? We're all supposed to make money from this. That's the point!'*

'*I thought the point was to make sure there are advances in medicine!*'

Theo had given up. He knew by then that Malachy Walsh would do anything to protect his star, Declan. Whether or not Walsh was involved in the corruption, he clearly wanted the college's partnership with big pharma to succeed.

Theo is on his own.

He's taken everything he can find from Declan's initial trial proposal and saved it in a file on his laptop. He knows Declan has already received direction from Amarita Medical discussing what they'd like the trial to return. He also knows Declan himself flagged some concerns about the drug, but reassured Amarita Medical that he has research students he can work with to make sure those concerns are 'ameliorated'.

Theo has contacted the Fox. They haven't spoken properly in years but he's always felt Louis liked him. And he knows the Fox might be able to act as a conduit to fix things with Alexandre. Theo's father might be disappointed in him but he is a man of integrity.

Between them, they must be able to find a way to take on these people. These powerful, powerful people.

Theo has been careful. Ever since he expressed his concerns about Declan, he's been aware he might be under surveillance. He doesn't think that's paranoia. He knows how much money these drug companies put into their products. St Edmund's might only be playing a small role in this, but it's still a role.

He hasn't booked any flights. He hasn't phoned anybody. Bar that one ambiguous contact with the Fox, he's not alerted anybody else to his suspicions. He'll wait until he's out of Ireland.

And then he'll ring Dani and tell her why he left and what he suspects. He wishes he could have told her already. He feels so guilty for keeping secrets from her. He's taken to writing that down. In his books, on his computer. He can't say it out loud, so typing it and scrawling it is his only outlet.

I'm sorry, Dani. I love you. I'm just trying to protect you. You mean everything to me.

Theo is almost out of the courtyard when he hears his name being called, softly.

'Theo.'

His blood runs cold.

It's Declan.

He's come down from his room on the other side of the court-yard.

Theo can't be sure, but he has a feeling Declan was waiting for him.

'A late one in your girlfriend's?' he says.

Theo nods.

'Are you heading back to your room?'

'Yeah. I want to hit the library tomorrow.'

'Sure. Look, is there any chance I can have a chat with you? I had a call from the provost this morning and it's left me really worried. I think there's been a big misunderstanding.'

'Eh, yes. Of course. Can it wait until tomorrow?'

'Maybe I can walk you over to your room?'

Theo hesitates. He's not going to his room. He's leaving the college completely.

'Um, you know what, let's chat now,' he says. 'I've got a lot on tomorrow.'

'Absolutely. I understand. I think it would help if I could show you what I'm talking about. In one of the labs?'

Theo can't see the point of going to a lab but all he can think of is how to keep this man happy and off his back. Let him spin him his tale. Theo will pretend to understand and retract his suspicions.

As soon as they're done, Theo will leave. He'll head to the airport and book a last-minute flight.

He has no way of knowing that when he goes into the lab with Declan, Declan will try to convince him to stay on board.

That Declan won't believe him when Theo claims he gets it and apologises for being paranoid.

That Declan's fear that Theo is about to ruin his career will get the better of him and make him so angry he'll lash out.

That Theo will be sent flying into the corner of one of the lab desks.

That he'll crack open his skull and bleed to death while Declan stands over him and panics.

That Declan will hide Theo's body, using plastic sheeting from the renovations upstairs and in the office that Declan will inhabit for the rest of his lecturing years in St Edmund's.

And that he'll make it look like Theo took his own life.

If Theo had known any of that . . .

He'd have stayed in Dani's bed.

2024

Dani's disciplinary hearing doesn't go on for very long.

The task force took two days to establish her theory about renal failure was correct. The 'Alpha' file she found had never been sent to the FDA.

With Declan Graham, the head of the trial, facing a charge of murder, Turner Pharmaceuticals had already begun to distance itself from St Edmund's. They also dropped their claim that the information was retrieved illegally. Murder tops confidentiality and it was blatantly obvious that the research school was adulterating the trial results.

Now Turner is setting in motion a fresh submission to the FDA and preparing responses to queries from the American Department of Justice. Turner claims it had no idea Declan Graham was in any way corrupt. The man is a psychopath, a killer, they are happy to run the trial again and to bring in their own experts to show that Glatpezil is safe.

They were never intentionally misleading the FDA.

That was all Declan Graham.

Dani doesn't care. The drug won't go to market any time soon.

She's emptied all of the drug she stole into the toilet. Whether her mother would be one of the kidney failure statistics or not, there's no way she'd ever consider giving her the tablets now.

But she has mixed feelings about it. She remembers Patrick from the video shown at the medical conference and how well he did on Glatpezil.

She doesn't know if he'll continue to have access to the drug.

Her heart bleeds for him and for everybody who thought it was a saviour drug.

The task force aren't going to let Turner abdicate responsibility. She suspects they'll move next on the company executives. George has told her that Sharona has compiled a folio of candid email exchanges and recorded phone calls between Declan Graham and senior Turner execs about the real trial results. Declan was so busy focusing on Dani and the task force, he never saw Sharona coming.

Turner will also have to explain the actions of their security guard.

Ron Perry was on a plane to the States before the Irish police force had anything to charge him with. Dani's not worried about him. The FBI were ready to meet him at his landing gate.

It might take some time, but there will be justice for Cecelia Vargas, the woman who first raised concerns about Glatpezil.

Malachy Walsh has been suspended by St Edmund's board for failing in his duty of care to the college. That, combined with the sexual harassment complaints against him, means his career is ruined.

Dani is happy about all of this but she can only focus on one thing.

What Declan did to Theo.

He's still refusing to tell the truth, but the weight of DNA evidence is against him.

Evidently, he assumed the body would never be found.

George sits with her during her hearing.

She has to explain why she didn't disclose her previous encounters with Graham, or her suspicions about what happened to Theo.

By the end of it, facing the panel of two women and one man, she knows what the outcome is going to be.

She'll get a slap on the wrist, but it'll be for form's sake.

The task force is too happy with the results to undermine the officer who brought them in.

She met Lucia this morning, in the corridor in HQ. The Italian woman said nothing, she just hugged Dani.

When she left, Dani smelled of Versace perfume and felt nothing but a calm sense of achievement.

Afterwards, George walks her to her car.

'Two weeks' suspension,' he says. 'Not a bad little holiday.'

She smiles.

'What are you going to do?' he asks.

Dani considers this.

'I'm going to take Theo's ashes to his father,' she says. 'His aunt and uncle are coming up to Paris. We're going to have a funeral of sorts. Which should be fun because his aunt and his father haven't spoken in decades. And they're religious nuts who have a problem with suicide, though at least that's not a problem now. Plus, the father's fixer will be there, no doubt asking me a million questions about Declan Graham and planning how to get to him in an Irish prison.'

'That's, eh . . . closure for everybody, I guess,' George says. 'Are you okay?'

Dani wonders how she's supposed to answer that.

'Not really,' she says. 'I keep thinking of the times I was in that office. When I think of the effort that he went through to convince me Theo was alive and then that he'd killed himself. All those things he used against him. Looking up that B&B in the town Theo had mentioned his aunt lived in. Then planting his stuff by that lake. And to let me sit there, so near his body. Knowing what he'd done. Jesus.'

'The man is evil,' George says.

'I wish you'd met Theo,' she says. 'He was such a beautiful man, George. And really fucking smart. He knew, even then, what St Edmund's planned to do.'

Dani stops walking for a moment.

'All these years later,' she says. 'It's like he's died all over again.'

Her voice cracks.

George pulls her in for a hug.

'I'm so sorry, Dani,' he says. 'For you and for Theo.'

When he releases her, her face and his shoulder are wet.

'Thank you,' she says. 'For supporting me in there.'

'You earned it.'

'Will we get Colm Ahern?' she asks.

George frowns.

'I don't know,' he says. 'We have to prove Declan had assistants helping him alter the trial data. I suspect, when Declan's against the wall, he'll name names. Turner isn't going to help him. Why would he help them?'

Dani is satisfied.

'The trip to France won't take too long,' she says.

George nods.

'I don't know if I've completely blown it with you. But when I come back, would you like to go for that drink?'

George doesn't answer for a few moments.

Dani is about to speak, to spare him the awkwardness of turning her down. But before she can, he reaches his hand out and touches her cheek.

'I would love to go for that drink,' he says.

She turns her face into his hand and inhales him.

It doesn't feel strange or weird in any way. It's like she was meant to be this close to him. She sighs, content, and she feels him do it, too.

This is going to be something, she thinks. Me and him. It's going to be big.

Dani is about to tell him that when her phone rings.

She takes it out.

Rose Hill Residential Centre.

'Gimme a sec,' she says.

George nods and she answers the phone.

'Dani here,' she says.

'Hello, Danielle. It's Sini.'

Dani doesn't even need Sini to tell her what comes next.

She can hear it in her voice.

Cora is gone.

And in that moment, Dani realises something.

Cora must have been waiting.

She'd been waiting for Dani to find Theo.

That's what she'd hung on for.

Dani closes her eyes.

She should feel alone in the world, but she doesn't.

Dani feels George's hand in hers.

He squeezes it as he looks at her with concern.

She has him.
She has friends and work colleagues.
She has a life.
She's not on her own.
Theo would be so proud of her.

Acknowledgements

This is my thirteenth novel, and along the way, I've met so many wonderful people in the publishing industry and the reading world. Some say thirteen is unlucky but I'm hoping to buck the trend. So, if you've got this far and are thinking of leaving a bad review, help a writer out.

A huge thank you to my editor Stef Bierwerth and the team in Quercus and Hachette Ireland for all their hard work over the last nine years of my publishing journey. And thank you, also, to Nicola Barr and the Bent Agency for everything they've done and continue to do for my novels. Much love to Sharona, my copy editor, who got her own character in this one. You're a joy to work with.

Thank you to my brilliant screen co-writer Dave for reading an early iteration of the mess that became *The Trial* and offering up helpful suggestions, tea and, when needed (often needed), wine. I'd be lost without you.

And a final, very important thank you to Keith O'Neill for his expertise in all things medical. I'm so grateful for the guidance.

This book was written during a tumultuous year but I'm grateful, as always, for the support of my family and friends, especially Martin and our beautiful children, Isobel, Liam, Sophia and Dominic.

I've dedicated this book to my grandmothers, Maureen and Julie, who both suffered with dementia before they left us. They were two strong, classy, fascinating women who left a mark on me. I hope I've made them proud.

Along with Kathleen, who I've finally found. May she rest in peace.